AT FI... COULD NOT DETECT ANYTHING AMISS.

He listened for the screams of panicked citizens, but, unlike before, there appeared to be no rampaging creature running amuck in the streets below. He searched the sky for what Sue had alluded to, yet all he spotted was a TV news-copter in search of a scoop. The cameraman aboard the copter gave the Torch a friendly wave as he turned his lens on the blazing super hero. Johnny started to wave back.

Then a blast of bright yellow energy blew the copter out of the sky.

FANTASTIC FOUR®
WAR ZONE

a novel by
Greg Cox

based on the
Marvel Comic Book

POCKET STAR BOOKS
NEW YORK LONDON TORONTO SYDNEY

This book is a work of fiction. Names, characters, places, and incidents are products of the author's imagination or are used fictitiously. Any resemblance to actual events or locales or persons, living or dead, is entirely coincidental.

An *Original* Publication of POCKET BOOKS

A Pocket Star Book published by
POCKET BOOKS, a division of Simon & Schuster, Inc.
1230 Avenue of the Americas, New York, NY 10020

MARVEL, the Fantastic Four and all related character names and likenesses thereof are trademarks of Marvel Characters, Inc., and are used with permission. Copyright © 2005 by Marvel Characters, Inc. All rights reserved. www.marvel.com. This novelization is produced under license from Marvel Characters, Inc.

ISBN-13: 978-1-4165-0965-3
ISBN-10:   1-4165-0965-8

First Pocket Books printing August 2005

10 9 8 7 6 5 4 3 2 1

POCKET STAR BOOKS and colophon are registered trademarks of Simon & Schuster, Inc.

Cover art by Glen Orbik

Manufactured in the United States of America

For information regarding special discounts for bulk purchases, please contact Simon & Schuster Special Sales at 1-800-456-6798 or business@simonandschuster.com.

You don't have to make a speech, big shot!
We have to use our powers to help mankind, right?

—Benjamin J. Grimm

A GREEN-SKINNED SKRULL WARRIOR showed them to their table. "Here are your menus," he said, the latex wattles upon his lower jaw wobbling somewhat as he spoke. "I'll be back to take your orders in a moment."

"Thank you," Susan Richards replied. She made sure her baby daughter, Valeria, was safely tucked into her high chair, then smiled at the wide-eyed little boy seated next to her. "Isn't this fun, Franklin?"

The SkrullWorld Café was the latest theme restaurant to hit New York, attracting families and tourists who wanted a little extraterrestrial atmosphere with their over-priced burgers and salads. Waiters and waitresses made up to resemble various alien species circulated among the seated patrons. From where she was sitting, on the ground floor of the split-level eatery, Sue spotted blue-skinned Kree soldiers, lizardlike Badoon, a feathered Shi'ar empress, and even a fairly convincing replica of a Stone Man from Saturn. Sue pitied the poor, semi-employed actor sweating inside that bulky, foam-rubber costume.

Talk about paying your dues, she thought.

A sparkling electric starfield, complete with glowing

nebulae and supernovas, adorned the high, domed ceiling, while model spacecraft, built with varying degrees of accuracy, hung on wires above the ground floor. Life-size busts of iconic cosmic entities such as Galactus and the Watcher peered down on the patrons from opposite sides of the mezzanine. Dry-ice fog tumbled from luminous craters scattered throughout the restaurant. Sci-fi music and sound effects played in the background.

"Pretty cool!" Franklin enthused. The towheaded eight-year-old looked about him eagerly, craning his neck to check out the miniature space cruisers suspended overhead. "Look, there's Daddy's old rocket ship!"

Glancing upward, Sue located the model her son was excitedly pointing at. Sure enough, a toy-sized duplicate of Reed's original spacecraft, complete with an old-fashioned booster rocket, hung from the ceiling above them. The stylized numeral **4** inscribed on the hull of the cylindrical, silver vessel was not quite historically accurate, but clearly indicated exactly what ship the model was intended to represent: Reed Richards's first experimental spaceship, the one that had changed their lives forever.

A pang of bittersweet nostalgia struck Sue. It had been aboard that original rocket that Reed, Ben, Johnny, and she had all been exposed to the cosmic rays that had transformed them from a quartet of first-time astronauts into the superheroic Fantastic Four. The extraordinary abilities they had gained on that fateful flight had proved both a blessing and a curse, drawing them closer together while simultaneously propelling them into a life of never-ending danger and excitement.

If not for that fragile spaceship, she reflected, *I might still be plain old Sue Storm—and not the Invisible Woman.*

But that was not what today was about. Right now she

just wanted to spend some quality time with her children, like any other devoted wife and mother. Malevolent super-villains and insane alien conquerors could wait; it was a beautiful fall morning and she intended to make the most of it.

"I see, honey," she told Franklin. "We'll have to remember to tell your father about it later."

"How come he couldn't come with us?" her son asked. He looked away from the model starships and started to flip through his menu.

"Daddy had to work in his lab this morning," she said, "but he and Uncle Johnny and Ben are all going to join us for a picnic in the park later on today. Won't that be fun?"

She made a mental note to page Reed later on, just to remind him to meet them in Central Park around three-thirty. Sometimes, when he was caught up in his experiments, he could be maddeningly absentminded about such things. It wasn't that he didn't enjoy spending time with his children; he just needed a little nudge now and then, especially when he was closing in on yet another revolutionary new discovery or invention.

The dangers of marrying a supergenius. Good thing I'm used to it by now.

"You bet!" Franklin replied. In his enthusiasm, he accidentally kicked the base of the table, toppling a bottle of fluorescent purple ketchup, which rolled over the edge of the table before anyone could grab it. The glass bottle plummeted toward the tile floor.

No problem. Concentrating, Sue quickly visualized a spongy cushion between the bottle and the floor. Her cosmically mutated brain responded by generating an invisible force field of precisely the desired size and shape. It had taken her years to master this strange new ability, but now

Sue could project her force fields with but a moment's thought—and with near pinpoint accuracy.

The falling bottle landed snugly in the unseen cushion, which Sue mentally lifted to the level of the tabletop before replacing the ketchup where it belonged. "Careful, honey," she urged Franklin, as though nothing miraculous had occurred.

"Thanks, Mom," he replied.

A waiter dressed as the Space Phantom passed by their table, bearing a tray of steaming entrées. "Mmm, the food here smells delicious," Alicia Masters commented from across the table. She ran her fingers over the special braille menu she had requested. "I can't decide what to order. It all sounds good."

"I know," Sue agreed, glad that Alicia had been able to join her and the kids this morning. The blind young sculptress was one of the Fantastic Four's oldest friends, practically a member of the family. "If I don't watch myself, I'm going to need a whole new wardrobe just to accommodate my expanding waistline."

"I'm sure that's an exaggeration," Alicia insisted with a smile. Her striking, pale blue eyes stared sightlessly at the other woman, unable to perceive Sue's lustrous blond hair and still-svelte figure—stylish civilian attire helped Sue blend in with the rest of the crowd, despite her being a world-famous superheroine. "So, how did this place turn out?" Alicia asked. "I admit I'm curious as to what it looks like."

Sue recalled that Alicia had personally sculpted the huge busts of Galactus and the Watcher overlooking the mezzanine, and Sue generously described the restaurant's sci-fi decor to her friend. "The Kree wannabes aren't quite the right shade of blue, but nobody else seems to be noticing."

"Well, most people haven't run into the real thing quite as often as you have," Alicia pointed out.

"This is true," Sue conceded. As the Invisible Woman, she had encountered more than her fair share of aliens and otherworldly life-forms over the years. If it was strange and unusual, then the Fantastic Four had surely run into it, probably more than once. That was just the way their lives were, ever since those cosmic rays had changed everything.

All the more reason to appreciate peaceful mornings like this, she resolved, happy to see her children enjoying themselves, just like any other kids, and not in jeopardy from any vengeful archfoe. She took a moment to bask in the warmth and companionship of the moment and hoped that the rest of the team was enjoying the morning as well, each in his own way. *After everything we've been through lately, we deserve a day off.*

She prayed nothing would happen to spoil it.

Located in the heart of Greenwich Village, many blocks south of the SkrullWorld Café, Washington Square Park was playing host to the city's annual "New York is Book Country" festival. Rows of temporary stalls and kiosks had been set up along the park's paved walkways, showcasing the literary wares of assorted large publishers, small presses, and antiquarian booksellers. A folk band composed entirely of local authors and poets performed on an elevated stage near the large concave fountain at the center of the park. A towering plume of water rose from the fountain, which had been turned on for the occasion, even though it was late October. Skeletal trees looked on silently as a chilly autumn wind scattered crunchy brown leaves across the ground. An imposing marble arch, over seventy-five feet tall, loomed over the northern end of the square, facing the historic redbrick town houses on the opposite side of the street.

Despite the blustery weather, a large crowd had turned out for the outdoor festival, joining the usual crowd of NYU students, street performers, dog walkers, and joggers. Old men played chess at concrete pedestals set up near the southwest corner of the park. Mounted police officers patrolled the perimeter of the square. Lines formed at several of the book stalls, where well-known authors and celebrities signed their latest tomes.

One of the longest lines led to a table occupied by a blond young man in a distinctive blue uniform. A large, embossed **4** was emblazoned upon his chest. Johnny Storm, also known to the world as the Human Torch, sat behind the table, upon which were stacked multiple copies of the official "2006 Fantastic Four Calendar." A glossy color portrait of the team, taken by a friendly neighborhood photographer named Peter Parker, adorned the calendar cover. Next to Johnny, on the other side of the piled calendars, a festival worker accepted cash and credit cards, leaving Johnny free to autograph calendars for his adoring fans.

The proceeds were going to promote literacy programs, so Johnny was happy to donate his morning to the cause. His line being largely composed of attractive, young NYU coeds was a highly welcome bonus.

What can I say? he thought, smiling at the latest beauty to approach the table, a statuesque brunette wearing jeans and a snug pink sweater. *I'm a true humanitarian.*

"Hi there!" he greeted her as he accepted a newly bought calendar from the woman. His boyish expression matched the one in the cover photo. "Who should I make this out to?"

"My name is Holly," she answered, blushing, "and this is my roommate, Candace." She tugged the woman behind her, a perky-looking redhead whose studious glasses failed to conceal her inquisitive green eyes, up to the table. "We each bought a calendar."

"This is *so* exciting!" Candace gushed. She glanced down at Johnny's hands as he positioned Holly's calendar in front of him. "Er, don't you need a pen or something?"

He gave her a mischievous wink. "Not really." He held up his gloved index finger, the tip of which suddenly took on an incandescent glow. He pressed his finger to the calendar and effortlessly seared an inscription into the glossy cardboard cover: *To Holly, with blazing affection, Johnny.* "See? Works just like a laser printer . . . and I don't even need to plug it in."

The two women were suitably impressed. "Wow!" Candace blurted. "That could save me a fortune in pens."

"That's nothing," Johnny bragged, although, to be honest, it had taken him years to gain that degree of control over his flame powers. He handed Holly her calendar and then took Candace's. "You should see me when I really heat things up."

"I think I'd like to," Holly said coyly. A frigid gust of wind blew past them and she hugged herself to keep warm. She nodded at Johnny's tight blue uniform. "Aren't you cold in that outfit?"

He laughed good-heartedly. "Hey, I'm the Human Torch. I'm *never* cold." He signed Candace's calendar and stood up behind the table. "Step closer. Let me show you something."

While the pair of roommates looked on, Johnny mentally adjusted his internal thermostat, raising his body temperature several degrees in a matter of seconds. Not enough to generate a full manifestation of his powers, but enough to generate a toasty aura through the thin fabric of his uniform, which was composed entirely of "unstable molecules." The latter were a singularly useful invention that allowed the uniforms of the Fantastic Four to adapt to the distinctive powers of Johnny and his teammates; as a result, his clothing was in no danger of catching on fire— until Johnny himself did.

Waves of soothing heat radiated from his body, warming the two coeds with his personal incalescence. But even though his present temperature would have alarmed any reputable physician, Johnny felt in no way feverish. He hadn't even broken a sweat.

"Too cool!" Holly said, leaning toward Johnny with her palms held out in front of her. "Boy, we could sure use you on a cold night. You should come by our dorm room sometime."

Life is good, Johnny thought. "Sounds great to me."

Candace glanced up at the full-color poster of the Fantastic Four pinned up behind Johnny. "Is the rest of team here today?"

"Er, maybe," he said hesitantly. Peering past the two women, his eyes picked out a large, stocky figure lurking in the midst of the crowd, several yards away. A hat, scarf, shades, and bulky trench coat concealed the individual's features. No one around him appeared to be giving the solitary figure much thought, which was probably just the way he wanted it. "I wouldn't be surprised if another member of the gang dropped by the park at some point, but I'm pretty much the feature attraction today." He feigned a moment of insecurity. "Hope you're not too disappointed."

The delectable roommates wasted no time assuring him that this was far from the case. Behind them, many of their fellow students were now growing impatient for their own chance to meet the Human Torch in person, but wouldn't even think of leaving their place in line. For himself, Johnny was more than willing to keep signing calendars for as long as it took to satisfy every one of his fans. *All for a good cause,* he reminded himself. Holly and Candace aside, of course.

Too bad Ben didn't seem to be having as much fun. . . .

Less comfortable with being gawked at, Benjamin J. Grimm did his best to keep a low profile as he trudged through Washington Square Park, gloomily taking in the happy people all around him. His voluminous trench coat was drawn tightly shut, all the way up to his chin, with the collar turned up to further conceal his appearance. A wide-brimmed fedora rested low upon his craggy brow, while a thick wool muffler covered his face from the nose down. Opaque sunglasses and a pair of mittens the size of boxing gloves completed his disguise, which appeared to be working, at least for the time being. He hadn't noticed any curious and/or horrified looks coming his way.

Yet.

From a distance, he watched Johnny flirt with the college girls and felt a stab of envy. *Kid doesn't know how lucky he is,* Ben thought. There had been a time, back during his football-hero days, when Ben had enjoyed the same kind of attention.

But not anymore. Not since the Change.

A melancholy mood descended upon him. The festive atmosphere only heightened Ben's sense of being cut off from all the normal, everyday people surrounding him. Carefree laughter and conversation bounced off his stony hide like radio signals from a world that no longer held any place for him. Smiling couples, both young and old, walked past him hand in hand, taunting him with their casual intimacy. Frazzled parents struggled to keep up with their kids, who ran from booth to booth, usually several steps ahead of their folks. A would-be entrepreneur hawked a self-printed pamphlet, "150 Sure-Fire Pick-Up Lines."

Yeah. Right.

A face-painter transformed eager children into cats, dogs, clowns, devils, and even a couple of miniature Hulks and Spider-Men. Their brand-new faces could easily be washed off at the end of the day. Ben wished he could say the same.

Aw, get ahold of yerself, he thought irritably. *Ain't like this is anything new.* For better or for worse, he'd had years to come to terms with his present condition. He flexed his muscles beneath his heavy garments, feeling rocky plates slide over the surface of his massive torso and limbs. *And it ain't like you got nobody at all in your life. There's always Reed and Suzie and the little squirts, even the hotshot over there,* he thought, peering at Johnny through his tinted sunglasses. *It's just that it still gets to me sometimes, that's all.*

Even after all this time.

Not wanting to torture himself anymore, he forced himself to look away from Johnny and his horde of admirers. He lumbered through the crowd, his heavy tread cushioned somewhat by the fallen leaves carpeting the pavement. A display of used coffee-table books caught his eye, and he wandered over to take a closer look, mostly for lack of anything better to do.

The oversize tomes were laid out atop a long rectangular table, protected from the elements by a plastic canopy. The majority of the books featured glossy reproductions of classical art, a bit highbrow for his tastes, but one title struck his fancy: *Fighter Jets from A to Z.*

"That's more like it," he muttered to himself. His voice was deep and gravelly, with an accent that betrayed his roots in Manhattan's Lower East Side; Yancy Street, to be exact. A former test pilot, Ben had never lost his interest in cutting-edge aircraft, no matter how much one particular flight had cost him. He reached out for the book, wanting to inspect the contents, only to be hampered by the clumsy mittens engulfing his hands. "Aw, fer Pete's sake."

He glanced around furtively, checking to see if anyone was looking. The proprietor of the booth appeared to be engaged in a lively conversation at the other end of the table, and nobody else seemed to be watching, so Ben decided to take a chance. He shucked off the cumbersome mittens, exposing his hands to view.

Freakish and inhuman, the hands were the size of a bull gorilla's, but with only four stumpy digits on each hand. Thick stone segments, separated by intersecting cracks and crevices, encrusted every inch of his appendages, so that they appeared to have been assembled from broken rubble, not flesh and blood. Granite chips took the place of fingernails. The rough, weathered surfaces were a dull, rusty orange in color.

He picked up the book again, but the pages were thinner than he had anticipated; his lumpish fingers made leafing through them difficult. Just another simple pleasure that his monstrous form denied him. "The hell with it!" he grumbled, putting the book back down in disgust. 'Ain't worth the trouble."

"Is there a problem, sir?" the owner of the booth asked. A elderly man with thick bifocal glasses, he approached Ben from the far end of the table. "Perhaps I can assist you with some . . ."

His words trailed off as he caught sight of Ben's exposed

hands. The bookseller's eyes bulged behind his corrective lenses and he gulped audibly, his skinny Adam's apple bobbing like a yo-yo.

What's the matter? Ben thought, scowling behind his heavy muffler. *Ain't you ever seen a bona fide cosmic mutation before?* He hastily tugged his mittens back on, before the old guy had a heart attack. "Forget about it," he grunted, and stalked away from the table, immersing himself back into the relative anonymity of the crowd. Within seconds, he had left the booth behind.

His brief encounter with the spooked bookseller had done nothing to lift his mood. He eyed the other fairgoers with an increasing sense of isolation and loss.

This was a bad idea. I should've never let Torchie talk me into coming to this shindig. He headed for the outer fringes of the festival, wanting to put some distance between himself and the lighthearted civilians flocking to the event. *I don't belong here. This is a place fer ordinary folks, not fer someone who's just . . . a Thing.*

The sun beat down on the grassy shore of what would someday be known as Lake Turkana in East Africa. A tribe of primitive ape-men busied themselves upon the shore's pebbly edge, at the fringe of a sprawling savanna dotted with acacia trees. Birds squawked overhead, occasionally swooping down to snatch a fish from beneath the glassy surface of the lake. Wildlife rustled in the tall grass beyond the tribe's temporary camp. In the distance, a smoking volcano towered above the horizon.

Two million years in the past, Reed Richards viewed the prehistoric scene with fascination. It was not every day that he got to observe his own evolutionary ancestors at their daily routine. The naked ape-men before him were prime specimens of *Homo habilis*—"Handy Man"—the earliest known human species, and the first to develop the use of tools. No more than five feet tall, with the females considerably smaller, the dwarfish hominids had long arms like chimpanzees, but walked erect on two legs. Protruding jaws and brow ridges betrayed their lineage from earlier species of primates. Throats not yet developed enough for human speech emitted various hoarse articulations that fell short of constituting an actual language.

Dark-skinned children splashed along the shore of the lake while some of their elders rooted for edible roots and tubers, digging at the ground with pointed sticks. Warier tribe members watched the tall grass, keeping an eye out for any lurking predators. Another sucked the marrow from the scavenged bones of a dead antelope. Not far from Reed, an adult male meticulously chipped away at a rounded chunk of basalt, creating a sharp edge at one end of the rock. A younger hominid carefully scrutinized the process, learning from his elder. No campfires burned upon the beach; humanity was still hundreds of millennia away from mastering fire.

The early humans paid no attention to the tall, distinguished-looking *Homo sapien* standing in their midst. This was because Reed had set the time machine on Observe mode only; as a result, he existed slightly out of phase with the primeval environment, rendering him both invisible and intangible to the ape-men. *Just as it should be,* he reflected. *The last thing I want to do is risk disturbing the timeline by altering the past.*

So far the experiment was going well. Although the Fantastic Four had captured their original time machine from the villainous Doctor Doom years ago, Reed continued to improve on the basic technology, extending its

range and targeting capacities. Today's expedition into the
Pliocene era was a test of a new cross-temporal search engine that he had programmed into the machine's navigational system. Based on radiometric dating, electron spin
resonance, geomagnetic polarity, Earth's shifting position
within the expanding universe, and a myriad of other fac-
tors, the new program was intended to refine the time machine's targeting apparatus, theoretically making it easier
to locate events whose exact time and place had been lost
to history . . . say, a *Homo habilis* encampment roughly two
million years ago.

He scanned a nearby rock outcropping with a handheld sensor of his own invention. Isotopic levels of potas-
sium and argon gave him a precise determination of his
present bearings, both in time and space. *Not bad,* he
thought, pleased with the results. He still couldn't go
straight to the moment when mankind's ancestors had first
employed tools, but he was getting closer. *Perhaps if I factor
in probabilities at the quantum level?*

But that was an experiment for another day. For now
he was content to look on invisibly as the adult hominid
turned an ordinary rock into a primitive blade. As a scientist, Reed found the moment both intriguing and inspira-
tional. "Handy man" indeed; Reed knew that he was
witnessing the first halting steps along a road that would
someday lead to electron microscopes, fusion reactors . . .
and even time machines.

Mimicking his elder, the younger ape-man picked up
two stones of his own and began striking them together.
Reed watched intently, eager to behold the transference of
acquired knowledge from one generation to another. *The
triumph of education over instinct,* he mused. *The very essence
of humanity.*

Would the hominid youth successfully manufacture a cutter of his own? Reed held his breath. . . .

Beep!

A buzzer sounded from the comm link in his chest insignia. Reed looked up to see a glowing, two-dimensional plane of light appear a few feet above his head. This, he knew, was the time platform returning for him. The luminous square, approximately ten-feet by ten-feet, rapidly descended toward him, passing over his body like a ghostly elevator. Reed felt the peculiar tingling sensation he had come to associate with time travel.

What on earth . . . ? His high forehead wrinkled in confusion—he had not summoned the time platform to retrieve him. Irritation and puzzlement gave way to concern as he realized that something must have triggered the machine's emergency recall function. *This could be serious.*

Technically, Doom's invention was a time-space transporter, not merely a time machine; thus Reed found himself instantly transferred from primeval Africa to the Baxter Building, the Fantastic Four's high-rise headquarters in modern Manhattan. Rising thirty-eight floors above Madison Avenue, only a few blocks away from Times Square, the skyscraper was a Manhattan landmark, not to mention a favorite tourist attraction, complete with a gift shop in the lobby.

The time-travel chamber, however, was not open to the public at any time. Gleaming steel walls enclosed the empty vault on the building's thirty-fourth floor. A blastproof window separated the chamber from the adjacent control room. Reed Richards saw himself reflected in the transparent Plexiglas: a lean, thirtyish male with brown hair and prematurely graying temples. His blue uniform fit snugly to an athletic figure that was in better shape than many of his scientific contemporaries, thanks to the benefits of good nutrition and an unusually adventurous lifestyle.

He waited until the glowing platform faded beneath the soles of his boots, then rushed to find out what was amiss. "Sue? Johnny?" he called out, wondering if perhaps one of them had summoned him back from the Stone Age. "Ben? Franklin?"

No answer. The control room appeared to be empty, suggesting that this was an automated recall after all. A warning Klaxon testified to the existence of some urgent crisis requiring the immediate attention of the Fantastic Four.

With no time to lose, Reed's arm literally *stretched* across the chamber to unlock the reinforced steel door guarding the chamber. An elastic twang, like the sound of a rubber band being snapped, echoed throughout the chamber as the elongated arm contracted suddenly, yanking the rest of his body forward and through the now-open doorway. Only the unstable molecules in "Mr. Fantastic's" uniform allowed the garment to stretch along with its wearer.

Reed sprung to the control panel, which was linked to the Baxter Building's unified computer network. "Password: four to the fortieth power," he hailed the voice-activated system. A distended finger pressed a touch pad two feet away, silencing the Klaxons. "Emergency report."

A holographic display manifested above the control panel. Reed quickly scanned the readout and was alarmed to discover evidence of a matter-antimatter interface. It could only mean one thing.

The Negative Zone. Not again.

Reed had discovered the Zone himself years ago. He had been searching for a way to achieve faster-than-light travel by bypassing conventional space, only to discover a route into what he later discovered was an entire universe composed of "negative" antimatter, a parallel dimension of unearthly wonders and dangers. Using a portal of his own invention, the Fantastic Four had traveled to the Negative Zone on numerous occasions, each time barely escaping with their lives. It was teeming with deadly hazards and hostile life-forms, many of the latter insanely malevolent. More than once, the power-hungry denizens of the Zone had attempted to invade Earth's own positive-matter universe—with near-catastrophic results.

"Blast it," he murmured to himself. There were times he wished he had never discovered how to access that forbidding dimension, which was the main reason he had kept the technology a closely guarded secret; although the Negative Zone offered a whole new realm of existence to explore, there were too many dangers lurking there to keep the gateway open between Earth and the Zone.

If I knew then what I knew now, he asked himself, *would I still build the portal?* As a scientist, he instinctively resisted the idea of declaring any field of inquiry off-limits; the expansion of human knowledge was inherently good. Yet he could not deny that his discovery of the Negative Zone had yielded dire consequences for both universes. Not only had he unwittingly alerted hostile intelligences to Earth's existence, but invaders from Earth had sometimes wreaked havoc on the Negative Zone as well, creating yet more strife and hostility between the inhabitants of both dimensions. *And all because of me.*

Still, like so many troubled scientists before him, Reed knew there was no way to undiscover what he had learned (at least not without severely damaging the timeline). For better or for worse, the genie was out of the bottle. Now the only responsible thing to do was to deal with the consequences of his discovery, by keeping a close eye on the Negative Zone itself, and by guarding the Negative Zone portal as best he could.

Had someone managed to penetrate the intense security guarding the Nega-Portal?

It was, in fact, located on the same floor as the time machine, behind thick, nearly indestructable adamantium doors, yet Reed did not need to check on the location physically. A quick look at the building's internal diagnostics revealed that the portal remained undisturbed. Whatever had set off the emergency systems, it had not originated there.

A closer inspection of the data indicated that the trigger events were taking place outside the Baxter Building, as detected by the building's external sensors and other monitoring devices that the Fantastic Four had set up throughout the world to detect unusual electromagnetic activity and phenomena. In the past, these monitors had served as a valuable advance warning system with regards to hazardous time warps, telekinetic assaults, and cloaked extraterrestrial warships—a benefit clearly not lost on Reed in this case. The readouts now alerted him to the presence of first one, then another rupture in the space-time continuum, emanating from somewhere deep within the Negative Zone.

All thoughts of prehistoric hominids forgotten, Reed blinked in disbelief at the information the sensors were screaming at him.

The ruptures were indeed originating from the Negative Zone. But they were also terminating right here—in the very heart of Manhattan.

2

"HERE YOU ARE," THE WAITER ANNOUNCED, deftly transferring early lunches from his tray to the table. "One Blastaar Burger, with Cosmic Fries; the Sub-Mariner Seafood Salad, with Creamy Atlantean dressing on the side; an Inhuman Turkey Wrap, hold the mayo; and a kid-sized portion of Impossible Man Poppup-Tarts . . . all from the furthest reaches of the galaxy!"

Sue Richards couldn't help but be critical of the glaring inaccuracies. *Actually, only the Impossible Man is from outer space. Those other beings are from Earth or another dimension.* She appreciated the waiter's spirited delivery, however, and resolved to leave him a good tip.

Plus, the food smelled great.

"I'll be right back with your drinks," the waiter promised, as Sue made sure Valeria's bib was in place. Franklin grinned at the sheer enormity of his burger, while Alicia felt for her silverware. Sue looked forward to sampling her salad as soon as Valeria was taken care of. She hadn't realized until this very moment just how hungry she was.

"Dig in," she told the others.

But before anyone could take a single bite, a bizarre,

overpowering disturbance caught the attention of everyone in the restaurant. A loud crackling noise, like an enormous electrical discharge, accompanied the sudden appearance of a bright emerald flash in the empty air above them, about level with the mezzanine. At first Sue thought that the brilliant burst of light might simply be a special effect intended as part of the restaurant's ambience, but then she noticed that the staff looked just as startled as the patrons.

This is no act, she realized, instinctively tensing for action. The air suddenly smelled of ozone. *Whatever this is, it's for real.*

Instead of dissipating, the initial flash gave way to a streak of coruscating green energy, hovering approximately thirty feet above the ground floor. Before the wondering eyes of the dazzled spectators, the streak rapidly expanded, like a growing tear in the very fabric of reality, until it was roughly the size of an opened pair of double doors. Through the glowing aperture, Sue glimpsed a riotous swirl of shapes and colors that looked distinctly familiar. *I've seen something like that before . . . but where?*

No doubt Reed would be able to expound sagely on the precise nature of this phenomenon. Sue simply knew trouble when she saw it. She instantly activated a concealed signal device on her belt buckle, summoning Reed and the others. Hopefully, they would respond immediately.

So much for our quiet Saturday morning . . .

"What is it?" Alicia asked anxiously, hearing the loud gasps and exclamations of the people nearby. Her face turned upward toward the rift, drawn by the violent crackling sounds. The mysterious occurrence roiled the atmosphere within the restaurant. Freak winds buffeted those inside, knocking over glasses and table settings. Sue's blond tresses whipped about wildly, as did Alicia's long, reddish-brown hair. "What's happening?!"

"I'm not sure," Sue replied, raising her voice to be heard over the general clamor. She hastily lifted Valeria from her high chair and handed the infant over to Alicia. Thank goodness Alicia was here; despite her handicap, there was no one else in the world Sue trusted more to take custody of the children. Besides, Sue suspected that the Invisible Woman was going to be needed any minute now. "Be ready for anything."

Are we under attack? she fretted. Had Doctor Doom or one of their other foes chosen this very moment to seek revenge upon the Fantastic Four? She prayed that wasn't the case—far too many innocent bystanders were present. She glanced at a table only a few yards away, where a fourth-grade birthday party had been in progress until this unexpected interruption. Nearly a dozen children sat around the table, looking up with a mixture of fear and wonder, all potential targets for whatever danger the luminous rift posed.

Sue stared intently at the gap, half-expecting Doom to emerge at any second. As if to confirm her dire suspicions, a dark shape appeared within the tumult of colors at the center of the aperture. The shape grew larger by the instant as it seemed to hurl across an immeasurable void toward them. A thunderclap shook the entire restaurant, and the shape burst from the gap with an ear-piercing screech.

The unexpected intruder was not Victor Von Doom, but rather a grotesque bat-winged creature with a leathery, purple hide and large, flared ears jutting from its oversize skull. Bestial black eyes peered from sunken sockets, above a pair of flattened nostrils. Yellow fangs protruded from beneath its lips, while jagged talons turned the creature's fingers and toes into lethal weapons. Its wings flapped loudly overhead.

Sue recognized the monster at once—it was a Scavenger, one of the many hostile life-forms native to the Negative Zone. The Fantastic Four had encountered such creatures before, on various perilous expeditions into the Zone. *Of course,* Sue thought. She realized now why the eldritch light show within the gap had seemed so familiar; it looked just like the so-called Distortion Area that separated one universe from the other. She had passed through the same disorienting panoply of colors on her way to and from the Negative Zone.

But what on earth was a Scavenger doing here now? In the Negative Zone, the Scavengers were the minions of an alien conqueror named Annihilus, who used them to capture other life-forms for his own purposes. Annihilus claimed to have genetically engineered the Scavengers to serve him. From what Sue had seen in the past, the creatures possessed little intelligence or initiative of their own.

Was Annihilus behind the creature's appearance? Or was this just some sort of freak accident?

There was no time to speculate on the reason for the creature's shocking arrival. Shrieking like an enraged demon, the creature flapped toward the roof, slashing angrily at the hanging wires obstructing its path. The Scavenger's razor-sharp claws sliced through the thin metal strands, causing heavy model starships to plummet toward the crowded floor below. Frightened patrons screamed in alarm as they stood frozen beneath the rain of chrome-plated models.

Sue acted instantly, visualizing a protective canopy over the endangered bystanders. The falling models bounced harmlessly off the unseen barrier, yet the crisis was hardly over, not while the berserk Scavenger was still creating havoc within the restaurant. Screeching angrily, it dove at a table on the mezzanine, causing the diners there to scatter in fear. She glanced fleetingly at the dimensional warp that had disgorged the creature, fearful that yet more Negative Zone monstrosities might be on their way . . . perhaps even Annihilus himself?

The very thought sent a chill down her spine.

To her relief, the glowing rift collapsed into itself, vanishing as though it had never existed. The turbulent atmospheric disturbances subsided, and Sue's hair fell loosely back into place. Whatever had birthed the phenomenon, opening up a temporary gateway between Earth and the Negative Zone, it appeared to be over . . . at least for now.

Good, she thought. *I've got enough on my hands right now without dealing with any more unwanted visitors.*

"What is it?" Alicia asked. Cradling Valeria against her chest, she reached out with her free hand to draw Franklin closer to her. "What's making that squawking sound?"

"We have company," Sue said tersely. Remembering how Alicia and Franklin had once been severely injured by Annihilus, she decided to hold off mentioning the intruder's origins. The memory of her friend and son lying in their hospital beds, bandaged and battered by the Scavengers' master, came back to her with painful clarity. "Some sort of flying monster."

"A Scavenger," Franklin said helpfully. His large blue eyes were wide with fear. "From the Nega-Zone!"

"What?" Alicia gasped.

At the moment, Sue wished that her young son was not quite so well-versed in his parents' exploits. "It'll be all right," she promised. "Just look out for each other."

Sue mentally dissolved her force shield, letting the toy

spaceships drop to the floor with considerably less momentum, then went on the offensive. Trying to lock onto the flying Scavenger with her eyes, she attempted to trap the monster inside a projected invisible-force bubble, but the creature was moving too fast and erratically to focus on. It swooped and soared, veering first this way, then another, as though confused and disoriented by its new environment. Customers on the upper tier of the restaurant screamed and ducked their heads as the Scavenger flapped toward them. One man shrieked in alarm as the creature's claws grazed his head, tearing a bloody gash across his scalp. He threw himself to the floor and started crawling away on his hands and knees.

By now, even the dimmest customers realized that the airborne monster was not an intended part of their dining entertainment. Pandemonium erupted as terrified patrons grabbed their children and bolted from their seats. They shoved and pulled at each other in their desperate attempts to reach the exits. Tables and chairs were knocked aside, adding to the chaos. Screams and angry curses competed with the inhuman screeching of the flying Scavenger, who slashed and kicked at the fleeing humans. A distraught father tried to ward the monster off with an aluminum chair, but the Scavenger yanked the weapon from the man's hands, then knocked him aside with a single sweep of his wings. The man went tumbling across the mezzanine into the wall, then disappeared beneath a rush of injured and terrified customers.

The panicky stampede posed almost as great a threat as the monster itself. Sue feared that helpless innocents would be trampled in the mob's headlong rush for the doors. She watched in dismay as people fleeing the mezzanine tumbled upon the stairways leading down to the first floor. Battered bodies landed in a heap at the bottom of the steps, where their anguished cries failed to stop their fellow humans from treading over them. Bones shattered beneath frantic boots and shoes.

Sue didn't think anyone had yet been killed, but she recognized a tragedy in the making. Trusting Alicia with her children, Sue leaped onto the lip of a fuming fiberglass crater. She crafted a force field in the shape of a funnel and held it to her lips like an invisible megaphone.

"Attention, everyone! Please remain calm! This is Sue Richards of the Fantastic Four." Using another of her superhuman abilities, she turned her street clothes invisible, revealing the skintight blue uniform she wore underneath her civilian attire. The FF's trademarked 4 adorned her chest, while a wide black belt encircled her slender waist. Black gloves and boots completed the ensemble. "I've signaled the rest of my team and they should be here shortly. In the meantime, I'm here to protect you!"

Unlike, say, Spider-Man or the X-Men, the Fantastic Four enjoyed a generally good reputation among their fellow New Yorkers. Sue was counting on that positive image now, if only to restore a degree of order to the situation.

Her amplified pleas also attracted the attention of the Scavenger, who now dove at Sue with its front claws extended. "Watch out!" someone yelled, and Sue dissolved her funnel just in time to form an invisible force field around her. The creature slammed into the barrier like a meteor, sending a wave of painful psychic feedback through her skull, but the shielding remained intact.

Shaking off the effects of the collision, the Scavenger immediately took to the air once more. Frustrated by the unyielding force field, the bat-winged gargoyle sought out easier prey. Sue watched in horror as the Scavenger swooped down on the nearby birthday party and snatched up a defenseless youngster with its hind legs.

No! she thought. *Not a child!*

A fenced-in dog run occupied a portion of Washington Square Park, several yards distant from the teeming book festival. Ben Grimm stood outside the fence, being careful not to rest his prodigious weight against the fragile chain-link, and watched the playful canines cavort with their human companions and each other. The high-spirited antics of the pooches lifted some of the darkness hanging over his soul.

Maybe I oughta get a dog, he thought. *A pug-ugly bulldog, maybe, that won't mind the way I look.*

But as he considered the pros and cons of moving a dog into the Baxter Building, a sudden chime came from beneath his trench coat. An emergency signal from the comm link on his belt. The distinctive tone of the chime immediately informed him who had sent the alert. *Suzie's in trouble!*

Before he could respond, however, an unexpected change came over the canines in front of him. All at once, every one of the dogs started barking and yapping to beat the band, as if a whole passel of cats had just materialized on the other side of the fence. Fur bristled and teeth were bared. Angry growls issued from multiple snouts.

What the heck? Ben wondered. The dogs' respective owners looked equally puzzled by their pets' strange behavior. Ben noticed that all of the dogs were pointing north, toward the upper end of the square, and turned around to see what might be agitating them. A sense of foreboding came over him and he feared that the distress signal might have to wait.

I gotta bad feeling 'bout this.

At first, he couldn't discern anything unusual, just the Washington Memorial Arch overlooking the park as always. Then an intense burst of emerald light flared in the open space beneath the arch, about six feet above the pavement. Ben blinked in surprise, spots appearing before his eyes despite his sunglasses. Violent winds whipped up the air around the arch, causing dead leaves to whirl madly about. A mounted police officer struggled to contain his steed, who appeared just as worked up as the yowling dogs.

Ben's jaw dropped as the initial flash expanded to reveal some sort of screwy hole in reality. The psychedelic display of colors inside the gap bore a suspicious resemblance to Distortion Area between Earth and the Negative Zone. Thunder boomed from somewhere inside the rift.

Uh-oh. This don't look good.

Sure enough, a bizarre alien life-form lunged out of the rift onto the pavement. A scaly, green-skinned biped, the invader had a head like a dragon, with a curved, hooklike snout that was over a foot long. A bony crest ran across the top of its skull. Reptilian eyes glared from the depths of monocular, side-facing sockets. Jagged claws sprouted from its hands and feet. All in all, the monster looked like a cross between a crocodile and the Creature from the Black Lagoon.

A Borer!

He had run into this creature or its twins on numerous jaunts into the Negative Zone. Despite their vaguely humanoid proportions, the Borers were nothing more than mindless eating machines, capable of chewing their way through solid rock and metal. They lived in the barren asteroids surrounding the Zone's central vortex, where they posed a frequent menace to anyone who ventured into

their domain. Their feeding frenzies made piranha appear
anorexic by comparison.

But what was a Borer doing here? And in Greenwich
Village, no less?!

Reed would have to be the one to figure that out
later—for now, there was a perpetually hungry monster
on the loose. Already, the Borer's abrupt manifestation had
thrown the north end of the park into a tizzy. Strident
shouts and squeals of terror greeted the creature's arrival,
joining the frantic yapping of the dogs. An unearthly wail,
sort of like an angry foghorn, blared from the Borer's
throat.

"Get outta here!" Ben shouted at the people nearest
the monster. He had seen a pack of Borers rip apart a
spaceship in a matter of minutes; he didn't want to think
what the creature's voracious jaws could do to a bunch of
innocent New Yorkers. "Lemme handle this ugly sunnu-
vagun!"

He hustled toward the Borer, shedding his sartorial
camouflage as he ran. Coat, hat, scarf, and mittens littered
the park grounds as the Thing revealed himself to startled
onlookers.

Like his hands, Ben's entire body was covered by plates
of rocky, orange armor. More or less impervious to the
weather, he wore only a pair of blue trousers and large
black boots. The 4 logo on his belt buckle matched the
one on his fellow team members' chests. Six feet tall, and
more than five hundred pounds, his brutish form bulged
with superhuman strength, enough so that he would have
been plenty intimidating even without his craggy, granite
exterior.

Not even Ben's face had escaped the effects of the cosmic rays that had transformed him into the Thing.

Irregularly shaped chips of rock were layered over his hairless face and cranium. His nose was nothing more than a flattened lump of stone above a pair of bulging jaws, while his ears were no longer visible at all. Only the concerned blue eyes peering out from beneath his heavy Neanderthal brows revealed Ben Grimm's inner humanity.

His impromptu striptease, and monstrous aspect, provoked gasps from those he stampeded past, his heavy tread pounding against the pavement like an elephant's hooves. "Omigod!" a middle-aged woman blurted. Her souvenir T-shirt and baseball cap pegged her as a tourist. "Another one!"

Sheesh, Ben thought, annoyed to be equated with the subhuman Borer, even by a clueless out-of-towner. *Don't she recognize the idol of millions?*

In motion, the Thing sounded like a rockslide rolling downhill. His burly form belied his speed, however, and he made good time crossing the length of the park. "Outta my way!" he bellowed, clearing a path through the fleeing pedestrians. His booming voice rang out like a bass drum. "Comin' through!"

By the time he reached the shadow of the arch, the dimensional warp had already vanished from sight. *Thank heaven fer small favors,* he thought. One Borer on a rampage was more than enough.

As if famished by its inexplicable voyage through the Distortion Area, the insatiable beast had already started chomping away at one of the thick marble columns supporting the arch. The dense stone proved no match for the Borer's powerful jaws. Powdered rock and chips of marble went flying as the Borer tunneled through the rectangular shaft like a living engine of destruction. The police officer fired at the monster from atop his steed, but the bullets bounced off the Borer's impenetrable hide, winging a woman pushing a stroller. She screamed and dropped to the pavement. A heroic passerby rushed to assist her, while the horrified cop stopped shooting at once. He looked anxiously at the Thing, obviously desperate for assistance.

Don't sweat it, Ben thought. *I got ya covered.*

He snatched up a sturdy metal bench, intending to swing it like a club at the distracted Borer, but a more urgent threat suddenly made itself known. Ben's eyes widened at the sight of the monumental arch tottering unsteadily as the Borer ate away at its support. Cracks spread along the top of the arch, defacing the sculpted marble frieze. The whole edifice looked as if it was about to collapse onto the injured woman and the Good Samaritan tending her. A few feet away, a crying toddler was still strapped into its stroller.

Ben dropped the bench and raced forward, positioning himself in the cavity beneath the right-hand column just as the Borer emerged from the other end of the shaft. Ben threw up his arms and caught the truncated base of the column before it could crash to the ground.

Several thousand tons of sculpted marble settled upon the Thing's arms and shoulders as he strained to keep the column steady. Like Atlas supporting the weight of the world, he spread his legs to brace himself against the colossal weight pressing down on him. "Wotta revoltin' development this is," he muttered through clenched teeth.

By now, more cops had converged on the scene. Mounted police officers tried futilely to manage the flood of frightened pedestrians fleeing the vicinity of the arch, while the original cop jumped down from his horse and rushed toward the wounded mother and her baby. He and the Good Samaritan hurried to get the endangered pair clear of the arch's shadow, but too many confused people were still in the vicinity. "Hey, Officers!" Ben hollered at the cops. "You gotta clear this area! Keep everybody away!"

Ben wasn't sure how much longer the battered monument would hold together. "The street, too!" he added, worried about boulder-sized chunks of marble raining down on Washington Square North. The cops got the message, and immediately stopped traffic on the busy side street. Uncomprehending taxi drivers honked in protest.

But while he and New York's Finest coped with damage control, the Borer charged into the crowded book fair. Thankfully, the creature appeared to have more of an appetite for metal and concrete than flesh and blood; ignoring the screaming pedestrians (for now), the insatiable monster chewed through a wrought-iron fence before turning a streetlamp into a midmorning snack. Sparks flew from the tottering steel pole, but the exposed wires and high voltages did nothing to discourage the Borer's feeding frenzy. The lamp pole fell into the fleeing crowd, smashing fragile human bodies beneath it. Sparking cables hissed like cobras, alive with electric venom.

Stuck holding up the arch, Ben stewed in frustration, unable to grapple with the monster for the time being. Hell, he couldn't even activate the comm link in his belt buckle, leaving only one other possible option.

"Hey, Torchie!" he bellowed. "You're up!"

"Perfect," the teenage fanboy said, holding up Holly's cheap disposable camera. An authorized Fantastic Four sweatshirt protected his scrawny frame from the autumn chill. He squinted through the camera's viewfinder. "Smile!"

Try and stop me, Johnny thought. Grinning from ear to

ear, he posed between Candace and Holly, with an arm draped over each woman's shoulders. Heat poured off him like a radiator, tempting the sexy coeds to press themselves ever more closely against him, the better to take advantage of his toasty physique. *Man oh man, it doesn't get any better than this.*

The fanboy snapped the picture and Johnny made a mental note to write something nice on the kid's calendar, for being such a good sport and waiting so patiently for his own turn to talk to the Human Torch. Johnny felt a responsibility to all his fans, not just the ones of the gorgeous female persuasion. "Thanks, pal!" he said sincerely. "I really appreciate your help."

"Sure thing, Mr. Storm, sir!"

The kid handed the camera back to Holly, who nevertheless seemed in no hurry to tear herself away from Johnny's side. The hot-blooded super hero was about to invite the girls back to the Baxter Building for a private tour when the raised logo upon his chest emitted a sudden chime.

Sue? he thought, recognizing the tone of the distress call. He winced at his sister's lousy timing, but knew that she wouldn't have sent the alert unless it was truly an emergency. *Hang on, Sis. I'll be right there!* "Excuse me, ladies," he began, "but I'm afraid something's come up."

Just then, some disturbance broke out beyond the book fair, at the northern end of the park. An incongruous clap of thunder—on a clear blue day?—was followed by raised voices and the sound of running footsteps. A police whistle sounded and a mob of panicked citizens came storming through the book fair, knocking over tables and kiosks in their terror. "Run! Run, Beth!" someone shouted to a woman standing on Johnny's line. "It's a monster!"

Monster?

For a second, Johnny wondered if Ben was somehow responsible for the uproar. This seemed like an extreme re-action, however, even to the Thing's grotesque appearance—everyone knew who he was anyway. Then a low-pitched howl echoed across the park, followed by the unmistakable sound of metal being ripped apart. Johnny tried to peer past the crowd to see what was happening, but too many booths and milling people blocked his view. Frantic screams added to the cacophony. He heard gunshots and more anguished cries.

Does this have anything to do with Sue's distress signal? he wondered. As far he knew, she and the kids were many blocks uptown, yet he couldn't imagine that this was just a coincidence. *Some sort of coordinated attack on all four of us?*

Alarmed by the sudden chaos, Holly and Candace clung to Johnny more tightly, but he reluctantly disengaged himself from the lithesome coeds. "Stand back," he warned them. Heat waves rippled the air around him. "Things are about to get pretty hot around here."

"Cool!" the teenage fan exclaimed.

Johnny stepped away from the booth, then glanced around to make sure that nothing combustible was nearby. Satisfied that he wouldn't burn the book fair to the ground when he ignited, he clenched his fists and looked to the sky.

"Flame on!" he shouted, setting himself on fire. A blazing sheath of red-hot flames rushed over his body, turning the blond-haired youth into the Human Torch. His uniform, composed entirely of unstable molecules, ignited as well. A rush of intense heat, as from a blast furnace, drove Holly, Candace, and the other autograph seekers back. The girls looked as if they were having second thoughts about getting up close and personal with this walking inferno. The licking flames crackled loudly. A smell like burning magnesium filled the air.

Too bad, Johnny thought. *I didn't even get their phone numbers.*

Duty called, however, and he directed a burst of super-heated plasma through his legs at the ground beneath him. He blasted off into the sky like an ascending missile, leaving a blackened scorch mark on the pavement. He rocketed upward, a tail of flame trailing behind him, until he was over a hundred feet above Washington Square, looking down at the entire park.

Lambent yellow flames veiled his eyes. Through the shimmering glow, he immediately took in the scene below, where an all-too-familiar monster was busy consuming a toppled lamp pole from the bottom end up. Injured people, apparently struck down when the pole had hit the ground, were being frantically dragged out from beneath the heavy iron rod by anxious friends and strangers, only seconds before the casualties could vanish into the creature's greedy maw along with the metal pole. Scaly green jaws worked overtime.

Johnny couldn't believe his eyes. *A Borer! How'd that get here?* The Torch had never before seen a Borer anywhere except the Negative Zone, and Reed's Nega-Portal was nearly forty blocks away. His brainy brother-in-law had been working in his lab earlier, Johnny recalled. *Has something gone wrong back at the building?* Lord knew this wouldn't be the first time someone had tried to hijack the Nega-Portal for his own nefarious purposes. . . .

Growing more concerned by the second, the Human Torch circled in the air, scanning the park and city streets below. He didn't see any other Negative Zone denizens running amuck, but injured people already littered the grounds of the park, while a handful of overwhelmed cops tried to cope with the crisis. *Where's Ben during all of this?* the Torch wondered. It took him a moment or two to spot the Thing, who looked as if he had his gargantuan hands full trying to keep the Washington Arch from collapsing.

Looking away from Ben, the Torch's eyes widened in alarm as he spied the hungry Borer advancing toward an elderly man in a wheelchair. In one of the most heinous acts of cowardice Johnny had ever witnessed, the old gent's attendant had apparently bolted, leaving the disabled man to face the insatiable monster on his own. "Help me!" the man shouted. He tried to roll away from it, but was no match for the creature's speed. Scaly legs chased after the tantalizing wheelchair and its defenseless occupant. "Help, please!"

The Torch dived like a meteor toward the Borer and its intended prey. A globe of burning plasma ignited within his hand, and he hurled the fireball at the Borer's thick green hide. The flaming sphere smacked against the back of the monster's skull, exploding into a burst of red and yellow sparks. The creature howled and jerked its head around, glaring up at the Torch with angry saurian eyes. Its hooked jaws snapped furiously at the blazing figure above it.

In the weightless void of negative space, the Borers had been capable of propelling themselves through the empty air. The Torch was glad to see that, here on Earth, they appeared subject to the laws of gravity. "Hah! That got your attention, didn't it?" he taunted the earthbound monster. He fired off another salvo of fireballs, anxious to divert the Borer away from the old man in the wheelchair. "Have some more fireworks on me!"

Tough enough to pass through shredded steel without

being cut, the Borer's dense hide withstood the Torch's fireballs as well. The fiery missiles barely scorched the creature's emerald scales as they exploded against the monster, one after another. Still, Johnny knew from experience that the Borers, like most mindless beasts, were somewhat afraid of fire.

I can live with that, he thought.

By now, the enraged Borer had completely forgotten its prospective victim. It turned and ran from the barrage of fireballs, pursued by the flying Torch, who attempted to herd the monster away from the mass of fleeing park visitors, while simultaneously seeking to avoid setting the deserted book festival ablaze. *This is trickier than it looks, especially with all these books and posters strewn about.* Washington Square Park was a bonfire waiting to happen. . . .

He had to keep it confined to the park, though; the last thing he wanted was to let the Borer loose on the rest of Manhattan. In his mind's eye, he could see the unstoppable omnivore gnawing away the foundations of some towering skyscraper until the building crashed to the ground, killing thousands.

I can't let that happen. But how do you trap a creature that can eat through anything?

Intent on escaping the raining fireballs, the Borer instinctively headed for the fountain at the center of the park, which rested inside a concrete bowl roughly fifty feet in diameter. A plume of glistening white water rose above the fountain, attracting the besieged monster, as did the chilly spray carried by the wind. The Borer clambered over the lip of the bowl and ran down the slope until it reached the fountain itself, whose frothing geyser temporarily kept the Torch at bay.

Okay, Johnny thought. *Now what?* The fountain

seemed as good a place as any to hold the Borer, but how long would the ravenous beast be content to stay put beneath the cascading water?

The distress signal buzzed again, this time using Reed's tone, and the Torch took advantage of the lull to activate the fireproof comm link built into the 4 on his chest. "Johnny here," he reported. "What's the scoop?"

Maybe Reed will have an answer, he thought hopefully. Not to mention an explanation as to why a monster from the Negative Zone was currently tearing up the West Village.

The bottom of the column was slick with Borer drool. The corrosive saliva stung Ben's hands even through his rocky armor, making him wince. The oppressive weight of the marble shaft bore down on his back and shoulders, and he could already feel the strain in his lower back. His boots were planted firmly on the arch's foundations, but his knees sagged beneath the tremendous load. His arms and legs started to cramp.

Reed's distress signal sounded from his belt, but he was in no position to respond. *Sorry, Stretcho. I'm kinda busy right now.*

Moving carefully, he eased himself toward the edge of the shaft until he was mostly out from beneath it, supporting the marble edifice with his outstretched arms. He felt the massive column begin to slip from his grasp and he gently lowered it onto the ground, yanking his lumpy fingers back at the last minute. The opposing column cracked apart near its base, and the entire arch tilted forty-five degrees to the right. Ben held his breath as the right-hand support thudded against the concrete.

He half-expected the whole structure to collapse into a

heap of rubble. *At least all the bystanders are safely out of the way by now,* he mused. Only the mounted police officers remained nearby, albeit at a prudent distance. To Ben's relief, however, the lopsided monument appeared to be holding together as it rested squarely on the ground.

"You did it!" a cop exclaimed from atop her horse. "I can't believe it."

"Yeah, how 'bout that," Ben grunted. He cracked his neck, which sounded like continental plates scraping against each other, and wiped the Borer's acidic spit from his hands. Wisps of steam rose from his scorched palms, which looked as though they had been sandblasted. "Just the same, don't let nobody get too close." He didn't want anybody near the arch until it could be checked out and secured by a qualified engineer.

Not that this was likely to be problem. Looking around, Ben saw that the park had pretty much been evacuated, the frightened crowd spilling out into the surrounding neighborhood. Only the injured remained, and the few brave souls looking after them. Sirens blared as emergency vehicles arrived on the scene. Ben doubted any of the mobilized cops and EMTs were equipped to deal with something like the Borer.

That's where we come in. Ignoring the pain from his smarting palms, he snatched up the bench he had discarded earlier and stomped off in search of the alien monster. *Lemme at that overgrown termite.*

Following the trail of destruction was no challenge, especially with Johnny blazing in the sky above the creature. Ben caught up with his high-flying teammate as the Torch circled the fountain, keeping watch over the Borer below. Despite the emergency, the Thing chuckled at the way the mindless monster had circumvented Johnny's flame powers. "What's the matter, punk?" he hollered. "You get out-smarted by a Borer? Or are ya just afraid of gettin' yer feet wet?"

"You wish!" Johnny shouted back. "I could boil off every drop if I wanted to." He flared up to near nova intensity for emphasis, then let his flame die down to a less blinding level. "I just hate the smell of steamed Borer!"

"Yeah, yeah, that's what they all say," Ben retorted. Bench in hand, he hopped over the edge of the bowl around the fountain and descended toward the creature. "Lemme show you how it's done."

The monster was making a meal of the fountain itself. Jets of water sprayed in all directions from the mangled pipes and nozzles. Ben resigned himself to getting soaked as he approached the Borer from behind, holding the ten-foot bench aloft like a baseball bat. *Let's get this over with,* he decided, *even if this whole ruckus did perk up my day a bit.* He shook his head at the realization that he was actually feeling a little less depressed. *Nuthin' like fighting a monster from another dimension to take yer mind off yer troubles, I guess.*

"Hey, Pac-Man!" he announced gruffly. He drew back the bench and swung it at the creature's head. "Guess what time it is?"

Before Ben could answer his own question, however, the Borer spun around and grabbed on to the oncoming bench with its jaws. With astonishing strength, it stopped the improvised weapon in midswing, then started gobbling its way down the length of the bench toward Ben himself. Painted iron slats disappeared down the monster's insatiable gullet, reduced to metal confetti by the Borer's snapping jaws. Ben could smell the creature's hot, caustic breath.

He yanked back his hands, letting go of what was left

of the bench, and determined to stay out of gnashing range of the Borer's jaws, which could probably chew right through a certain rocky orange epidermis. The Thing raised his mammoth fists before him, daring the monster to step closer. "Come an' get it, ya metal-munching garbage disposal!"

With a savage roar, the Borer charged at Ben, only to stagger back in surprise as a searing bolt of flame shot down from the sky, producing an eruption of scalding steam between the monster and the Thing. "There you go, Ben!" the Torch called out from above. "Don't say I never did you a favor!"

"Who asked ya?" the Thing said indignantly. He wasn't about to look a gift Borer in the mouth, though. Taking advantage of the creature's momentary confusion, he delivered a haymaker that sent the Borer flying across the concrete bowl. Ben bounded over the damaged pipes, through a gauntlet of jetting water, in hopes of putting the Borer down for the count. Meanwhile, Johnny pelted the dazed monster with fireball after fireball.

Outnumbered and under fire, the Borer looked for a change of scenery. Rolling over onto all fours, the creature started gnawing at the concrete floor of the fountain, its powerful jaws tearing open an escape route even as the Thing came running up behind it. "Hold on a sec!" he bellowed in protest. "You ain't goin' nowhere!"

But he was already too late. Before his eyes, the Borer disappeared down a tunnel of its own making. Ben came to a halt right on the edge of the gaping pit, which descended at an angle through God only knew how many tons of solid concrete and bedrock. A stench like a broken sewer wafted up from the murky tunnel, and Ben could hear the racket made by the Borer's voracious progress.

The Torch zipped down from the sky, hovering only a few yards above the tunnel entrance. The heat from his flames dried the excess water soaking the Thing's stony hide. "What are you waiting for?" Johnny asked impatiently. "Let's go get him!"

"Not so fast, hot stuff," Ben rumbled. "What if there are broken gas lines down there? One spark and ya could blow up this whole neighborhood." He marched toward the yawning cavity. "Leave that critter to me."

"But . . . but. . . ," Johnny stammered, unable to refute Ben's logic, but reluctant to be left behind. Red and yellow flames crackled restlessly. "What am I supposed to do in the meantime?"

The Thing glanced back over his shoulder. "Get hold a Reed." He hadn't forgotten about those distress signals earlier, nor stopped worrying about the rest of their team. "Find out what's up with him and Suzie."

"I just did!" Johnny said. "He says that the Negative Zone is breaking through all over town. He's on his way to help Sue now!"

Ben nodded grimly. *Shoulda known Reed would be on top of this mess.* He felt a tremor of anxiety as he recalled that Alicia and the kids were supposed to be with Sue this morning; even though he and Alicia weren't a couple anymore, he didn't like the idea of her being stuck at ground zero of another Negative Zone incursion. She had already suffered enough once when that had happened. *Suzie's there, too,* he reminded himself. *She can look after Licia and the rug rats.*

Or so he hoped.

"First things first," he muttered, descending into the waiting abyss. He'd worry about the big picture later. "Right now I got a Borer to round up."

His footsteps echoed ponderously as he entered the pit. Deep gashes, left behind by the Borer's destructive jaws, scarred the walls of the tunnel, which resembled an abandoned mine shaft. Quickly leaving the sunlight behind, he activated the searchlight built into his belt buckle. A bright white beam probed the darkness ahead.

Ben recalled that, back in their native habitat, deep within the Negative Zone, the Borers lived in similar tunnels, carved into the asteroids floating in the Debris Belt. No doubt this Borer felt at home in this dark, subterranean burrow. *Kinda spooky,* Ben thought. He felt like Captain Kirk in that old *Star Trek* episode about the rock monster that could eat through solid stone. *'Cept I look more like the monster than I do William Shatner.*

The Borer's escape route intersected with some sort of underground service tunnel. Rats squeaked and scurried away from Ben's search beam and pounding tread. Brackish-smelling water dripped from the ceiling. The Thing splashed through greasy, iridescent puddles, wondering why he got all the glamorous missions. He trailed the Borer by the sight and sound of the damage it was inflicting on the city's infrastructure. Judging from the clamor up ahead, the monster wasn't far away. Piles of molten slag littered the floor of the tunnel; Ben tried not to think about where they had probably come from. He took care not to step in the metallic droppings.

A sudden vibration shook the tunnel, accompanied by a distant roar. *Must be near the subway*, he realized. *Probably the F train.* Would the rampaging Borer stay clear of the subway system and its unsuspecting passengers?
Ben doubted he would be so lucky.

• • •

"Gretchen!" a nameless woman shrieked as she watched the little girl being carried aloft in the claws of the Scavenger, who flapped away from the disrupted birthday party, leaving the child's now-empty chair behind. Gretchen herself looked petrified with fright, her small face turning white as she hung beneath the soaring monster, gripped tightly by the taloned feet of the gargoyle. Within seconds, both the Scavenger and its pintsize hostage were forty feet above the floor and climbing higher. "Save her!" the woman cried out hysterically to the Invisible Woman. "Please, save my baby!"

Sue knew all too well what the distraught woman was going through. *I can't let anything happen to that child.*

Her eyes anxiously tracked the Scavenger, which continued to flap randomly about the restaurant, like a trapped bat frantically trying to find its way out of an attic. An idea occurred to Sue; if the crazed Scavenger was so desperate to escape the premises, why not make things easier for it—sort of?

Sue concentrated on a five-by-ten-foot section of the ceiling, turning the solid plaster and masonry invisible. An entire chunk of the ceiling appeared to vanish, exposing a swath of clear blue sky. The miraculous exit instantly attracted the Scavenger, which headed straight for the gap and the freedom beyond. Dangling from its hind legs, little Gretchen wept and cried out for her mother. In less than a heartbeat, or so it seemed, the Scavenger would escape with its prey.

But the ceiling was only invisible, not intangible. The Scavenger hit the underside of the dome headfirst, with a crack that could be heard throughout the entire restaurant. The impact stunned the creature, which automatically released its grip on its tiny hostage. Gretchen plummeted toward the floor, only to be caught by an invisible slide that deposited the child gently at the feet of her mother, who grabbed her daughter and hugged her as though she never intended to let her go. Unnoticed by either mother or child, the missing segment of ceiling reappeared, albeit now slightly dented.

No invisible slide eased the Scavenger's fall. Knocked unconscious, the monster dropped two stories onto the hard tile floor, where it lay silent and still.

For a second, Sue feared that the creature was dead. Glancing backward over her shoulder, to make sure that her own children were still safe with Alicia, she hurried forward to inspect the fallen monster, staying on guard just in case the Scavenger was only feigning unconsciousness. Her mental muscles were poised to throw up a force field at the first sign of an attack.

To her relief, however, it appeared to be both alive and genuinely out cold. *Thank goodness,* she thought, glad that the Scavenger was still breathing. She had only wanted to contain the monster, not destroy it. From what she had seen, the confused Scavenger had looked just as alarmed by its sudden appearance here as everyone in the restaurant. Small wonder it had gone berserk, transported against its will to an unknown new universe.

But what had created the dimensional warp in the first place? As far as Sue knew, the only way in or out of the Negative Zone around these parts was through the portal Reed had built at the Baxter Building . . . and that portal was hardly connected to the SkrullWorld Café.

Something is seriously wrong here.

She attempted to contact Reed again, only to discover that there was no need; he was already here.

"Sue!" he shouted from the entrance of the restaurant, shouldering his way past the exodus of diners pouring out of the café. His blue-clad torso stretched like a ribbon above the heads of the crowd so that his head and shoulders arrived several yards ahead of his legs and hips, his handsome face bearing a worried expression. "Are you and the children all right?"

"We're fine," she assured him quickly. She nodded at Franklin and Valeria, who were still in Alicia's attentive care. Valeria squirmed within the blind woman's arms, agitated by all the commotion but otherwise unharmed. A seemingly unfazed Franklin waved happily at his father. "Hi, Daddy."

Reed's anxious face relaxed somewhat and he directed his attention to the unconscious monster lying sprawled upon the floor. Now that the Scavenger had been subdued, friends and restaurant workers rushed to tend to the injured people sprawled upon the stairs and mezzanine. Pain-wracked moans and whimpers were answered by the sirens of emergency vehicles arriving outside. "I see you have the situation in hand."

"More or less." She scanned the restaurant; as nearly as she could tell, there were plenty of broken bones, lacerations, and bruises among the victims, but nothing immediately life-threatening. Satisfied that the wounded were getting the care they needed, she returned her attention to the downed creature. "Reed, what's going on? How did this happen?"

"I don't have an answer," Reed replied. With the crowd thinning out, the lower half of his body caught up with the rest of him, so that he resumed his ordinary human proportions. An elongated arm placed an adhesive patch against the Scavenger's throat. "This contains a sedative I developed some time ago, specifically designed to interact with the unique metabolisms of creatures from the Negative Zone."

As ever, Sue was impressed by Reed's foresight and ingenuity. She was quite convinced that he was the most brilliant man on Earth, and not just because he was smart enough to marry her. "But how did it get here?"

"I'm not certain," he said, retracting his arm. "But if the data I've received are correct, I fear that this particular specimen is not our only visitor from the Zone."

Sue's heart sank, fearful once more for her children's safety. "What do you mean?"

"No time for long explanations. Ben and Johnny need our help." He glanced down at the newly drugged monster on the floor. "The Fantasticar is parked outside. We'll need to take this Scavenger with us." He turned toward Alicia. "I hate to impose, but could you possibly look after the kids for the time being?"

"Don't worry about it," Alicia insisted. "We'll head back to my studio. You two do what you have to."

"Thanks," Sue said gratefully. Barring a citywide disaster, the children would be more than safe enough at Alicia's apartment in SoHo—dozens of blocks away from the Nega-Portal back at the Baxter Building. Noticing the nervous look on Franklin's face, Sue knelt to reassure her son. "It will be okay, honey. We're just going to help Ben and Uncle Johnny fix a problem. With luck, we'll be back in time for our picnic this afternoon."

The little boy did his best to be brave. This was not the first time his parents had embarked on some sort of scary adventure, and they had always come back before. "I understand, Mommy," he said. "You go whack some more monsters."

"You bet!" Sue promised. She kissed Franklin on the cheek, then rose to give Valeria a smooch as well. "You two be good. Don't give Auntie Alicia any trouble."

"We'll be fine," the other woman said.

Reed gave Sue's arm a gentle tug. "We should hurry. Johnny says there's a Borer loose in the Village."

A Borer? She vividly remembered those ferocious eating machines. An invisible force field lifted the Scavenger from the floor; to her relief, the winged monster was lighter than it looked. *What's next? Annihilus himself?*

"Let's go," she said.

3

THE TUNNEL RATTLED AS AN UNSEEN subway train passed by. The Thing listened to the vehicle depart, then resumed tracking the Borer. At least the hungry creature had not tried snacking on a train full of passengers yet, all the more reason to catch up with the Borer before it decided to add a little protein to its diet.

His search beam illuminated the murky service tunnel. Ben peered ahead, but could not catch a glimpse of the monster's squamous green hide. All he saw was evidence of the Borer's depredations: chewed support columns, missing pipes, shredded ventilation grates, and similar damage. Concerns about the tunnel's structural integrity crossed his mind, but he kept on going, glad that claustrophobia had never been a problem for him. *Compared to some of the Mole Man's tunnels,* he thought, *this is positively roomy.*

A solid wall appeared ahead and Ben feared that he had reached a dead end. "What the hell?" he muttered. Had he somehow lost the Borer's trail? Or had the alien beast just popped back into the Negative Zone the same way it had showed up in the park in the first place?

Nah, Ben thought. *It couldn't be that easy.*

Confused, he swung the beam of his searchlight from side to side, and the mystery of the Borer's apparent disappearance was dispelled; to his left, a ragged hole had been dug into the very wall of the tunnel, creating a new exit. The edges of the freshly carved portal were slick with saliva. Acrid yellow fumes rose from the disintegrating stone.

Guess the Borer decided to take a detour, Ben deduced. He found it worrisome that the monster had turned in the direction of the subway. Had the rattle of the passing train attracted the creature? If so, plenty of innocent commuters could be in immediate danger. *I gotta take that critter out before it gets a whole bunch of people killed!*

He stepped through the gap, taking care not to brush against the acidic drool, and found himself on the tracks of a subway tunnel. Rusty iron rails stretched away into the darkness, surrounded by windblown garbage and greasy puddles. He guessed that he was somewhere between the West Fourth Street and Fourteenth Street stations.

Ravaged and missing tracks indicated that the Borer was heading uptown, although a curve up ahead limited Ben's view. The electrified third rail of the tracks posed a potential hazard, but had apparently had little effect upon the hungry beast. Ben, on the other hand, reminded himself to be careful where he stepped. He could take a lot of damage himself, as any number of bad guys had discovered, but there was no need to endure a high-voltage shock if he didn't have to.

He started to head north, following the Borer's trail, only to feel a sudden gust of cold wind against his back, followed by the unmistakable roar of an oncoming train. He glanced back over his shoulder and saw a pair of headlights heading straight for him.

"Nuts!" Ben exclaimed. He looked down at the torn-up tracks in front of him, then up at the curve in the tunnel only a few yards beyond. He didn't need a brain like Reed's to grasp the enormity of what was about to happen; when the speeding train hit the missing tracks, it would almost certainly derail, slamming straight into the veering concrete wall ahead. A likely newspaper headline flashed through his mind: DOZENS KILLED IN FATAL SUBWAY ACCIDENT!

Not if I have anythin' to say 'bout it. A closet-sized alcove built into the wall of the tunnel offered refuge from the onrushing train, but Ben had no intention of getting out of the way. Instead he spun around to face the train, squinting into the glare of the train's high beams. A lighted orange circle at the front of the forward cab identified it as a northbound F train.

"*Stop!*" he hollered as the nearly four-hundred-ton train bore down on him. He flashed his own search beams and waved his gargantuan arms to get the conductor's attention. Cool air, pushed forward by the advancing train, blew against his face and chest. "Hey, you! Put on the brakes! The track's out!"

It was doubtful that anybody on the train could hear him, given the deafening racket being generated by the vehicle's approach, but the conductor must have spotted the Thing in front of him. An ear-piercing horn sounded, only to be drowned out by the squeal of the train's brakes. The train was coming too fast, however; Ben realized there was no way the speeding conveyance could slow to a stop before it hit both him and the stretch of mangled track beyond. *I was afraid of that,* he thought. *Guess all them folks are dependin' on me.*

Bracing himself against the coming collision, he threw

out his hands to meet the oncoming train. The front of the cab smashed into his rocky palms and he pushed back against the rushing train with all his might. The impact all but knocked the breath from his body, but he dug in his heels and refused to give ground. Solid steel crumpled around his hands and the overtaxed brakes shrieked like banshees. The train's relentless momentum pressed him backward, so that his heels dug deep ruts in the floor of the tunnel, yet the Thing made the train fight for every inch; he felt like a linebacker trying to block the charge of a 750,000-pound quarterback.

He could feel the train slowing, though, and kept on shoving back until the massive conveyance at last came to a halt, only a few feet short of the severed tracks. Ben breathed a sigh of relief. Disaster had been averted. The train, and everybody on it, was safe.

"Whew!" He stepped from the prow of the cab and wiped his cobblestone brow. His weary arms dropped to his side. Four-fingered handprints were impressed deeply into front of the train. *That was some workout.* "Ohmigod!" the conductor's voice exclaimed as he stuck his head out of the cab's side window. The man's face was pale and his eyes practically bulged from their sockets. Ben wondered what had shocked the poor guy more: the winded Thing or the ravaged tracks the train had been just about to hit. "Watch out!" the man yelled. "Behind you!"

What?

Before Ben could react, the Borer attacked. Claws scraped against his back and something hard and sharp took a chunk out of his shoulder. The Borer's jaws felt like a buzz saw digging into the tender flesh beneath his rocky armor. Blood streamed down the zigzagging crevices in his back.

"That's enough!" the Thing shouted, grunting in pain. He viciously elbowed the Borer in the gut, driving it backward. "I've had it with you and your blasted appetite!" Spinning around to face the monster, he ducked beneath the Borer's jaws and grabbed on to the creature's rib cage with both hands. He lifted the Borer high above his head, then hurled the beast back down onto the tracks, and away from the motionless train. *No more Mr. Nice Thing,* he decided, and kicked the prone monster in the side of the head, stunning it. The Borer emitted a squeal of pain, and its reptilian eyes rolled queasily in their sockets.

The monster tried to rise, but a fist like a boulder hammered it to the ground. Turning away from the dazed creature for just a second, the Thing yanked a length of iron rail from the broken tracks and wrapped it around the Borer's jaws like a solid-steel muzzle. The creature tried to roar in protest, but all that emerged from its clamped snout was a strangled squeak.

"Don't go away," Ben warned. "I ain't finished with ya yet." Securing another stretch of metal rail, he hog-tied the muzzled monster, twisting the metal rod as easily as he would a length of rope. With its jaws wired shut, there was no way the frustrated Borer could chew itself free of its bonds.

Leaving the monster spread out upon the floor of the tunnel, Ben stepped back to admire his work. He wiped the dirt and muck of the tunnel from his hands and looked down at the Borer with satisfaction. *That's more like it.*

A throb of pain reminded him of his injured shoulder. Wincing, he gingerly probed the wound with his fingers. His hand came away stained with red. *How 'bout that,* he thought. *Guess that critter really took a bite outta me.* He glanced down at his feet, where a trickle of blood gave the greasy puddles a crimson tint. *Serves me right for not payin' more attention.*

He stared at the sticky redness on his fingers. He didn't often see his own blood these days. It was kind of comforting to be reminded that, beneath his freakish appearance, his blood was still red like everybody else's.

"Thanks for the heads up," he said to the conductor, who had stepped down from his cab to join the Thing upon the tracks. Intent on stopping the train, Ben hadn't even heard the Borer approach from the opposite direction. "Buster there kinda caught me nappin'."

The conductor gazed uneasily at the captured Borer. "What in heaven's name is that creature?"

"Trust me," Ben told him. "Ya don't wanna know."

Only Johnny's arms were flaming as he stood by the tilted remains of the Washington Arch. A blast of superheated plasma erupted from his fingertips as he fused the lopsided marble columns to their bases, stabilizing the teetering monument until the city could repair the damage properly. As the chief financial officer of Fantastic Four, Incorporated (a position forced on him by his sister, in a shameless attempt to force him to "act more like an adult"), he made a mental note to make a substantial contribution to whatever fund was set up to restore the arch. The FF were hardly responsible for the damage, but it struck him as the right thing to do.

And tax-deductible, to boot.

Johnny killed the flame to let the heated marble cool. Thanks to Reed's unstable molecules, his uniform was none the worse for wear, despite having recently been set on fire.

"Nice work!" said one of the police officers on the

scene. By now, the park was crawling with cops and other emergency workers. Ambulances had carried away the worst of the casualties. Yellow crime-scene tape kept back a small horde of reporters and photographers, as well as plenty of thrill-seeking sightseers and paparazzi. There was even a rumor that the mayor was on his way. "Good thing you and the Thing—I mean, Mr. Grimm—were on hand today," the cop added. Although a number of people had been seriously injured, there had been no word of any fatalities. "Things could've turned out a lot worse."

"Yeah, I guess," Johnny said, distracted. His worried gaze kept returning to the shadowy entrance of the Borer's escape tunnel. *What's going on down there?* he wondered. *Has Ben caught up with it yet?* He considered trying to contact the Thing via their comm links, but what if he alerted the monster just as Ben was creeping up on it? *Don't be silly,* he told himself. *Stealth isn't exactly Ben's style.*

"Hey, look!" the cop said, pointing up at the sky. "Here come more of your buddies!"

Johnny looked up to see the Fantasticar cruising through the air toward the park. The streamlined silver vehicle, which operated using a form of magnetic propulsion Johnny didn't even pretend to understand, flew silently over the surrounding buildings as it headed in for a landing. The car's modular design allowed it to break apart into four separate aircraft, sometimes derisively referred to as flying bathtubs, but at present the Fantasticar remained in one piece. As the car descended, he spotted Reed and Sue behind the front windshield. The top of the car was open to the air, so that Sue's blond hair blew in the wind.

Executing a perfect vertical landing, the Fantasticar touched down on a grassy lawn several yards away from the broken arch. Johnny hurried to meet them, arriving

beside the vehicle before Reed and Sue could even un-
buckle their seat belts. Something stirred in the rear storage compartment, and Johnny was shocked to see a large,
purple gargoyle sleeping upon the floor of the car.
"Whoa!" Johnny blurted. "Is that what I think it is?"

"A Scavenger," Mr. Fantastic confirmed, stretching out
of the driver's seat and onto the lawn. His casual display of
elasticity provoked a smattering of applause from the excited onlookers. "Straight from the Negative Zone." He
glanced around the evacuated park grounds, while Sue exited the car as well. The paparazzi went into overdrive,
capturing shot after shot of the three of them together.
"Any word from Ben?"

Johnny shook his head. He had kept Reed and Sue ap-
prised of the situation via his comm link. "Nope." He
pointed toward the tunnel entrance over by the fountain.
"All I know is he went thataway."

Reed nodded grimly. "Come with me, Sue," he said,
striding decisively toward the waiting tunnel. Johnny realized unhappily that he was about to get stuck babysitting
the snoozing Scavenger. "There's not a moment to lose.
Your force field may be the only way to contain the Borer."

"What's the matter, big brain?" a gravelly voice called
out from the murky tunnel. The Thing stomped into daylight with a squirming Borer slung over his shoulder.
Rusty iron bands confined the beast's limbs and jaws.
"Ain't you never heard of a muzzle before?"

Mr. Fantastic smiled at the sight. "I stand corrected, old
friend."

"Ben!" Sue exclaimed. Her worried gaze went straight
to his bleeding shoulder. "You're hurt!"

Johnny gulped at the gory wound, which served as
an unnerving reminder of just how serious this whole

situation really was. He couldn't help feeling guilty that he hadn't been there to watch Ben's back. *This whole thing sucks.*

"Aw, don't ya worry about that," Ben insisted. Shrugging, he dropped the Borer onto the pavement. Blood continued to trickle from the gash in his shoulder. "It ain't nothin' but a nip."

"Even still," Reed said, "we should have that looked at." His arm extended to place an adhesive patch against the side of the Borer's throat; within seconds, the thrashing creature fell into a deep sleep. "Who knows what sort of extradimensional pathogens may have been transmitted by the Borer's bite?"

"Gee, thanks for that heartwarmin' idea, Stringbean," Ben replied. "I hadn't even thought of that yet."

"Hey, you think you've got problems," Johnny teased the Thing, knowing that his teammate wouldn't want anyone making a fuss over him. "I'll bet that poor Borer still hasn't gotten the taste of you out of its mouth."

"Least I managed ta get the critter under wraps," Ben said, glowering at the Torch, "which is more'n I can say for certain firebugs I know."

"That's enough, both of you," Sue scolded them. "Johnny, you go fetch the first-aid kit from the car."

Johnny knew better than to argue with his older sister. Running back to the Fantasticar, he quickly retrieved the kit, from which Sue extracted the necessary supplies. She cleaned out Ben's wound with an antiseptic swab, then spritzed the site with a germ-killing spray of Reed's own invention. "Watch it!" the Thing groused, flinching away from the spray. "That stuff stings!"

"Oh, don't be such a crybaby," she said, putting the spray bottle back into the first-aid kit, which Johnny held open for her. She removed a gleaming metal canister, unscrewed the top, and scooped up a handful of glistening orange goo. "Now hold still while I patch you up."

"Ah, not that glop, too!" Ben protested. His stubby nose wrinkled at the faintly medicinal smell of the gooey substance, a synthetic carbon-based plaster Reed had developed to repair gaps in the Thing's rocky armor until they had time to heal naturally. Sue applied the stuff liberally to Ben's injured shoulder, then smoothed it out with her gloved hands, like a master mason adding mortar to a brick wall. Ben shivered theatrically. "Yikes, that stuff is cold!"

"Johnny can take care of that," Sue stated calmly, stepping away from her work. She took the first-aid kit off her brother's hands. "Can't you, Johnny?"

"Whatever you say, Sis," the Torch replied. He placed his hand above the moist plaster and emitted a concentrated burst of heat that instantly baked Sue's repair job, causing the mortar to harden into place. "There! Looks just like the real thing, not that that's saying much."

"Thanks for nothin', squirt," Ben grumbled. He cautiously tapped the rock-hard patch and grunted in approval. "That'll do, I guess. Thanks, Suzie."

"You're welcome, Mr. Grimm," she said graciously. She turned her attention to her husband, who was examining the comatose Borer with a serious expression on his face. She walked over to join him, setting off another round of frantic clicking on the part of the paparazzi. She lowered her voice to avoid being overheard. "First a Scavenger, now a Borer. What's this all about, Reed?"

"I wish I knew, Sue." He scanned the vicinity with some manner of handheld sensor. "Where exactly did the Borer appear?" he asked Ben and Johnny.

"Over there, beneath the arch," the Thing informed

him. He nodded at the monster on the ground. "I hear you folks landed a Scavenger, too. So what're we goin' to with these jokers now that we've caught them?"

Mr. Fantastic tucked his portable scanner back into his belt. "Ultimately, I would hope to return them to their native dimension. In the short term, though, we can keep them in the reinforced holding cells underneath the Baxter Building."

"Even the Borer?" Sue asked.

"I believe so," Reed assured her. "The cell walls are made of a special vibranium–adamantium alloy, not unlike what Captain America's shield is constructed of, if not quite as indestructible. I designed those cells to hold the Hulk. They should be strong enough to hold these two specimens, especially if we keep them slightly tranquilized for the time being."

"Sounds good to me," Ben said. "Just as long as I don't hafta go traipsing through the sewers anymore. Not exactly my idea of a good time."

Johnny figured there had to a cheap shot there somewhere, but let it go. All kidding aside, he felt bad that Ben had been forced to face the Borer on his own, and relieved that the big lug had come out on top in the end. *I owe you one, pal,* he thought. *The next monster's mine.*

Reed was also thinking ahead. Concern deepened the furrows in his thoughtful face. "We may have coped with the present crisis," he reminded them, "but the larger question remains: How and why did these Negative Zone creatures appear here in the first place?"

4

LOCATED ON THE THIRTY-FOURTH FLOOR of the
Baxter Building, behind a pair of reinforced adamantium
air locks, the Negative Zone Chamber was the largest
compartment of Reed Richards's laboratories, about half
the size of a standard gymnasium. The bulk of the space
was consumed by the Negative Zone Explorer vehicle, a
compact, four-passenger spacecraft that was mounted directly above the Nega–Portal itself, a pit-shaped depression
in the middle of the stainless-steel floor. When not in use,
the Explorer rested atop the Portal like a chrome-plated
plug over a bathtub drain. The gleaming silver hull of the
ship was just as new as it looked; this particular Explorer
was only the latest in a series of vessels designed by Reed
to traverse the Negative Zone.

Sue was in no hurry to test it out.

A table-sized control console, sporting multiple lighted
gauges and digital displays, faced a wall-sized monitor at
the southern end of the chamber. The immense screen offered real-time images of the Negative Zone itself, transmitted via subspace relays. A desolate void, marked by
drifting asteroids and other flotsam, filled the screen. The

floating rubble was being drawn inexorably toward the
Debris Belt at the center of the Zone, a ring of broken
fragments that circled inward toward an even greater hazard: the dreaded Annihilation Vortex, where the shattered
chunks of antimatter exploded on contact with a transdimensional interface between the Zone and Earth. Brilliant
flashes deep within the Debris Belt marked the event
horizon of the Vortex, flaring up whenever another piece
of rubble was destroyed in a violent matter-antimatter reaction. An eerie purple glow emanated from the Vortex itself, lighting up the darksome void.

Sue gazed at the forbidding vista with apprehension.
She still remembered how Reed, after months of top-se-
cret experimentation, had first stumbled onto the
Negative Zone. He had nearly died on his first crude space
walk into the Negaverse, she recalled, and that had only
been the beginning of the Fantastic Four's long, and fre-
quently turbulent, relationship with that perilous realm. In
those early days, she had often stayed behind while the
men went exploring, and to this day she didn't know what
was harder: joining Reed and the others in that ghastly
place, or waiting anxiously to see if they came home alive.

*Seems that the Negative Zone isn't waiting for us to venture
there anymore.* She repressed a shudder at the thought. *Now
the Zone has come looking for us. . . .*

"Interesting," Reed murmured to himself. He stood in
front of the control console, perusing a virtual reality data
display. Statistics and graphics flashed above the console
too quickly for Sue to make any sense of them, even if she
had been conversant in the finer points of transdimensional physics, which she most certainly wasn't. "It's just as
I feared."

"What is?" Sue asked, trying to control the anxiety in

her voice. She was no shrinking violet, but the Negative Zone was far from her favorite subject; little Valeria had been conceived in the Zone, and the resulting complications had almost cost Sue the life of her daughter. The Negative Zone had played a part in Franklin's birth as well, another experience that both she and her child had barely survived. *That hits pretty close to home, so is it any wonder that the very mention of the Zone makes me uncomfortable?* At the moment, she felt grateful that both Franklin and Valeria were many downtown blocks away.

"Yeah, Stretch," Ben piped up. He leaned against the wall across from Sue, who stood beside Reed at the console, glancing occasionally at the door. Johnny was supposed to join them shortly, once he took care of another crucial task. "What's the scoop?" the Thing asked. "How come we're gettin' positively infested with Nega-Zone nasties?"

Reed pressed a touch pad and the holographic display blinked out of existence. "A detailed analysis of the sensor data confirms that the incursions in the city were not generated by any of the equipment here. Furthermore, it does not appear that the space-time rifts you both reported were caused by any sort of scientific activity here on Earth."

"So no one's gone and built their own version of our Nega-Portal?" Ben translated. "Like those Gideon Trust bozos?"

Although Reed had always kept the technology behind his Nega-Portal a closely guarded secret, unscrupulous scientists had occasionally found their own ways to access the Negative Zone, often with near-catastrophic results. Not long ago, in fact, a group of raiders sponsored by an organization known as the Gideon Trust had ruthlessly pillaged the Zone—until the Fantastic Four had put a stop to it.

"That doesn't appear to be the case this time," Reed acknowledged. "At least, as I said, not here on Earth."

It took Ben a second to grasp what Reed was implying. Ben's blue eyes widened in surprise. "Ya think mebbe someone's finally invented a Nega-Portal over on the other side? In the Zone itself?"

"Technically," Reed pointed out, "their equivalent of the Nega-Portal would be a Positive Matter Portal, but, yes, that's what I'm afraid of." A worried expression creased his face. "We're all too aware that the Negative Zone contains more than simply primitive monsters. The Zone is also home to a wide variety of intelligent beings, all with ambitions and agendas of their own."

"Few of them friendly," Sue said bitterly. Not for the first time, a disturbing thought occurred to her. "Reed, do you think either Blastaar or Annihilus is responsible?"

Two of the Fantastic Four's greatest foes—both of whom ruled over vast portions of the Negative Zone. While Blastaar was a power-hungry warlord feared by his own people, Annihilus was by the far the deadlier of the two, an inhuman monster possessed of near-limitless power and an undying enmity against all other life-forms. Each of them had attempted to invade the positive-matter universe on any number of occasions. *I wouldn't put today's attacks past either of them,* she thought. *Especially Annihilus.*

"We can't rule out that possibility," Reed said, "but there's no way to know for sure without further information." He stroked his chin pensively. "So far, each rift has only lasted for less than a minute, so that only one alien beast could manifest at a time, but their very existence is cause for concern. Whether accidental or deliberate, anything that weakens the walls between the Negative Zone and our own universe is too serious to be ignored."

Uh-oh. I think I know where this is going.

A loud hissing noise interrupted the discussion. The hydraulic doors of the air lock swung open to admit Johnny, who joined them around the control console. "Tough luck, folks. I tried getting in touch with some of our colleagues, to see if they knew anything about this weirdness, but I couldn't get hold of anybody. The X-Men and the Avengers are both out of town, maybe even off the planet. Ditto Dr. Strange." Johnny shrugged and threw up his hands. "Looks like we're on our own."

"So what else is new?" Ben grumbled. " 'Sides, the Negative Zone is our turf anyway."

"And our responsibility," Reed agreed. He quickly brought Johnny up to speed on his investigation. "I fear we may have to trace these incursions to their point of origin—somewhere within the Negative Zone."

I knew it, Sue thought glumly. *I knew he was going to say that.*

And the worst part was, she knew he was right.

"Maybe these are just random occurrences," she said optimistically. "A couple of freak events."

She had barely gotten the words out of her mouth when her hopes were dashed by an automated emergency alarm. Reed hurriedly called up his holographic readouts once more, while simultaneously silencing the siren with one flick of an elastic finger. "Another incident!" he reported. "Just like the first two. This one's centered around"—he swiftly performed the necessary calculations in his head— "the Times Square area."

Another finger stretched across the control panel and the images from the Negative Zone vanished from the visi-screen, to be replaced by live footage from CNN. Sue gasped out loud at what the TV coverage revealed.

What looked like a giant jellyfish, at least three stories tall, was oozing up Seventh Avenue. Like a mountain of slick, translucent flesh it dragged itself across the square by means of enormous pseudopods spreading out from its quivering base. Eyestalks atop the creature's towering bulk darted about wildly, trying to make sense of its new environment.

Talk about sensory overload. Sue couldn't imagine any place more different from the gloomy depths of the Negative Zone than the bright lights and giant billboards of Times Square. She almost felt sorry for the poor creature.

"Interesting," Reed commented. "It appears to be some variety of marine cnidarian. A medusa, to be exact."

The giant jellyfish's appearance had thrown the entire neighborhood into a panic. Hordes of tourists ran screaming from the boneless behemoth's slow advance. Drivers, stuck in traffic, abandoned their cars to join the fleeing pedestrians. It was like a scene from a Japanese monster movie.

"Whoa!" Ben exclaimed. "Since when did the Big Apple become the latest hot spot for Negative Zone monsters?"

"Not to worry," Johnny said quickly. "I'm all over this. Leave that overgrown sea slug to me."

Sue could feel the heat radiating off Johnny in his eagerness to confront the colossal invertebrate. He was halfway to the door by the time she shouted, "Johnny, wait! We need a plan!"

"You folks do the planning," he replied impatiently. "I'm going to deal with that creature before it flattens everything in sight!"

Sue was tempted to block the exit with a force field, but she had to admit that the situation in Times Square required immediate attention. On the screen, abandoned cars and trucks crunched beneath the weight of the titanic jellyfish as it headed north on Seventh, leaving behind a trail of mucus several traffic lanes wide. She was relieved that the monster had manifested uptown, and not down in SoHo where the kids were. Even still, it disturbed her to have this latest monster materialize so close to their home. *Practically next door.*

Johnny rushed out through the air lock, leaving his teammates behind. "Should we go after him?" Ben asked Reed. It was hard to tell if Ben wanted to help the impetuous Torch or beat some sense into him.

Reed shook his head. "No offense to Johnny, but we can't simply keep putting out fires. We need to address this crisis at its source—in the Negative Zone."

"But what if these monsters keep appearing here in the meantime?" Sue asked. "We can't just leave the city unprotected."

"True enough." Reed cast a concerned glance at the chaos in Times Square, then slowly let out his breath. On the screen, the mammoth jellyfish posed an immediate threat to the city and its people. "I'm afraid we have no choice but to adopt a two-pronged strategy. Ben and I will venture into the Zone, to locate the source of these incursions, while you and Johnny can remain here to deal with whatever creatures come through in our absence."

"Sounds like a plan to me," Ben said gruffly. He nodded at the waiting Explorer. " 'Bout time we took that new jalopy for a test-drive." He glanced at Sue. "Too bad you and the squirt can't come along for the ride."

To be honest, Sue was secretly relieved to have avoided another expedition into the Negative Zone. Still, she hated the idea of the team splitting up, even if there didn't seem to be any alternative.

"Promise me you'll be careful," she urged the two men. Despite the urgency of her own mission, she knew she wouldn't rest easy until both Reed and Ben were safely home again. Experience had taught her just how hard staying behind could be, especially where the Zone was concerned. "Please."

"Hey, it's just the Negative Zone," Ben joked. "What could possibly go wrong?"

"Flame on!"

Johnny Storm jumped out the open window, but it was the Human Torch who took to the skies. A sheath of fiery plasma enveloped his body, lifting him high above the city streets below. Below him, the Baxter Building rose thirty-eight stories above the corner of Forty-second Street and Madison Avenue: an imposing steel-and-glass skyscraper built to withstand just about everything short of the umpteenth coming of Galactus. The FF's distinctive 4 symbol was emblazoned upon the landing pad on the roof.

Without a backward glance at his home and headquarters, the Torch flew west toward Times Square at top speed. Within seconds, he spotted the giant jellyfish wreaking havoc upon the panic-stricken tourist trap. *Whoa!* he thought. His wide yellow eyes looked like twin headlights. *That makes that Borer look like a Beanie Baby!*

The monster, which Reed had called a medusa, was even more impressive in real life than it had appeared on the monitor back in the Negative Zone Chamber. Its bell-shaped body was big enough to ski down, with a fringe of tentacles spreading out onto the pavement beneath it. Milky, translucent flesh enclosed an apartment-sized digestive sac that was already filled with trash bins, potted shrubs, motorcycles, and other debris, but, thankfully, no human bodies that Johnny could see. Foot-high eyestalks vibrated frantically atop its glistening bulk. Loud squishing sounds accompanied its slow progress up Seventh Avenue. A fishy smell, like sushi gone bad, permeated the air. Viscous pseudopods lashed out violently at flashing traffic signals, gaudy neon signs, and slow-moving tourists. An empty taxi crumpled loudly as the heavy creature oozed over it.

The Torch gulped at the size of the creature, for the first time wondering if he had bitten off more than he could chew. *Maybe I should have waited for the others?*

But there was no time for second thoughts. Pandemonium reigned below him, as hundreds of frenzied men, women, and children clambered over each other in their desperate attempts to get away from the oncoming medusa. Despite the frantic efforts of the crowd, there was no way to evacuate such a teeming horde in a timely fashion. Bottlenecks formed at every intersection as people fought and clawed to make their way into the relative safety of the nearest cross street. Steadfast police officers, as well as more than a few trigger-happy civilians, fired at the medusa, but their bullets had no effect on the creature's gelatinous bulk. Stung by the medusa's tentacles, innocent victims lay strewn upon the streets and sidewalks, their mucus-covered bodies twitching spasmodically.

At least they're still moving, the Torch thought. In the chaos, it was impossible to tell if anyone had actually been killed yet. Someone else would have to take a toll of the casualties. *My priority is to stop this monster now.*

Even as the Torch hovered over the scene, held aloft by a cocoon of superheated air, the out-of-control creature sideswiped a large neon sign in the shape of a Campbell's soup can. Glass and plastic exploded, showering sparks onto the retreating crowd below. People shrieked in fear and pain as the sparks and debris rained down on them. Injured victims collapsed onto the sidewalk.

Agitated by the cascading sparks, the medusa struck out wildly with its tentacles. Windows shattered and chunks of shattered masonry rained down on the street, smashing through the hoods and windows of gridlocked cars that Johnny prayed were abandoned. Ruptured fire hydrants sprayed streams of water into the air. A cacophony of alarms and sirens assailed Johnny's ears. The smell of spilled gasoline and smoke competed with the briny stench of the colossal invertebrate. A police helicopter watched from above.

"Help!" a strident cry cut through the clamor. "Ohmigod! Please, somebody help me!"

Turning about in midair, the Torch spied a middle-aged window washer suspended outside an office building not far from the creature. The scaffolding supporting the man had been knocked loose by one of the medusa's flailing pseudopods and now dangled at a forty-five-degree angle at least six stories above the slime-covered pavement. The worker clung desperately to the bottom end of the platform, his legs kicking uselessly at the empty air. "Help!" he screamed again. "I can't hold on!"

The Human Torch dived to the rescue, but the man's panicky cries had attracted the medusa as well. A lengthy tentacle reached out and wrapped itself around the man's waist, yanking him free of the dangling scaffolding and pulling him down toward the creature. Beneath its bell-shaped dome, the creature's open mouth gaped hungrily.

Flying toward the screaming man, the Torch hurled a fireball at the offending pseudopod. The flaming sphere smacked against the tentacle and entire creature reacted in pain, quivering from top to bottom. The wounded tentacle thrashed about frenetically, flinging its terrified captive into the air. The man shrieked in fear as he tumbled through the sky, about to become a bloody splat on the sidewalk.

"Hang on, buddy! I've got you!" the Torch called out. Years of practice and training kicked in as he instantly retracted the flames from his arms and grabbed on to the man's outstretched wrists like the catcher in a high-wire act. A couple hundred pounds of panicky New Yorker tugged on Johnny's arms and shoulders, but his flames lifted both men as the Torch soared upward, away from the rampaging medusa. He kept the innocent civilian at arm's length, to avoid frying him, and looked about quickly for a safe place to deposit the poor guy.

A nearby rooftop caught the Torch's eye and he carefully lowered the rescued worker onto the tar-papered roof. "There you go," the Torch reassured the man, hanging in the air a few feet above the building. "Are you okay, dude?"

The man was coated with mucus from the waist down, and his face was slightly sunburned from his close proximity to the Torch, but he appeared to be pretty much intact. Johnny guessed that the man's heavy work clothes had protected him from the medusa's poisonous stingers. "I— I think so," he stammered, checking to make sure he still had the requisite number of arms and legs. "Thanks a lot, man!"

"No problem," the Torch said. Crackling flames distorted his voice. A blasted of concentrated fire melted the lock on a nearby stairway entrance. "Think you can handle it from here?"

"Sure thing!" the guy answered. Escaping certain death

seemed to have done wonders for his spirit. He cocked his head toward the street, where the huge medusa could still be seen looming over multiple lanes of motionless vehicles. "Go get 'im!"

"Will do!" the Torch promised, although he wasn't exactly sure how. Extending his flames back over his arms and hands, he rocketed after the monster. *Easier said than done,* he thought. *How'd you stop a three-story jellyfish anyway?*

By now, the oozing creature had made it to the intersection of Seventh Avenue and Forty-ninth Street. Determined to halt the medusa before it could cause any more damage or casualties, the Torch swooped down and left a trail of flame directly in the monster's path. A gooey tentacle grabbed for him, only to draw back abruptly from the intense heat generated by the flying figure.

Okay, Johnny noted, *at least we've determined that the darn thing's afraid of fire.* He kept safely above the gushing fire hydrants below. *That's something, I guess.*

Circling the medusa like a comet caught in a planetary orbit, he created a blazing ring of fire that trapped the creature right in the middle of the intersection. Its tentacles retracted inwardly, while its twitching eyestalks looked in vain for a way out. It lurched from side to side, unable to get past the burning halo, which was high in the air enough to block the enormous medusa without trapping any hapless refugees in with the monster.

That's better. But now what? The Torch could keep this up for hours if he had to, but that was hardly a workable solution.

Johnny considered his options. A full-scale nova-blast would probably fry the medusa for good, but he was reluctant to kill the creature if he didn't have to, especially since he had no idea how intelligent it was. A few years back, while exploring the Negative Zone, the Fantastic Four had inadvertently destroyed an artificially intelligent city that had turned out to be a sentient being in its own right. He wasn't about to make that mistake again.

I could always wait for the rest of the team. Given a chance, Reed could surely whip something up that could contain the monster. But, no, Johnny didn't want to pass the buck to his certifiably brilliant brother-in-law. Reed had more important things to figure out right now, like how to plug up whatever leaks in the space-time continuum were letting all these creatures through in the first place. *I need to take care of this myself.*

Still, he couldn't keep the medusa in midtown all day. Keeping up his fiery circuit around the frustrated jellyfish, he tried to figure out where he might able to herd the monster. To the west, about five blocks away, the Hudson River divided Manhattan from New Jersey. Johnny was sorely tempted to drive the medusa into the river and let it escape out to the sea (where it would then become the Sub-Mariner's problem).

Nah, he decided reluctantly. Just his luck, the alien creature would start laying eggs the minute it hit the water, and pretty soon the entire Atlantic Ocean would be overrun with monster jellyfish—and it would all be his fault. *That's no good.*

To the east then. It dawned on him that Rockefeller Center was only a couple blocks away. Maybe he could somehow trap the beast in the Center's world-famous ice-skating rink? That might be big enough to hold it. It wasn't a great plan, but it was the best he could come up with. *If nothing else,* he thought, *at least that will get the monster a few blocks closer to the Baxter Building, just in case I need to call in the rest of the team after all.*

Coming to a halt to the left of the medusa, he allowed the ring of fire to die out, then extended both arms and unleashed directed blasts of flame to either side of the monster. The fiery eruptions produced the desired result, sending the medusa heading east on Fiftieth Street. The Torch followed closely behind it, using alternating blasts from his right and left hands to keep the creature on the right track. "That's it!" he urged the fleeing medusa. "Keep on going!"

More empty cars and unlucky streetlights were crushed beneath the monster's path, but the Torch was relieved to see that the city's emergency response teams were beginning to clear the area of potential human casualties. Wooden police barricades closed the nearby streets for blocks in all directions. Flashing lights and blaring sirens testified that the Big Apple's civic defenders were striving to keep the situation under control, although fearful faces peered from the windows of every building. Johnny spotted snipers on the nearby rooftops and was grateful that, unlike certain other superpowered adventurers, he enjoyed a good working relationship with the NYPD, even if the current crisis was definitely out of their league.

Leave this to me, folks! he silently assured the vigilant cops. *I know what I'm doing . . . I think.*

Two blocks of slime-covered real estate later, the medusa oozed alongside Rockefeller Plaza. Ordinarily, at this time of day, the outdoor area would be packed with tourists and other visitors, but the alarming approach of the medusa had sent mobs of people fleeing from the center. Ground-floor doorways were jammed as people trying to escape the surrounding skyscrapers ran into equally desperate crowds seeking shelter in the very same buildings. Overturned tables and chairs crashed to the floor as diners poured out of the plaza café in a panic. Police whistles shrilly attempted to impose order on the bedlam.

Flags from around the world rose above the walls of the sunken skating rink, which was over a hundred feet long and about sixty feet across. Discarded skates littered the ice, as frightened people had fled the scene in their stockinged feet, not even sparing a moment to reclaim their shoes. It was too early in the season for the celebrated Christmas tree to be erected yet, but a gilded statue of Prometheus looked down on a smooth white sheet of ice. The gleaming titan was depicted in the act of stealing the secret of fire from the heavens.

Johnny could relate.

Okay. End of the line. Before the medusa could proceed any farther down Fiftieth, he did an end run around the monster and blocked its path with a scorching wall of flame. A blistering salvo of well-placed fireballs drove the medusa off the street and into the plaza, where it squished over decorative shrubs and benches before reaching the edge of the wall overlooking the skating rink. Flagpoles toppled downward onto the ice, snapped in two by the advancing medusa, which then sagged over the edge of the wall, as if reluctant to go farther. It extended a cautious pseudopod toward the ice below, then retracted it instantly.

How about that? the Torch observed. *It doesn't like the cold either, just like the Blob in that old movie.* An idea occurred to him and he smacked a flaming hand against his equally fiery forehead. *Why didn't I think of that before?*

"Go on!" the Torch shouted, shepherding the hesitant monster over the brink. A gout of red-hot flame, directed at the jellyfish's rear, gave the creature a little extra incentive. "Time to discover your inner ice princess!"

The medusa dropped twenty feet onto the waiting ice rink. It immediately drew in its tentacles and eyestalks, as though huddling from the cold. It tried to slide quickly across the ice, but its viscous mass froze to the rink's icy surface, like a gigantic tongue stuck to a lamp pole. The quivering jellyfish tugged strenuously at its base, leaving behind bits of frozen slime and protoplasm.

Could the medusa free itself in time? Johnny wasn't going to take that chance. *That's a start,* he thought, but putting the medusa on ice for the duration was going to take a lot more heavy-duty refrigeration than one admittedly famous ice rink could muster. He soared over the rink until he was directly above the struggling medusa. *Good thing I know just how to manage that.*

One of the Human Torch's lesser-known abilities, courtesy of the cosmic-ray bombardment, was the power to absorb heat from objects around him. Mostly, he used that talent to put out fires and such, but sometimes, when he really wanted to, he could turn that power up to the max.

Like now.

He closed his eyes and concentrated on sucking all the warmth out of the gelatinous entity below him. The fiery glow around his flaming body multiplied in intensity as thermal energy flowed from the stricken medusa into the Torch, causing the humongous jellyfish to freeze solid in a matter of minutes. Ice frosted over the medusa's translucent form as it grew still and immobile. All of a sudden, the rampaging creature resembled a tremendous mound of frozen yogurt.

His feat left the Torch burning even hotter than usual. He felt uncomfortably warm and feverish, even by his combustible standards. Opening his eyes, he raised his arms above his head and discharged the excess heat in a white-hot pillar of fire that briefly shot above the tops of the nearby skyscrapers. *Whew!* Johnny succumbed to a moment of fatigue. *Haven't pulled that trick for awhile.*

He flew over to the patio overlooking the rink and touched down upon the pavement. Letting his flames die out, he turned to inspect his work. From where he was standing, the frozen medusa didn't look as if it were going anywhere soon.

Works for me, he thought, relieved that he hadn't needed to incinerate the out-of-place creature. His sweaty body smelled of butane. In theory, the medusa could be kept frozen in suspended animation until Reed or somebody else figured out a safe way to unthaw it.

"Excuse me, Mr. Storm!" An attractive-looking Asian woman came running toward him, holding up a badge. A slew of uniformed cops and SWAT team members accompanied her. "Agent Lara Walker of SHIELD," she identified herself. "Can I be of assistance?"

"Definitely," Johnny informed her. SHIELD—the Strategic Hazard International Espionage Logistics Directorate—was exactly the kind of backup the FF could use right now, with qualified people and resources to spare. The Fantastic Four had often worked with SHIELD in the past. "I've got that thing on ice right now. Any chance you folks can keep it that way, at least until we have a chance to send it back where it came from?"

"Like in *The Blob*?" she said with a grin. "I think we can manage that."

Wow, Johnny thought. A SHIELD agent *and* a movie buff. He was tempted to ask for her phone number, except that it was probably classified. "Great," he said. "That's one less thing to worry about."

She peered past him at the gelid monstrosity on the ice. "So how exactly did that thing get here?" she asked him, her playful grin giving way to a more serious expression. "And, more importantly, what are the Fantastic Four planning to do about it?"

His chest insignia buzzed, alerting him to an urgent message from the Baxter Building.

"Hold that thought," he said.

5

"WATCH YOUR ARMS AND LEGS," Reed warned Ben as he prepared to seal the Explorer from the inside.

At present, the passenger module had unfolded like the petals of some immense cybernetic flower, revealing four padded seats radiating outward from the central control core. The Thing and Mr. Fantastic faced each other across the interior of the ship, while Sue and Johnny's seats remained unoccupied. All four seating enclosures were large enough to contain the Thing's bulky form, just in case they needed to switch stations.

"Sure thing, Reed." Ben adjusted the safety straps stretched across his chest. "Ready when you are."

"Very well." Reed turned his head to take one last look at Sue, who was standing behind the nearby control console with a worried look on her face. On the screen behind her, the monitor once more offered a panoply of views from inside the Negative Zone. *I'll be back before you know it,* he promised his wife silently, hoping that would indeed be the case. In truth, time flowed at varying rates throughout the Zone, making it all but impossible to predict how much time would pass on Earth while they were away. It could be minutes, or hours, or days.

No time to worry about that now, he realized. Looking away from Sue, he returned his attention to the launch controls. "Activating the hinge mechanisms now."

The metallic "petals" converged on each other, sealing Reed and Ben inside the bulb-shaped Explorer module. Visi-screens rose from the terminals in front of both men, allowing them to see outside the windowless vessel. Reed waited until the sensors indicated that Sue was safely outside the chamber, then began opening the portal beneath them. A metallic clang penetrated the titanium-steel walls of the Explorer as various security bulkheads retracted. "Internal systems A-OK," he reported, keeping a close eye on the diagnostic readouts. "Stand by for separation."

Automatic clamps released their hold on the Explorer and the capsule dropped into the now-open portal. The ship's downward acceleration tugged on its passengers as the Explorer plummeted down a vertical tunnel that felt as though it was at least a half mile long. One could be forgiven for thinking that the cylindrical shaft ran down the entire length of the Baxter Building.

In fact, however, only the first meter of the gateway existed in the same universe as the famous skyscraper. The bulk of the tunnel's construction extended into subspace, so that the Nega-Portal had no contact with the thirty-plus floors beneath Reed's laboratories. An efficient, not to mention prudent, use of the available real estate.

"Separation completed," Reed announced. Nimble fingers danced across the touch pad in front of him. Keen brown eyes tracked their progress through the portal. "Approaching the Distortion Area. T minus five seconds."

"Roger that," Ben acknowledged. "Stabilizers online."

Reed braced himself for the ordeal ahead. The Distortion

Area, so christened for its disorienting spacial and sensory effects, was a transitional plane between the positive and negative universes—and generally the most grueling phase of the journey.

"Hold on to your lunch," Ben muttered. "Here we go again."

The Explorer exited the bottom of the shaft with a sudden, jarring lurch. Mr. Fantastic's elastic physiognomy absorbed the brunt of the shock, but he felt sorry for the Thing's more rigid skeleton. Reed's center of gravity seemed to shift erratically, and time itself appeared to slow down. Their smooth descent grew choppier, as cyclonic forces buffeted the tiny vessel, causing it to rock violently from side to side, like a primitive raft atop a churning sea. Across the cockpit, Ben's face was scrunched in concentration as he worked the flight controls, fighting to keep the Explorer on course and not spinning like a top. Reed knew he was in good hands; Ben was one of the best pilots he had ever known.

Despite the Explorer's state-of-the-art shielding, a kaleidoscopic profusion of colors invaded the interior of the module, playing across the taut faces of both men. Unnaturally bright and vibrant, the colors seemed to belong to a spectrum beyond ordinary human perception. Reed theorized that the psychedelic display did not truly come from outside the ship, but was rather generated by his own overwhelmed optic nerves, as they attempted to cope with an nth-dimensional continuum they were not equipped to deal with. Even when he closed his eyes, the polychromatic chaos remained just as vivid and unsettling.

The sensory confusion produced all manner of strange, synesthetic effects. Reed *heard* the images flashing on his

monitors. He *tasted* the sound of his own breathing and
Ben's distracted grunts. He could *feel* the clean, antiseptic
smell of the cockpit upon his skin, *smell* the texture of the
gleaming steel control panel. He *saw* the taste of his own
dry mouth.

As unsettling as it was, however, the Distortion effect
was a vital part of his and Ben's transition to the Negative
Zone, in that the process converted every molecule in
their bodies from matter to antimatter. Without that crucial transformation, they would each be doomed to explode the first time their positive-matter bodies came into
contact with the substance of the Negative Zone, just as
the Scavenger, the Borer, and the immense jellyfish must
have been converted to positive matter during their own
trips through the Distortion Area.

Not that this knowledge made the turbulent passage
any easier to endure. Nausea threatened, but, thankfully,
Mr. Fantastic's control over his amazingly pliable body extended to his stomach. *I just need to hold on for a few more
minutes,* he reminded himself. *Subjective time, that is.*

"I hate this part," Ben said succinctly.

Then the frenetic shaking subsided and Reed's vision,
among other things, returned to normal. He glanced
down at his visi-screen, which relayed visual and auditory
data from the Explorer's external sensors.

Outside the module, what looked like the vacuum of
space stretched in all directions. Asteroids and diffuse, lu-
minescent gas clouds drifted across the monitor. Distant
stars, much more closely packed than in Earth's own universe, glittered in the distance. A weird amoeba-like creature, at least three football fields across, swam across the
void. As if sensing the Explorer's presence, it moved speed-
ily away in the opposite direction.

We made it, Mr. Fantastic realized. *We're in the Negative Zone.*

"Boy," Ben said sarcastically, "this place looks just as warm and invitin' as always." He peered at his own monitor, which offered him the same view as Reed's. A repulsor screen protected the Explorer from all but the largest pieces of space debris. "How'd we manage to stay away so long?"

Despite the danger, the scientist in Reed took more than a moment to marvel at the wide-ranging cosmos before them. Here was an entirely alien universe to explore, full of all-new wonders and discoveries just waiting to be probed. *What a shame,* he reflected, *that the hostile beings here have so seldom allowed us the luxury of pure scientific research and exploration. Who knows what amazing secrets the Negative Zone might still hold?*

Pressing a button on his control pad, Reed switched the image on the visi-screen to a view from the rear of the Explorer. Behind them, the outer fringes of the Debris Belt guarded the Annihilation Vortex. A crimson-scaled dragon soared past the Belt, reminding Reed that, unlike conventional space, the seemingly empty void outside in fact possessed a breathable atmosphere. As a result, sound waves propagated themselves readily through the universal ether. The wail of the departing dragon echoed across space.

Yet another way in which this cosmos is fundamentally different from our own, Reed thought. In the positive-matter universe, as governed by Einsteinian physics and the four fundamental forces, gaseous vapors were attracted by gravity to planets and moons of sufficient mass, so that atmospheres were concentrated around large solid bodies, leaving outer space a vacuum. But not in the Negative

Zone, which suggested the existence of some sort of repulsive force unknown to the positive universe. *Even time and gravity work very differently here.*

Although the entire Zone was immeasurably vast, the access shaft from the Baxter Building invariably deposited them somewhere in the vicinity of the Vortex. Was this because this particular region was somehow contiguous with Earth, Reed speculated, or did the Vortex's intense gravitational pull somehow attract his transdimensional probes? He leaned toward the latter theory; the Vortex appeared to be nothing less than a nexus of realities, the very crossroads of infinity.

We still have so very much to learn here. . . .

Ben was less inclined to rhapsodize on the unplumbed mysteries of the Negaverse. "So now what?" His deep voice echoed within the cramped confines of the module.

"We stick to the plan," Reed said tersely.

"Got ya." Rocky fingers manipulated a control panel that had been ergonomically designed to accommodate four-fingered hands with unusually blocky digits. "Sit back and enjoy the ride."

Photonic thrusters flared to life upon the Explorer's undercarriage, and the untested vessel began cruising away from the Debris Belt and out into the wider expanse of the Negative Zone. Artificial gravity kept Mr. Fantastic and the Thing oriented with respect to the floor, regardless of which way the capsule was pointing. As usual, Reed let Ben do the piloting, while Reed monitored the data streaming in from the Explorer's sensors. So far, he could not see anything that might account for the disturbing incidents back on Earth.

"Gotta hand it to ya," Ben commented. "This baby handles like a dream." A sizable asteroid blocked their path, but Ben deftly guided the Explorer around the obstacle. "Reminds me of a '57 Mustang I used to drive."

Reed remembered the automobile well. He and Ben went back a long ways, ever since they had been roommates at California State University. "I'm glad you approve," Reed said warmly. "Linked quantum processors improved the responsiveness of the navigational controls by a factor of—"

"Sheesh!" Ben exclaimed, interrupting Reed's explanation. "I was just tryin' to pay ya a compliment, not askin' fer a lecture on engineering!"

Reed did not take offense at his friend's outburst. He was well aware that, in his scientific enthusiasm, he tended to be long-winded at times; Sue had often teased him on this point. "My apologies," he said mildly. "I'll spare you the full details."

"Ah, it's no big deal," Ben said, shrugging his mountainous shoulders. "Prob'ly way over my head anyway."

A high-pitched beep intruded on the conversation. "The proximity sensors!" Reed announced. He called up the appropriate display on his console. "I'm reading one—no, two!—contacts on an intercept course with the Explorer. Sensor analysis indicates the presence of artificial alloys and a tachyon-powered star drive." His face assumed a grave cast. "These are ships, not asteroids."

"Sounds like we got company." Ben scratched unconsciously at the plaster over his wounded shoulder. "Wanna bet they ain't comin' just to check out our passports?"

"I suspect you're right." The only question was which hostile entity they were about to encounter. *Annihilus? Blastaar? Or some new menace we've never confronted before?* In any event, Reed was not too surprised by this tense turn of events. The Negative Zone had never been friendly to outsiders.

Within minutes, the alien vessels came within visual range. Identical in size and shape, they appeared to be eight-man scout ships, only slightly larger than the Explorer itself. The undercarriages of both ships bristled with armaments, while jagged fins sprouted from their dark red hulls, the better to slice through the pervasive atmosphere of this dimension's version of outer space. Intimidation seemed to have factored into the shipbuilder's designs as much as aerodynamics.

Reed recognized the design of the ships as Baluurian in origin. *Blastaar's people.* In the past, the oppressed citizens of the planet Baluur had attempted to banish Blastaar from their realm, but the tyrant had always managed to regain control of his empire eventually, thanks in part to his innate superabilities. As far as Reed knew, Blastaar was still in power in this sector of the Negative Zone, and it would foolhardy to assume otherwise. *If only a more reasonable Baluurian could someday assume the throne.*

"Hmmph. These mooks again," Ben grunted. He had evidently identified the design of the two spacecraft as well. "Shoulda known they'd be showin' up in no time." His craggy face took on a pugnacious expression. "Brace yerself, Stretch. Here comes the welcome wagon."

A flashing light on Reed's control panel indicated an incoming transmission. He activated the receiver, which instantly set itself to the correct frequency.

The alien face that appeared upon the visi-screen was unmistakably Baluurian. A leonine mane of dark gray fur framed a broad face whose bestial features hinted at feline descent. The being's skin was a lighter shade of gray. Sharpened canines added to the ferocious look of the other space traveler; the Baluurians were clearly not vegetarians.

"Attention, foreign vessel!" a deep, guttural voice

addressed them. An automatic translator converted the alien tongue to English. "This is Lieutenant Grajeer of the Baluurian patrol ship *Tyanna's Seed*. You have trespassed on the Empire of Blastaar the Supreme. Surrender at once!"

Well, that settles the question of whether Blastaar is still in charge, Reed thought. He attempted to reason with the aggressive patrol ships, even knowing it was likely to be a futile effort. "Attention, Baluurian ships. We are here on a peaceful mission of exploration. We mean you no harm. Please permit us to pass through your space unobstructed."

As there was no love lost between Blastaar and the Fantastic Four, he carefully avoided identifying himself. He sent only an audio transmission in order to reduce the chances of them being recognized by Blastaar's troops. Perhaps the patrol ships were unaware that the Explorer had emerged from the Distortion Area?

"Permission denied!" Grajeer responded angrily. "This is not a negotiation. Surrender or be destroyed!"

As if to drive home its commander's point, *Tyanna's Seed* fired a warning shot across the Explorer's path. A sizzling beam of ionic energy flashed through the ether, missing the module's nose by less than a yard. The second Baluurian ship fired as well, targeting the space behind the Explorer. For a moment, the earthship was caught between the destructive beams. Reed could hear the thrum of the interceptors' star drives.

"This is your final warning," Grajeer snarled. "Lower your repulsor screens and identify yourselves!"

"Nuts to this!" the Thing replied. He tapped decisively on the flight controls and a manual control stick sprouted from the console in front of him. He gripped the reinforced-steel stick with his right hand while working the control panel with his left. "Time to say bye-bye."

The nose of the Explorer swung upward ninety degrees, then the entire module shot out from between the two Baluurian patrol ships, which immediately took off in pursuit of the fleeing Earth vessel. Coruscating crimson beams chased after the Explorer as well, forcing Ben to resort to constant evasive maneuvers. The silver module veered and spun erratically, its random flight path keeping the Explorer one step ahead of the crimson beams, but making it harder to put any significant distance between the module and its determined pursuers.

"They ain't givin' up on us anytime soon," Ben predicted. The image on his visi-screen was divided between the space in front of them and the accelerating patrol ships on their rear. A high-intensity beam collided against their repulsor screens, causing the hull to vibrate alarmingly. Electrons clashed loudly outside. "How 'bout a little coverin' fire, if ya ain't too busy?"

"Understood," Reed said, calling up the Explorer's own weapons system. Part of him regretted that it had been necessary to equip the ship with arms in the first place, but, given the Fantastic Four's strife-filled history with the Negative Zone, it would have been beyond foolish not to be prepared for combat. Omnidirectional firing mechanisms telescoped out from the Explorer's streamlined steel hull. "Weapon systems engaged."

Necessity notwithstanding, the Explorer's weapons were strictly nonlethal. Reverse tractor beams, mostly, and focused electromagnetic pulses. Reed instructed the ship's computer to target both Baluurian vessels and watched on his monitor as amethyst-colored repulsor beams shot from four separate projectors, intersecting with the blasts from the enemy ships.

Unfortunately, the same evasive tactics Ben was using

to elude the Baluurian attacks made it equally difficult to get a good shot at their pursuers. Still, Reed was willing to put his own computerized targeting system up against any competitor. *Just try and match the sophistication of my algorithms,* he thought defiantly. *And the near-instantaneous speed of the computations.*

His first salvo of repulsor beams missed their targets, but forced both *Tyanna's Seed* and its sister ship to veer from their courses to avoid being hit. The Explorer pulled farther ahead of its foes as the Baluurian vessels were compelled to approach their prey cautiously. Their own beams continued to target the Earthship, however, striking glancing blows against the Explorer's shields. Flashing alert lights informed Reed that the periodic strikes were taking their toll on the ship's overtaxed repulsor screens. Primary systems shut down, forcing the backups to come online. *If this keeps up,* he realized, *we're going to be down to our hull plating soon.*

Taking a risk, Reed decided to concentrate all their weapons on one ship at a time. Ignoring *Tyanna's Seed,* which was lagging slightly behind the other Baluurian vessel, he directed a two-pronged attack at the nameless second ship.

First, a concentrated repulsor beam slammed head-on into the nose of the patrol ship, slowing its forward momentum. The noise sounded like a train wreck.

Second, Reed hit the stalled vessel with a coherent electromagnetic pulse that disrupted the ship's internal circuitry. Its ionic cannons fell silent and the entire ship slowed to a stop as the prismatic glow of its thrusters blinked out in an instant.

"Attaboy, Reed!" Ben enthused. "You really nailed 'em good!"

But for how long? Reed wondered. His past examinations of captured Negative Zone technology suggested that basic electrical principles held true on both sides of the dimensional barrier, but he knew that he couldn't afford to take anything for granted. *Who knows how quickly the power-dampening effects of the EMP will persist in this alien universe?*

Still, at least he had evened the odds a bit, if only for the moment.

Grajeer's voice exploded over the speakers. "How dare you fire upon a Baluurian warship? So much for your 'peaceful' pretenses! You will pay for this indignity with your miserable lives!"

Reed was tempted to point out that they had fired only in self-defense, but decided that would simply be a waste of breath. This Lieutenant Grajeer sounded almost as bellicose as Blastaar himself, if such a thing was possible.

"You and what army?" Ben challenged the remaining patrol ship. Now that they were no longer outnumbered, he turned the Explorer around to take on *Tyanna's Seed* head-to-head. Reed concentrated their repulsor beams on the oncoming ship, hoping perhaps to duplicate his success with the other Baluurian vessel, but the reverse tractor beams managed only a glancing blow against the starboard hull of *Tyanna's Seed,* knocking Grajeer's ship briefly off-course. The patrol ship quickly corrected its flight path and continued to charge, guns blazing, at the Explorer. Ben dipped and soared in response to the attacks, so that the crimson beams zipped past them harmlessly. "Missed again!" he taunted his opponent. "I've seen better shootin' from the pip-squeaks at Coney Island!"

Now there's *a reference that must be giving the automatic translator a workout,* Reed thought. Before he could comment as much, however, the Explorer was suddenly rocked by a plethora of blasts against its hull. At the same time, the proximity alarm went into overdrive, warning of multiple contacts arriving on the scene.

On the visi-screen, an armada of Baluurian warships, of varied size and configuration, zoomed into view. Ionic cannons and electron-torpedo launchers jutted from every exposed surface. The roar of dozens of powerful engines sent shock waves through the ether.

Reinforcements, Reed realized as he silenced the blaring alarm. For all he knew, Blastaar himself might be commanding one of newly arrived vessels. *Perhaps that imposing battle cruiser at the center of the armada?* The ship in question was over three hundred meters long, which made it at least twice as large as the nearest comparable vessel. Sharply pointed ailerons sprouted from the conical hull of the immense spacecraft, which tapered away from its bulbous prow, so the mighty warship resembled a flying mace. Smaller vessels zoomed ahead of the cruiser, leading the chase like a huntsman's dogs.

"What the—!" the Thing exclaimed. "Where did they come from?"

Sector 56-D, Reed thought. *Center of the Baluurian Empire.* He was impressed at how quickly Blastaar's forces had detected their presence in the Negative Zone. "We're seriously outnumbered, Ben. I recommend the better course of valor."

"Ya don't need to tell me twice, Stretcho!" Ben pulled sharply on the control column and the Explorer took off at right angles from both *Tyanna's Seed* and what seemed like the entire Baluurian navy. He opened up the throttle and the sudden acceleration put a strain on the module's vibranium-based inertial compensators, yanking Mr. Fantastic back into the padding of his seat. His malleable face and frame were momentarily stretched out of shape by the intense g-forces, but quickly snapped back into place with an audible twang.

Energy blasts continued to bombard the Explorer from all directions, and Reed monitored their destructive impact with increasing concern. Ever since that first spaceflight years ago, when he had failed to provide Ben and the others with sufficient protection against those fateful cosmic rays, Reed had never skimped on shielding; even still, he knew that the Explorer's hull and repulsor screens could not long withstand a barrage of this magnitude. Already, the screens were buckling beneath the onslaught. Warning lights flashed all over his control panel, as crucial systems threatened to go off-line. The artificial gravity shut down altogether, causing his stomach to lurch sickeningly. Beads of sweat peeled off his forehead and began floating about within the passenger compartment.

"Too bad we had to leave Suzie behind," Ben grumbled. "We could use a little force-field action right now."

The Explorer fired back with repulsor beams and EMP pulses, but the occasional strike did little to deter the enemy fleet; it was like trying to quell a riot with a single Taser. Reed winced at the damage being inflicted on the previously pristine module. One by one, searing blasts pruned the Explorer of its guns, leaving it unarmed. *Quite a maiden voyage this is turning out to be,* Reed thought ruefully. *Let's hope it's not a farewell cruise as well.*

Worse yet, the attacking ships were driving the Explorer back toward the Debris Belt—and the deadly Vortex beyond. Was this a deliberate strategy on their foes' part, forcing the Explorer and its passengers to choose between surrender and certain destruction? Reed almost admired the ruthless logic at work.

Ben saw where they were heading, too. "Dammit!" he exclaimed. "They're steerin' us right toward the Big Gulp." The Explorer pitched and yawed as he tried to veer off in another direction, but Blastaar's navy hemmed him in at almost every angle, leaving him nowhere to flee except toward the Annihilation Area surrounding the Vortex. "Can't break loose of this squeeze play!"

Another hit rocked the interior of the module. The smell of burning circuitry assailed Reed's nostrils. Smoke contaminated the cockpit, spreading outward like a vaporous globule in the zero gravity. A blinking yellow warning light turned solid red. "We've lost thruster control!"

"Tell me about it!" Ben said testily. Out of control, the Explorer spiraled helplessly toward the Debris Belt, which was now only fifty kilometers away. The Thing energetically worked the rudder, but to no avail. "The controls ain't respondin' at all! They're as dead as we're gonna be in about a minute or two!"

No exaggerating there. On their visi-screens, massive asteroids loomed directly ahead, growing larger with every passing heartbeat. Without the ability to maneuver, there seemed to be no way Ben could keep the Explorer from slamming into one or more floating hunks of rock. And, even if by some miracle, they managed to avoid being pulped by the maze of shifting rubble, there was still the Vortex to contend with. In his mind's eye, Reed could readily imagine the battered Explorer exploding into atoms the second it reached the event horizon of the Vortex. No doubt Blastaar would rejoice at the sight.

The Debris Belt was only minutes away. If they were

going to act, it had to be now. "Abandon ship!" Reed ordered. "Eject!"

He pressed the Emergency Release button and his entire seating enclosure burst free of the Explorer, propelled by explosive bolts. Reed tumbled head over heels through the ether while he hurriedly fumbled with his safety straps. He disengaged himself from the attached seat until only his emergency flight harness remained strapped to his body. He took a deep breath of the Negative Zone's peculiar atmosphere, grateful that he had not been ejected into the deadly vacuum of ordinary space.

But what about Ben? Mr. Fantastic used his flying harness to gain control of his zero-gravity cartwheeling and maneuvered himself until he had a clear view of the Explorer as it spiraled into the outer fringes of the Debris Belt. The silver capsule was missing one slice—and one slice only. Ben's seating compartment had not yet ejected from the doomed vessel.

"Ben!" Reed activated the comm link on his chest. "Where are you? You need to eject now!"

"I'm tryin' to!" The Thing's irate voice was broken up by bursts of static, possibly due to electromagnetic interference from the Vortex itself. "The stupid button ain't workin'!"

"Use the manual override!" Reed shouted. He caught his breath as a space boulder the size of Plymouth Rock narrowly missed colliding with the Explorer. His right arm stretched toward the speeding module, as if wanting to reach in and activate the release himself, but the Explorer was already too far away. At about fifteen hundred feet, the attenuated limb hit its limit and could go no farther. Grimacing in pain, Mr. Fantastic retracted his arm, helpless to save his friend from what appeared to be certain annihilation. "Hurry, Ben, while you still have a chance!"

Drifting asteroids obscured his view. The Explorer disappeared into the cluster of debris, while Reed looked on from several kilometers away. Even though he knew what had to be coming, he still flinched involuntarily as a sudden conflagration flared somewhere inside the Debris Belt. The enormous fireball billowed up midway through the Belt, visible through the gaps between the boulders. A thunderous din reached Reed's ears. A shock wave rippled across the ring of asteroids. "Ben!" he called out hoarsely. *"BEN!"*

Only silence and static came through the open comm link.

Mr. Fantastic found himself floating alone in the blackness of interstellar space. The violet glow of the Vortex, along with the explosive matter–antimatter reactions along its event horizon, illuminated his abysmal surroundings. Across the ether, he could hear the rumbling of heavy boulders crashing against each other. The air smelled faintly of smoke and ozone. The ambient temperature, although chilly, was enough to sustain human life. His flying harness carried him away from the Debris Belt, toward the enemy armada.

He stared bleakly at the deadly ring of rubble that had apparently claimed the life of his oldest friend, but the Baluurian ships allowed him little time to mourn. "Attention, intruder!" a raspy voice addressed him via his comm link. "This is the imperial flagship, *Burstaar's Revenge.* Your ship and comrade have paid the price for your unlawful defiance. You will now be taken into custody, to await the judgment of Blastaar the Supreme. If you are wise, you will offer no further resistance."

A dozen or more search beams converged on Mr. Fantastic, all but blinding him. Seconds later, he felt the pull of a tractor beam lock onto him. A swift assessment of his situation convinced Reed that there was little point in attempting to escape. Where could he go, what could he accomplish, stuck out in space, light-years away from the nearest inhabited planet? At worst, he would end up sucked into the Vortex himself, once the propulsion unit on his harness lost power.

If Blastaar or one of his minions was behind the incursions back on Earth, this might be his best and only chance to get to the bottom of the mystery.

If only Ben were here to join him . . . !

Reed switched off his flying harness, conserving its power, and submitted to the demanding pull of the tractor beam. Countless gunports aimed their weapons at Reed, prepared to blast him to atoms at the first sign of resistance. Squinting into the glare of the search beams, he was not surprised to find himself being sucked toward the imposing battle cruiser he had noticed earlier. The imperial flagship, he presumed. A heavily armored bay door slid open in the dark red hull of the ship, exposing a gaping maw toward which Reed was irresistibly drawn. He wondered if Blastaar himself would be among the welcoming party.

Could be worse, he consoled himself. At least he hadn't fallen into the hands of Annihilus instead.

Blastaar was merely a barbaric warlord, fond of enforcing his will through brute force. Annihilus, on the other hand, was a threat of a distinctly higher order of magnitude. *If we're lucky, he has nothing to do with this entire affair.* The shadowy bay opening filled Reed's view, before swallowing him up completely.

6

"THEY'VE LEFT ALREADY? WITHOUT US?"

Johnny couldn't believe what Sue had just told him. Standing here in Rockefeller Plaza, on a sunny Saturday afternoon, it was hard to grasp that Reed and Ben were already a universe away, somewhere inside the Negative Zone. He glanced at the frozen medusa, still safely immobile upon the ice-skating rink. At Agent Walker's instructions, New York cops and SHIELD technicians stumbled out onto the ice, toting a combination of both high-tech cryogenic units and old-fashioned fire extinguishers. Johnny was impressed by the female agent's efficiency.

"What's the deal?" he asked his sister, annoyed at being left behind. "They couldn't wait for me to finish up here?"

Sue's voice emerged from the **4** on his chest. "It was nothing personal, Johnny. This was the only plan that made sense. Ben's the pilot and Reed's the scientist. It's logical that they be the ones to take the Explorer into the Negaverse. You and I need to stay here to cope with whatever comes through the rifts in the meantime."

"Well, when you put it that way . . . ," Johnny conceded. A few feet away, Lara Walker listened in on the conversation while occasionally barking orders into her own communicator. "Sounds like we've got the easier job."

"Knock on wood," Sue said. An alarm sounded in the background and he could hear her voice grow tense. "Hang on! Sensors are detecting another incursion. Let me call up the coordinates." Johnny and Walker exchanged a worried glance as, seven blocks south, Sue fiddled with the sensor controls. "I've got it. Down in the Flatiron District, around Twenty-third Street."

"I'm on it!" Johnny told his sister. He turned to Lara Walker. "Got to split. You okay here?"

"Go to it, hero," she told him.

Content to leave the medusa in the agent's capable hands, Johnny stepped away from the woman and indulged in a little spontaneous human combustion. "Flame on!"

The Human Torch took to the sky, quickly clearing the buildings surrounding the plaza. Trailing a tail of fire behind him, he jetted downtown as fast as his superheated plasma could carry him. The Flatiron District was less than thirty blocks south—he would be there in seconds.

In the meantime, he maintained an open comm link to Sue. "Any word on our latest visitor?"

"Not yet," she reported, her voice sounding as though she were flying right there with him. "Just the usual reports of a bright green flash, followed by thunder." He could hear her monitoring the local news reports. "Wait! Someone's claiming to have spotted some sort of winged creature over the Flatiron. Details are sketchy. There's no footage yet."

"Never mind," he told her. "I'm almost there."

Why fuss over the news when he could check things out for himself?

"Be careful, Johnny."

"Don't worry about me," he said, rolling his eyes. Sometimes Sue forgot that he wasn't a kid anymore, and that she didn't need to be his overprotective older sister. *I took care of that jumbo jellyfish, didn't I?* He wondered what kind of freakish creature had come through the rift this time.

Another Scavenger?

That shouldn't be too tough to handle.

Madison Square Park stretched beneath him as he approached the Flatiron District, named for the landmark building looming directly ahead. Located on a triangular wedge of real estate at the intersection of Fifth Avenue and Broadway, the Flatiron was New York's oldest skyscraper, erected way back in 1902. At one time the tallest building in the world, the twenty-two-story structure had long since been dwarfed by its successors, but remained a favorite of photographers and architecture buffs.

And apparently, Negative Zone monsters as well.

At first, the Torch could not detect anything amiss. He listened for the screams of panicked citizens, but, unlike before, there appeared to be no rampaging creature running amuck in the streets below. He searched the sky for what Sue had alluded to, yet all he spotted was a TV newscopter in search of a scoop. The cameraman aboard the copter gave the Torch a friendly wave as he turned his lens on the blazing super hero. Johnny started to wave back.

Then a blast of bright yellow energy blew the copter out of the sky.

The Torch froze in midair. "Oh my God!" he gasped. Nothing was left of the copter except for a few blackened ashes that rained down on the streets below. It had all happened so quickly that for a moment it hardly seemed real; it took Johnny a second or two to accept that the copter and its occupants had been literally disintegrated before his very eyes.

Who? How?

The fatal blast had come from the roof of the Flatiron Building. Staring down at the roof in horror, he spotted a winged figure standing atop the Flatiron, where the angled prow of the building pointed uptown past the park. He had briefly mistaken the figure for a gargoyle before, but now he remembered that, wait, the Flatiron didn't have any gargoyles. The Torch descended toward the roof below, feeling a growing sense of apprehension. No mere Scavenger had produced the blast that had destroyed the helicopter.

Please, he prayed, *don't let it be* him!

But a closer look at the creature confirmed his worst fears.

"Oh my God, Sis," he whispered. "It's Annihilus!"

The dreaded creature, known throughout the Negative Zone as the Living Death Who Walks, was of roughly human height and proportions, but any resemblance to *Homo sapiens* ended there. An armored exoskeleton, tinted in various shades of green and purple, protected every square inch of his body. Vicious spikes protruded from the heavy plates draped over his shoulders, while a raised purple collar shielded his neck and skull. Scalloped batwings, not unlike those of his loyal Scavengers, flared from his back, so that he looked like a demon freshly escaped from hell.

Which was a pretty accurate description.

Unlike conventional armor, his exoskeleton was not constructed from metal but rather looked to have been grown from some sort of chitinous material, like the carapace of an enormous insect. Annihilus claimed to have

evolved centuries ago from a primitive arthropod on a remote planet in the Negative Zone, and his vaguely insectile appearance seemed to bear that out. To be honest,
Johnny had always been a little fuzzy on where Annihilus
ended and his armor began.

His jade-green mask was insectile as well. Dark green
eyes peered out through bulging, convex lenses, above a
set of hinged mandibles. Antennaed audio receivers concealed his ears. Overlapping strips of nacreous shell transformed the faceplate into an armored helmet. As far as
Johnny knew, only Alicia Masters had ever been shown
the face beneath that noseless mask, and, of course, the
blind sculptress had been deprived of (or spared) the
sight.

Lucky her.

Mounted to the bottom of Annihilus's collar, directly
below his chin, was a six-inch-long cylinder, approximately two inches in diameter. This was the Cosmic
Control Rod, the source of the invader's omnipotence and
his prized possession to boot. Even without the golden
Rod, the insectoid was a dangerous adversary. With it, he
was damn near unstoppable.

This is a nightmare. I mean, this is the worst *thing that could
happen right now.*

No surprise, Annihilus quickly spied the blazing figure
in the sky above him. "Johnny Storm!" he intoned. His inhuman voice lacked any sort of human warmth or feeling.
Unnerving clicks and buzzes hinted at a larynx more bug-
like than mammalian. "Once more we meet! But this time
we clash within your unsuspecting universe, not my own!"

"Oh yeah!" the Torch challenged him. He longed to
avenge the murdered helicopter crew, but knew better
than to charge carelessly at the powerful alien. *I need to be*

smart about this. Annihilus claimed to be more than a thousand years old, and Johnny had no reason to doubt him—the homicidal monster hadn't lasted that long by being a pushover. "What are you doing here?!"

With a single flap of his mighty wings, Annihilus rose to meet him. The searing flames enveloping the Human Torch appeared to deter the invader not at all. "Annihilus requires no invitation, mortal! I go where I please, and death goes with me!"

Johnny knew Annihilus was not exaggerating. The ultimate paranoid, Annihilus was driven to destroy everything and everybody that threatened his own precious immortality. The insectoid lived in fear of having the Cosmic Control Rod stolen from him and therefore sought to wipe out every other sentient life-form first. He took this radical doctrine of preemptive war to an insane, genocidal extreme.

And now he was here on Earth.

"You didn't have to kill those people! What do you want here, anyway?" the Torch demanded, afraid that he already knew. Part of him was just trying to put off the inevitable battle for a few more minutes; he wasn't looking forward to facing Annihilus all on his lonesome.

A dry, raspy cackle escaped the insectoid's throat. "Are you playing the fool, Johnny Storm, or are you truly feebleminded?" His wings flapped indignantly, over seven feet wide from tip to tip. "Have you forgotten all the times you and your accursed clan have threatened my dominion over the Negative Zone? And how others of your species nearly destroyed me?"

Oh, that, Johnny remembered. He knew Annihilus was referring to the so-called N-Raiders, a group of rival explorers who had used their own Nega-Portal to try to exploit the untapped resources of the Zone, eventually capturing Annihilus in an attempt to drain the power from his Cosmic Control Rod. Although Annihilus had ultimately freed himself from the N-Raiders' trap, his ordeal had weakened him enough that another human warrior, who called himself Hellscout, had been able to inflict what had seemed like fatal injuries on the vulnerable insectoid. *Too bad they didn't take,* Johnny thought. Hellscout had stabbed Annihilus through the thorax and even chopped off the insectoid's head, but Annihilus had still managed to regenerate himself over time. Just as he always did.

"That wasn't our fault!" the Torch insisted. His temperature rose as his voice grew more heated. "The Fantastic Four had nothing to do with that. We wanted to *stop* the N-Raiders!"

Annihilus dismissed Johnny's protests with an imperious wave of his hand. "What do I care of your insignificant squabbles and divisions? Time and again, your universe has proven itself a mortal threat to my own existence. I cannot—will not—rest until I have subdued the positive universe—and destroyed your entire miserable species!"

Without warning, he turned his Cosmic Control Rod against the Flatiron itself. The golden cylinder flashed brightly—and an incandescent burst of energy smashed through the roof, blowing apart the floors below. Windows all along the top five floors of the building exploded outward, showering glass on the streets below. Smoke, flames, and anguished screams rose from the blackened crater at Annihilus's feet. From what he glimpsed of the devastation, Johnny was surprised there was anybody still alive to scream.

"You bloodthirsty freak!" he raged. He didn't want to think about how many lives had just been snuffed out by

Annihilus's outburst. Dozens of people killed, solely to punctuate the monster's maniacal threats. "No more!" the Torch shouted over the flames crackling over his body.

Annihilus wasn't the only one who appreciated the value of a preemptive strike. Summoning up his own power, the Human Torch unleashed a scorching blast of white-hot flame at the bat-winged insectoid. He knew better than to waste time with any measly fireballs; this burst was hot enough to melt concrete. *Take that, you murderer!*

But the scalding flames splashed over Annihilus like so much dishwater. "Ignorant mortal!" he mocked Johnny. "My Cosmic Control Rod has kept me alive for more than a millennium. See how it shields me from your pitiful assault!" He flapped toward the Torch, heedless of the hero's spectacular pyrotechnics. "The only reason I have not slain you yet is that I require certain information from you first. Tell me now, human: Where can I find what is known as . . . the Baxter Building?"

What? The Torch jetted away from his enemy to stay safely out of Annihilus's reach. What did the monster want with the Baxter Building, except perhaps revenge on the rest of the Fantastic Four? Johnny was surprised that Annihilus apparently needed directions, but perhaps that wasn't so odd once Johnny stopped and thought about it; the FF had managed to keep the fiendish insectoid confined to the Negative Zone for years now, with his rare incursions into this universe seldom spreading beyond the reinforced steel walls of the Baxter Building itself. No wonder he wasn't familiar with the layout of New York City. *It's not exactly like he can look us up in Fodor's.*

"No way!" he hollered at Annihilus. He flew higher, trying to put as much distance as possible between Annihilus and the innocent people below. *As long as he's after me,* the Torch thought, *he's not blasting away at anyone else.* Still, the last thing he wanted to do was show his foe the way back to the Baxter Building and Sue, especially if that was where Annihilus wanted to go. His recent brush with death seemed to have left Annihilus even more murderously crazed than ever. "You're not getting anything out of me!"

"Spare me your meaningless bravado!" Annihilus hissed. His wings carried him upward at surprising speed; it was all the Torch could do to keep one step ahead of him. Outstretched purple gauntlets reached for their prey. "I shall wring the truth from you with my own hands!"

"First you've got to catch me!" Johnny taunted, but his gibes rang hollow to his own ears. He was already winded from freezing the medusa earlier, while Annihilus was endowed with near-limitless cosmic energy, thanks to that damn Rod of his. *I've got to find some way to level the playing field!*

Snatching the Cosmic Control Rod was his best shot, but it was risky, in that it meant coming close enough to Annihilus to make a grab for it. *This could go south really fast,* he thought. But what other choice did he have? Nobody ever said being a super hero was going to be easy.

First, he needed to catch Annihilus off-guard. A blinding flash sounded like just what the doctor ordered, so the Torch marshaled his strength and put all his effort into generating light instead of heat. For a second, he flared up brighter than the sun, emitting an incandescent brilliance that lit up the sky. At the same instant, he squeezed his own eyes shut, just to avoid dazzling himself.

His tactic appeared to pay off. "My eyes!" Annihilus keened, throwing his hands up in front of his face. Johnny had hoped that the insectoid's vision, accustomed to the murky depths of the Negative Zone, would be vulnerable to a blinding flash of light. "Vile creature! Your trickery will not save you!"

Who knew how long the effect would last? Seizing his chance, the Torch dived at his disabled foe. He zipped right past Annihilus, so near that he could hear the monster's dry, insectile buzzing, smell an odor like formic acid from Annihilus's breath and carapace. The golden casing of the Cosmic Control Rod glinted in the sunlight and Johnny grabbed for it with his right hand. He didn't bother to extinguish the flames around his fingers; past experience had taught him that the Rod could not be harmed by a little fire. His fingers came within an inch of the gleaming cylinder— only to be repelled by a force field that emitted bright blue sparks upon contact. An electric jolt stung his fingers, and he yanked back his arm empty-handed. "Damn!"

"Thieving human!" Chitinous gauntlets grabbed blindly for Johnny, missing him by inches. "Did you think that I would not anticipate your cowardly attempt to claim my treasure? A shield of repulsive energy is sufficient to defend myself from your larcenous ways. Such is the power of my Cosmic Control Rod!"

The Torch sped away from the gloating insectoid. *You know,* he thought sourly, *maybe Annihilus wouldn't have to worry so much about his beloved Rod being stolen if he would just stop bragging about it all the time.*

The alien invader flailed about in the sky, snatching angrily at the empty air. "Answer my question, Johnny Storm, and perhaps I will prolong your life for a short time more!" Annihilus's mandibles clacked together loudly. "Where is the Baxter Building?"

His inhuman profile tracked the Torch's flight, suggesting that his vision was returning to him. Johnny tried to figure out what to do next. Annihilus way outmatched him in both power and endurance, so his only hope was to outthink his enemy. *This isn't over by a long shot,* the Torch thought defiantly. *I'm not out of tricks yet.*

Annihilus blinked behind his convex lenses, then scanned the sky for his blazing prey. Surprise showed upon his masklike face as he saw that the air was filled with Human Torches, each identical in appearance to the others. Over a dozen fiery youths zipped about in all directions, throwing off tendrils of flame like so many Fourth of July skyrockets. "What base deception is this?" Annihilus railed indignantly. "Show yourself, mortal!"

All but one of the many Torches were duplicates, composed solely of burning plasma. Hidden among the profusion of decoys, the real Torch admired his handiwork and tried to repress a telltale smirk. *This should slow Bugface down,* he thought smugly, *at least for a minute or two.*

"Bah!" Annihilus spat. Johnny's ploy backfired as, apparently deciding that the Torch was not worth the bother, the winged invader changed course and swooped down toward the crowded city streets below. "I shall dispose of you later, trickster," he promised. "For now I have more pressing matters to attend to."

No! Johnny thought, aghast. The busy intersection in front of the Flatiron Building was packed with pedestrians, many of them craning their necks back to gawk at the airborne spectacle taking place high above their heads. *Damn it!* Didn't all those rubberneckers realize they were in danger? Scores of terrified survivors poured out of the Flatiron, adding to the crowding and confusion. Annihilus would have his pick of victims to choose from.

"Come back here!" the Torch cried. He dove after Annihilus, pitching fireballs at his departing adversary in a

feverish attempt to recapture the insectoid's attention. Too
many people had died already. He couldn't let Annihilus
inflict his madness on the packed streets below. "We're not
finished yet!"

Ignoring him, Annihilus glided downward like a hawk
until he was only seven or eight feet above the intersection.
Destructive blasts rocked the streets and sidewalks, sending
helpless bodies flying. Panicked spectators and pedestrians
screamed and ran for cover. Would-be commuters bolted
from the bus stops and shoved at each other in their desperate attempts to gain the safety of the nearby buildings,
even trying to get back inside the smoking Flatiron.
Revolving doors were wedged shut by an excess of flailing
human bodies, while some idiot with a videophone tried
to catch the whole thing on film. A Doberman on a leash
barked shrilly as its horrified owner fought strenuously to
pull it beneath the shelter of an awning. A moment later,
only a charred crater remained where the dog and its
owner had been. A street vendor abandoned his hot dog
stand and took off down Fifth Avenue at a sprint, only to be
obliterated by yet another burst of cosmic fire.

"No!" the Torch cried in despair. The Living Death
Who Walks was living up to his name, creating carnage for
its own sake. Startled drivers hit their brakes, causing other
cars and trucks to rear-end them. Honking horns and the
sound of crashing metal added to the chaos. New York cab-
bies swore profusely, until another blast from the Cosmic
Control Rod sent taxis and limos tumbling through the air.
An upside-down cab smashed through the plate glass of
window of an upscale clothing shop on Broadway. A mangled Mercedes crashed down on top of a bicycle messenger
who couldn't scoot out of the way fast enough. A double-
decker bus, packed with tourists, exploded into pieces.

Flames and shrapnel claimed yet more victims. A kid on a skateboard was tossed six feet into the air, before slamming to earth somewhere amidst a no-man's-land of demolished bodies and vehicles.

Fifth and Broadway had become a war zone.

Heedless of the flying metal, Annihilus descended toward the streets, his greedy claws outstretched before him. A well-groomed businesswoman, toting a briefcase in one hand and a cell phone in the other, scurried across Broadway, weaving desperately between the wrecked and overturned vehicles. Her erratic course caught the questing gaze of Annihilus, who grabbed her beneath her arms and lifted her effortlessly from the street. Her cell phone and briefcase slipped from her fingers, crashing to the street below. The cheap phone shattered into pieces. Briefing papers spilled out onto the asphalt.

Having claimed his prize, Annihilus flapped back into the sky, swiftly climbing to nearly a hundred feet above the pavement. One of the woman's shoes came loose and fell toward the sidewalk. The Torch incinerated it in midair as he flew by in pursuit of Annihilus and his hostage. Zooming to the rescue, only a yard behind his quarry, the Torch could hear the woman's hysterical screams.

"Silence, female!" Annihilus snapped. He cruised upward at over one hundred miles an hour. "Answer my questions if you value your worthless life! Where is the Baxter Building?"

"Up north!" the woman blurted fearfully. She pointed uptown with a shaking finger. "That way!"

"Excellent!" Annihilus declared, veering in the direction indicated. "Then I no longer have need of you."

Over three hundred feet above the city, he callously tossed the woman aside. She would have fallen to her death had not the Human Torch been there to catch her before she hit the ground. Remembering once again to extinguish his arms, he scooped her up and carried her back down to the sidewalk. *That's one less life lost,* he thought grimly. Every minute he spent rescuing the woman gave Annihilus an even larger head start on him, but what else was he supposed to do? Impatience gnawed at him as he hastily determined that the former hostage was more shaken up than anything else.

"G-good Lord!" she exclaimed. She was trembling like a leaf, possibly in shock. "What *was* that thing?"

"Trouble," he told her. Glancing around, he spotted a couple of harmless–looking people standing nearby. "You there!" he ordered them curtly. "Get this woman to a hospital!"

No one wanted to argue with the burning man. "Er, okay," one guy said, stepping forward. His initiative inspired others to approach the rescued hostage as well. "We'll take care of her."

"Thanks." Entrusting the woman to the care of her fellow New Yorkers, the Torch launched himself skyward after Annihilus. He hated to leave all the carnage and destruction in the Flatiron District, but until Annihilus was stopped, no one was safe. The armored gargoyle wasn't hard to spot; Johnny quickly spied the invader flapping over the midtown area, up around Forty–second Street. To his alarm, he realized Annihilus could hardly miss the huge blue 4 painted on top of the Baxter Building.

Sue! he thought. His sister was all by herself at the FF's headquarters, which occupied the top five floors of the skyscraper. Pouring on the speed, he simultaneously activated the comm link on his chest. "Sue! Watch out! Annihilus is heading right for you!"

7

THE CARGO BAY DOOR SLAMMED SHUT behind Reed Richards. The tractor beam released him and he dropped onto the scuffed steel floor as the ship's artificial gravity asserted itself. After the bright lights of the search beams, it took his eyes a moment to adjust to the relative dimness of the cargo hold. He blinked at his welcoming party: a squadron of armed Baluurian soldiers. High-tech body armor and helmets encased the warriors' stocky frames, which were essentially humanoid, right down to the usual number of fingers. The muzzles of their energy rifles were pointed at the prone human. Reed instinctively distended his body, the better to absorb any enemy fire.

"On your feet, outzoner!" one of the soldiers barked. He appeared older than the captain of the patrol ship, but no less belligerent. Streaks of silver had infiltrated his charcoal-gray mane. Deep creases lined his bestial snout. Reed guessed that he was the ranking officer in the party. An automatic translator embedded in Reed's chest symbol bridged the language gap between them. "In the name of Blastaar the Supreme, you are a now a prisoner of the Empire."

Mr. Fantastic rose to his feet, moving slowly as to avoid provoking the armed contingent. He held up his black-gloved hands to show that he was unarmed; he rarely carried weapons, preferring to rely on his unique abilities when it came to self-defense. "All right," he said. "There's no need for threats. I'm willing to cooperate."

The officer turned to one of his subordinates. "The adhesion suit," he demanded.

"Yes, Commander Vatriin," the soldier said. He stepped forward, bearing a bundle of black, metallic fabric and hurled his burden at Reed's feet.

"Put that on," Vatriin instructed Mr. Fantastic. "Quickly."

What's this about? Reed wondered. He inspected the bundle, which appeared to be a baggy garment consisting of an all-over bodysuit and matching hood. The matte-black fabric was thick and exceptionally durable; he wondered if even Ben would be able to tear it. Reed would have liked to examine the sturdy material under an electron microscope.

He swiftly donned the so-called adhesion suit, which struck him as a cross between a straitjacket and a bee-keeper's outfit. To his surprise, the pieces of the suit bonded together seamlessly when pressed together. He ran his finger along the bottom of the hood, where it joined the rest of the suit, but could no longer feel any division between the two components of the costume; it was as though the entire garment were made of a single, unbroken piece of material, with Reed sealed inside. Even his hands and boots were enclosed inside the claustrophobic costume. A translucent plate in the hood allowed him to see.

No wonder it's called an adhesion suit, he realized. The separate pieces appeared to have bonded together on a molecular level. *At least I can still breathe.* Apparently oxygen molecules were somehow capable of penetrating the dense fabric. *Likewise sonic waves, since I can hear as well.*

Experimentally, he tried to stretch his fingertips, but, unlike his gloves of unstable molecules, the unyielding black fabric refused to stretch with him, nor could Reed detect a single gap in the garment through which he might be able to stretch free. The all-enclosing suit effectively negated his elastic abilities.

The conclusion was obvious. His captors clearly knew who he was—and what he was capable of. "Very well," he said. "You can lower your guns now."

Commander Vatriin laughed harshly at the very notion. The weapons remained pointed at Reed as the subordinate who had brought the suit carefully inspected the garment to make sure that no seams or gaps remained. "He's sealed up tight," the Baluurian reported to his commander. "A Mantracorian sand-mite couldn't slip out of that suit."

"Good," the officer grunted. He seemed to relax slightly now that Mr. Fantastic's powers no longer posed a threat. The soldiers parted to reveal an open doorway behind them. "Come with us, human."

The soldiers escorted Reed into a wide corridor outside the cargo bay. Although this was hardly his first time aboard a Baluurian warship, Reed could not help examining his surroundings as the squad led him at gunpoint through the bowels of the massive vessel. Riveted steel walls and bulkheads gave the interior the feel of a battleship or submarine. The look was stark and utilitarian, built for strength and durability rather than ornamentation. Signs and directions were posted in blocky Baluurian script. Reed could translate just enough of the markings to get the impression that they were heading toward the prow of the ship, perhaps to the command deck?

"Where are you taking me?" he asked Vatriin.

"Hold your tongue, human!" the aging soldier snapped. He bared his fangs. "You're a prisoner, not a guest. Take care not to forget that!"

The corridor smelled of animal musk and perspiration; apparently Baluurian standards of hygiene varied from the human norm. The artificial gravity felt slightly higher than Reed was used to, perhaps one-point-three times Earth standard. The temperature was warm and muggy, quite a change from the chill of the interstellar atmosphere outside. Reed soon felt hot and sweaty inside the stifling adhesion suit.

The throbbing of powerful tachyon engines vibrated through the walls and floor of the flagship. Baluurian military personnel passed them in the branching corridors, sometimes pausing to gape at the human prisoner. Both male and female Baluurians seemed to serve aboard *Burstaar's Revenge,* although only the males seemed equipped with full armor and weaponry. Perhaps the females served primarily as support staff? Unlike the lions of the African veld, the female Baluurians possessed manes as well, although the shaggy beards and tresses of the alien women were lighter in color than those of the males. *Fascinating,* Reed thought. *A provocative case study of divergent evolutionary patterns across dimensional barriers.*

Just a quick look around sparked a thousand questions and theories in Reed's mind. He was tempted to try to pump his escorts for more information, but the Baluurians seemed in no mood to satisfy his scientific curiosity. Hopefully, there would be an opportunity to learn more at some later point. *Just remember,* he reminded himself, *you're*

here to close a gateway between Earth and the Negative Zone.
That had to be his first priority.

Along with staying alive, that is.

Reed tried to keep track of the various turns taken by
his escorts as they navigated the interior of *Burstaar's
Revenge.* Sloped ramps led toward the upper decks, bypassing large sections of the gigantic flagship. He looked for
any sign of a laboratory where transdimensional experiments might be conducted, but nothing immediately pre-
sented itself. Of course, a battleship was hardly a likely
venue for such research; the actual source of the incursions
was almost surely elsewhere.

At length, the armed procession approached a pair of
reinforced double doors at the end of yet another hallway.
A pair of guards in gilded, impeccably polished armor
flanked the door, energy rifles cradled against their chests.
An imperial seal, depicting an exploding atom, was emblazoned upon the closed steel doors.

The older officer stepped forward to address the guards.
"Commander Vatriin, reporting with the prisoner," he said
stiffly. A soldier behind Mr. Fantastic shoved Reed forward
roughly.

One of the gilded sentries nodded. "You are expected."
He pressed a button upon his gauntlet and the double
doors slid open with a hiss of released air. Vatriin led the
procession into the chamber beyond, which was revealed
to be a combination observation deck and throne room.
An enormous curved visi-screen dominated the far end of
the spacious chamber, looking out on the swirling Vortex
at the center of the Debris Belt. Colorful tapestries, depicting historic battles and massacres, adorned the adjacent
walls. A carpet of thick, turquoise fur covered the floor.
Taken as a whole, the sumptuous furnishings gave the

chamber a luxurious atmosphere quite at odds with the Spartan decor Reed had observed elsewhere aboard the ship.

A veritable cornucopia of exotic dishes and drinks were piled high atop a polished marble table running along the left side of the chamber. Desks and computer consoles ran along the opposite side, leaving a broad path down the middle of the chamber, which led to the back of a large, platinum-colored throne facing the visi-screen beyond. The pungent aroma of the alien delicacies both tantalized and revolted Reed, sometimes at the same time.

A hubbub of conversation fell silent as the soldiers and their prisoner entered. Reed spotted stern-looking Baluurians clustered in groups all around the chamber. From their elegant robes or unusually ornate armor, he guessed that many of those present were high-ranking ministers or generals. Aides and attendants mingled among the dignitaries. Non-Baluurian servers, belonging to various subject species, quietly cleared away dirty plates and goblets. Reed recognized many of the alien servants from past expeditions into the Negative Zone. A Kestoran drummer beat out a martial rhythm upon a tambour constructed from the bones and hide of some unknown beast. A pathetic-looking Scavenger, missing its wings, was chained to a post just beyond the table of refreshments. It rattled its chain and groveled for scraps of food, reduced to either a court jester or a pet. A robot from the planet Krysok manned a computer console.

The milling court parted to allow Commander Vatriin to approach the back of the central throne. He nervously cleared his throat before declaring, "The Earthman is here as you demanded, sire."

A deep, malignant chuckle arose from the other side of

the throne. Mr. Fantastic knew that heartless laugh too well. He was not at all surprised when the throne spun around to reveal that its titanic occupant was none other than Blastaar himself.

Like his fellow Baluurians, the savage monarch had a fulsome mane, gray skin, and a mouth full of jagged fangs. Yet he was larger and more physically imposing than his subjects, with broad shoulders, a wide neck, and heavily muscled limbs. At six-feet-six-inches, he was half a foot taller than the Thing and just as powerful. A metallic cuirass, lacquered a deep indigo blue, exposed his bare arms and legs. Matching boots and wristbands completed his imperial attire.

A half-eaten shank of meat was gripped in Blastaar's right fist, while his left held the stem of jeweled goblet. A trickle of chartreuse wine ran down his chin, streaking his beard.

"Richards!" he roared. His deep, baritone voice was less gravelly than the Thing's, more like a growl than a rock-slide. "How dare you have the audacity to invade my realm once more?"

On one level, Blastaar was within his rights to protest, Reed realized. *I'm the intruder here, not he.* Reed would have felt more guilty about his uninvited arrival, however, had not Blastaar attempted to conquer Earth on numerous occasions. Indeed, the Fantastic Four had first become aware of Blastaar's existence when he had attacked the Baxter Building via an early version of the Nega-Portal. That initial battle had been the FF's first encounter with intelligent life from within the Negative Zone, and sadly, it had set the tone for too many of their later contacts with the Zone and its denizens.

Blastaar rose from his throne, towering over his subjects

and prisoner. His black eyes gleamed with cruel amusement. "That adhesion suit fits you well," he taunted Mr. Fantastic. "My own people once attempted to confine me within such a suit, not long before we met. But such paltry restraints were no match for the power at my fingertips."

This was no mere hyperbole, Reed knew. Unique among his people, Blastaar possessed the ability to project powerful atomic blasts from his bare fingers. How exactly Blastaar had gained this power, whether it was a result of genetic mutation or some other event, remained a mystery, but Reed's past analysis of the blasts had suggested that they were composed of a cascade of high-velocity neutrons, possibly generated by heavy lepton/baryon particle interactions within the cells of the warlord's body. The resulting bursts, as the Fantastic Four and other heroes had learned from experience, were capable of smashing through solid titanium. Reed had been on the receiving end of Blastaar's attacks before and was in no hurry to endure them again.

Yet that might be unavoidable, he realized.

"I'm not here to challenge you," Mr. Fantastic explained. "I'm investigating a phenomenon that may pose a threat to the integrity of both our universes."

"So you say," Blastaar replied. He did not bother to ask Reed about the nature of the phenomenon in question, perhaps because he was already aware of the incursions? "My people were monitoring your transmissions. It seems your ill-advised expedition has already cost you the life of your brutish companion." Blastaar grinned broadly at the thought of the Thing's demise. "I only wish I could have witnessed his destruction with my own eyes!"

Blastaar's attitude infuriated Reed. "You have no right

to make light of his sacrifice!" He clenched his fists within the adhesion suit. "He was worth a hundred of you!"

The tyrant laughed at Mr. Fantastic's anger. "But I am still alive and you are at my mercy!" A thought crossed Blastaar's mind and his face took on a warier expression. "We detected only two life-signs aboard your spacecraft. Where are the rest of your infamous clan, the Human Torch and your alluring mate?"

Far from here, thank heavens, Reed thought. He wondered briefly how Sue and Johnny were faring back in Manhattan. Had any other creatures crossed over from the Negative Zone? *How much time has passed on Earth since Ben and I left in the Explorer?*

"That's none of your affair," he said defiantly. Why let Blastaar know just how outnumbered Reed was at the moment? "What should concern you is my mission here. I have reason to believe that something in the Negative Zone is breaking down the wall between our two universes. What do you know of this?"

Reed was counting on Blastaar's enormous ego. If the Baluurian conqueror was indeed behind the incursions, surely he wouldn't miss an opportunity to gloat over his accomplishment.

Or would he?

A sly smile stretched across Blastaar's broad face. *"That,"* he said, echoing Reed's own words, "is none of your concern." His fangs tore a juicy bite of meat from the hefty drumstick in his hand, then he threw the half-eaten shank to the chained Scavenger, who fell upon it hungrily. Blastaar washed down the morsel with one last gulp of wine before speaking again. "You are in no position to demand information."

"But we've joined forces before," Reed reminded him,

"when faced with a common threat." Granted, Blastaar had invariably attempted to betray them in the end, but he *could* be reasoned with, at least on occasion.

Blaastar tossed the empty goblet carelessly over his shoulder. A pale yellow serving girl from the ruins of Ootah scurried to retrieve the cup.

"Perhaps this so-called threat does not worry me," he said cryptically, in a tone that convinced Reed that the warlord knew more than he was telling. "As to why, that you will learn when the time comes—and not before."

Damn, Reed thought. He had underestimated Blastaar's sadistic pleasure in keeping him in the dark. What better way to torment a mind like Reed's than by depriving him of much-needed data?

Rapid footsteps pounded the floor behind him. Reed swiveled his head in time to see (through the faceplate in his hood) a Baluurian underling hurry past him. Judging from the newcomer's relatively slight proportions and lack of armor, Reed guessed that he was some manner of technician.

"Sire!" the man blurted breathlessly. "We've received a coded transmission from Hethael. The second stage of the operation has been effected. The Death-Bringer has—"

"Silence!" Blastaar bellowed angrily. "How dare you interrupt me while I'm interrogating a prisoner?" He raised his hands and flexed his fingers in a menacing fashion. The pads of his fingertips glowed ominously. "You will hold your tongue until I call upon you, is that clear?"

The unfortunate messenger cowered at the sight of his monarch's explosive digits. "Of course, Supreme One!" He backed away fearfully. "A thousand apologies, my liege!"

Mr. Fantastic observed the exchange with interest. What exactly had provoked Blastaar's outrage? Had he merely been irked by the messenger's intrusion, or had the messenger been about to say too much? Reed quickly reviewed what he had just overheard.

Hethael? He didn't recognize the name from his previous explorations of the Negative Zone. Nothing too surprising there; the Zone was a universe unto itself. Even after all these years, the Fantastic Four had barely begun to map its myriad planets and galaxies. *And "the Death-Bringer" . . . could that be a veiled allusion to Annihilus, aka the Living Death Who Walks?* The fearsome insectoid and Blastaar had been both enemies and allies at various points in their histories, depending on the ever-shifting balance of power within the Zone.

Reed frowned. He didn't like the idea of Annihilus being involved in this affair as well. Blastaar and his Baluurian legions were dangerous enough.

"So, Richards," Blastaar addressed him, dismissing the terrified messenger from his mind. He lowered his hands to his sides, where the infernal glow around his fingertips began to fade away. "Where were we before we were so impetuously interrupted? Perhaps you were about to beg for your worthless life?"

Mr. Fantastic eyed the despot's faintly luminous fingertips, and an idea occurred to him. "Hardly," he declared. "Moreover, I don't care what ridiculous new scheme you may have devised. Have you forgotten how many times the Fantastic Four have defeated you in the past, not to mention the Avengers and others?" Contempt dripped from Reed's voice as he sneered scornfully at his captor. "In fact, when I consider your endless failures, I'm surprised that you even had the nerve to bring me aboard this pitiful flagship of yours."

"What?!" Blastaar roared. His gray face flushed with

anger. "You mock me before my very throne?!" Like an old-fashioned quick-draw artist, his hands leaped up from his sides, the thick fingers splayed wide before him. His minions gasped loudly and dived for cover. The militant drumming fell silent as the Kestoran musician ducked behind his instrument. The Scavenger tugged fruitlessly on his chain. "Feel my wrath!"

With a thunderous boom, a burst of unleashed energy exploded from Blastaar's hands, straight at Mr. Fantastic. Roughly five hundred kilonewtons of concussive force slammed into Reed like a battering ram, knocking him off his feet. Only the extreme elasticity of his body kept his rib cage from shattering; as it was, the breath was driven from his lungs and every inch of his torso ached. Reed suspected that his uniform wasn't going to be the only thing on him that was black and blue, provided he came out of this confrontation alive. His ears rang and his limbs felt even more rubbery than usual. *Good Lord!* he thought. Blastaar's volcanic detonations were more powerful than he remembered.

But had his daring gambit succeeded? Shaking off the impact of the blast, Reed hastily inspected the front of the adhesion suit, whose heavy-duty fabric had provided him with a degree of protection from the attack. Probing the suit, his hands found just what they were looking for: an open gap in the material, at least three inches across.

That's all I need, Mr. Fantastic thought. Relaxing the molecular bonds of his own flesh and blood, he flowed out through the tiny rent in a feat that would boggle the mind of even the most accomplished contortionist. Within a heartbeat, he was outside the adhesion suit, clad only in his own blue uniform. *Just as I had hoped.* Provoking Blastaar had proven remarkably easy.

The furious monarch instantly realized his mistake. "Seal the chamber!" he shouted. At his command, heavy blast doors slammed down, blocking the exit. Baluurian soldiers, who had only moments before sought shelter from their leader's destructive blasts, ran toward Reed, drawing their weapons. "Do not let the cursed Earthman escape!"

But Mr. Fantastic had no intention of fleeing. He had not come this far only to leave empty-handed. Springing into action, he stretched his body across the length of the throne room while dodging the sizzling bolts from the guards's guns. Aides and ministers squawked in alarm, unable to escape the violence. A stray shot connected with a computer console, which exploded in a geyser of white-hot sparks. Marble chips flew from the banquet table. Platters of food and bottles of liquid refreshments tumbled onto the carpet. Scorch marks defaced the visi-screen.

I need to end this quickly, Reed realized, *before some innocent servant gets hurt.* His elongated body zigzagged in midair to avoid the energy bolts, then wrapped itself around Blastaar like a boa constrictor. Mr. Fantastic's legs and lower body pinned Blastaar's arms to his sides, while his chest encircled the warlord's bull-like throat, strangling him. Reed's own neck lengthened by a couple of feet, so as to keep his head at a safe distance from Blastaar's snapping fangs. The despot's fetid breath, redolent of fresh meat and strong spirits, came out in gasps.

"Surrender, Blastaar!" Mr. Fantastic demanded. Extracting a tranquilizer patch from his belt, he stuck the patch onto tyrant's forehead in hopes of diminishing his foe's superhuman vitality. "Tell me what I want to know!"

"Never!" Blastaar spat. The adhesive patch seemed to have no effect on his atomically charged metabolism. Veins bulged atop his brow as he strained to free himself from Mr. Fantastic's coiled body. "Release me, you spineless mortal, or suffer the consequences!"

The armed guards hesitated, for fear of hitting their unforgiving ruler. "Hold your fire!" Commander Vatriin ordered. "For Tyanna's sake, don't shoot!"

In truth, Blastaar's invulnerable frame could probably shrug off a few energy bursts, but Mr. Fantastic couldn't blame Vatriin for his caution. If he was one of Blastaar's subjects, he wouldn't want to risk incurring the tyrant's wrath either. *All the better for me,* Reed thought. *At least I'm not being blasted from all sides by trigger-happy guards.*

"You will pay for this, Richards!" Blastaar snarled hoarsely, his thickly corded throat muscles resisting Mr. Fantastic's pythonlike squeeze play. Spittle sprayed from his lips. "You and your entire wretched planet!" He struggled to free his arms, exerting every ounce of his Thing-like strength. Reed gritted his teeth in exertion, uncertain how long he could hold on against Blastaar's might. He tightened his grip on the conqueror's throat, but was unable to keep Blastaar from shouting at his guards. "Get this treacherous maggot off me!"

Heeding their ruler's command, the soldiers raced forward and began tugging on Mr. Fantastic with their bare hands and gauntlets. Reed's fists and boots whipped about like weighted bolas, bloodying Baluurian noses and lips, but it was hard to repel the guards and contain Blastaar at the same time. Snatching up a discarded rifle, Commander Vatriin joined the scuffle, trying to hit Mr. Fantastic in the face with the butt of the weapon. Bobbing at the end of his rubbery neck, Reed's head darted back and forth, keeping one move ahead of the cold steel butt. "Hold still!" the Baluurian officer spat. He grabbed on to the human's neck, which simply thinned out enough to slip between Vatriin's fingers. "Outzoner freak!"

The guards, pulling at Mr. Fantastic's body despite the pummeling they were receiving from his fists and feet, managed to loosen his grip on Blastaar. It was by less than an inch, but that was all the struggling warlord required.

"Enough!" he roared, breaking free of the constricting coils. He reached up with both hands and grabbed onto Mr. Fantastic's shoulders, which were currently wrapped around Blastaar's throat. Reed clenched his elastic muscles, but the irate tyrant was too strong. Stretching Mr. Fantastic like taffy, Blastaar pulled Reed away from him and hurled Mr. Fantastic against the nearby visi-screen. "Away with you!"

Rolling himself into a ball, Reed rebounded off the screen, then ricocheted around the observation deck at high velocity. Startled Baluurians, as well as their down-trodden servants, scampered to avoid the sentient sphere as he bounced off the floor, walls, and ceiling. Long accustomed to this unorthodox mode of travel, Mr. Fantastic had no trouble controlling his bounces, nor remaining aware of his surroundings; even when his face collided with a solid surface, his malleable features readily absorbed the impact. *Keep moving,* he told himself. *You're not out of the woods yet.*

"Richards!" Blastaar bellowed, angrily peeling the useless patch from his forehead. Heedless of the alarmed bystanders, he raised his hands and fired wildly at the bouncing human. Ear-shattering booms shook the chamber as one explosive blast after another reduced the once opulent throne room to a debris-strewn battleground. The caroming blue ball made a difficult target, however, and Mr. Fantastic managed to keep one bounce ahead of his frothing adversary.

But for how long? As far as Reed knew, Blastaar's stamina and energy reserves were virtually inexhaustible. Mr. Fantastic's mind raced feverishly, evaluating his alternatives. *I can't keep up this pace forever,* he knew. Blastaar's initial blast, and the subsequent struggle with the mighty warlord and his guards, had already taken their toll. Adrenaline could only overcome fatigue for so long. *So, what next?*

Taking a hostage was not an option. Blastaar was too ruthless; Reed had no doubt that the brutal despot would gladly sacrifice a subject or two to capture a hated enemy. That left a swift escape as the most promising objective.

Bounding over to the sealed exit, Mr. Fantastic flattened himself to the width of a single sheet of fine paper and attempted to slide beneath the massive blast doors. *Maybe I can still locate a lab or computer station,* he thought, *and search for a lead regarding the incursions back home.*

But the doors' airtight seal was too tight for even him to pass through. A protection against gas attacks, perhaps? In any event, there was clearly no escape to be found there.

Meanwhile, a quick-thinking guard stamped his boot onto the pancaked Earthman, hoping to hold Mr. Fantastic in place. "I have him!" he shouted to his fellows. "Over here!"

"Not so fast," Reed replied. The guard had sorely underestimated the fugitive's capabilities. Mr. Fantastic effortlessly yanked himself out from beneath the soldier's foot, causing the flummoxed guard to fall backward onto his rear. "I'm afraid I only look like a doormat."

Reed compacted himself back into a ball and propelled himself straight into the unyielding doors, bouncing away from the site only seconds before another atomic blast left a dent in the adamantine barrier. "You cannot get away!"

Blastaar ranted, enraged by Mr. Fantastic's evasive tactics. The shock wave from his blast knocked over guards and dignitaries like tenpins. "None can escape my fury!"

Reed feared that Blastaar's arrogant boasts were not far from the truth. Brown eyes peered from an animated blue globe, searching for a ventilation shaft of some sort. It didn't have to be very wide; Mr. Fantastic could stretch through the eye of a needle if necessary. Back at the Baxter Building, he often saved time by navigating a network of narrow conduit tubing embedded in the walls for his personal use.

But in the general chaos, with Blastaar's neutron bursts reducing everything in sight to rubble, it was hard to make a thorough inspection of the unfamiliar chamber, especially while dodging energy bolts and volcanic blasts. Smoky fumes rose from shattered control stations, adding to the difficulty. Deafening booms competed with the shrieks of the panicked court. An emergency Klaxon wailed in reaction to the live weapons fire upon the deck.

"Run all you can!" Blastaar threatened. A hellish radiance enveloped his hands as burst after devastating burst erupted from his fingertips. "My power will find you before long! Then will you know the full force of my hatred!"

Reed felt himself slowing down. A seething ball of atomic energy rocketed at his face and he expanded outward into the shape of a torus, letting the bomb-burst zip through the hole at the center. The blast's passage battered his inner circumference, making him wince in pain. *That was a close one,* he realized. *Too close.*

Hitting the floor, he rolled across the scorched blue carpet like a hula hoop, with the bravest of Blastaar's guards chasing after him. Another blast tore through the air and he barely retracted himself in time. The burst passed over the suddenly smaller hoop, missing Mr. Fantastic by less than an inch.

A strangely electronic-sounding cry reached his ears, following almost instantly in the wake of another thunderous explosion. *What in heaven?* Reed thought. He spun around on his axis to see the enslaved robot sprawled upon the floor next to the smoldering remains of his workstation. The robot's right leg was missing below the knee joint. Sparks flared from the truncated limb. Exposed wires and rotors flailed about like torn human flesh. Power lights flickered alarmingly. Static filled the robot's pitiful moans.

Guilt stabbed at Reed's conscience. *This is no good,* he thought. *I'm accomplishing nothing, excepting endangering all these trapped bystanders. Even if Blastaar doesn't care about the safety of his people, I do. None of them asked me to invade their universe.*

Looking around quickly, he spotted Commander Vatriin, still clutching the rifle he had tried to pummel Reed with. Launching himself off the floor, Mr. Fantastic bounced off the surprised officer's breastplate, grabbing hold of the rifle as he did so. "Mind if I borrow this for a moment?" Reed quipped. Human hands, extending from a energetic blue hoop, wrenched the weapon from Vatriin's grasp and held on to the rifle as Mr. Fantastic straightened himself out, then stretched toward Blastaar's throne.

Time to end this, he thought. *One way or another.*

The imposing platinum seat was about the only piece of furniture that its owner's fearsome energy blasts had left intact. Reed ducked behind the throne and lifted the rifle, resting the barrel upon the chair's tall back. Blastaar himself was only a few yards away, turning toward the throne as he tried to keep his elusive foe in sight. Reed had a perfect view of the tyrant's brutish profile.

A quick glance confirmed that the firing mechanism was simple enough, so Reed took aim at Blastaar's head and pushed down the trigger. His ductile shoulder absorbed the recoil as a crimson energy bolt struck Blastaar at point-blank range.

"Hah!" the undaunted warlord laughed. As the glow of the energy bolt faded, Reed saw that Blastaar's dark mane was not even singed. The Baluurian monarch turned to face his human adversary head-on. "Is that the best you can muster? Have you forgotten that I can withstand any extreme?" He sneered at the rifle in Reed's hands. "You cannot even begin to harm me with so paltry a weapon."

True enough, Reed thought. He recalled how, in their very first encounter with Blastaar, the rampaging invader had shrugged off the full force of Johnny's flame powers. *Which is why I knew this gun couldn't kill you. . . .*

Blastaar did not wait for Reed's reply. Happy to have a stationary target, if only for the moment, he aimed both hands at Mr. Fantastic and let loose a fresh eruption of atomic power. The blast ripped the heavy throne from the floor, driving it straight into Reed's gut and pinning him between the uprooted chair and the screen behind him. Any normal human would have been broken in two by the blow, but Mr. Fantastic's body spread out to absorb the impact, leaving him merely stunned. His compressed abdomen was as thin as film where the throne pressed against him.

Given a moment to recover, he could have slid out from between the throne and the wall, but Blastaar didn't give him that minute. Another blast struck Reed, rattling every bone in his body.

And another.

Reed felt as if one of the Mole Man's enormous cave

monsters had stepped on him. His head was ringing, and darkness began to encroach on his vision. He sagged limply against the visi-screen, all but dissolving into a boneless puddle of blue and pink gelatin. He struggled to hold his head up, stay conscious, but the darkness would not be denied. He could feel himself slipping away.

"Shall I kill him, sire?" Commander Vatriin placed the muzzle of a energy pistol against Reed's forehead. He sounded eager to repay the human for the assault on his dignity. His voice seemed to come from very far away.

"Not yet," Blastaar declared. "His clever human brain may still be of use to me." Reed's eyelids fell shut, cutting off his view, but he could still hear the warlord's booming voice, before he blacked out completely.

"Notify the captain. Set course for Hethael!"

8

RISING NEARLY ONE THOUSAND FEET above Forty-second Street and Madison Avenue, the Baxter Building was a rectangular skyscraper with a gleaming steel-and-glass exterior. Mirrored windows, composed of an unbreakable carbon poly-lattice, guarded the residents' privacy, while the walls themselves were woven from a state-of-the-art carbon-aramid polymer thread that rendered the structure nearly impervious to superpowered assaults. A five-story rocket silo, attached to the upper northeast corner of the building, distinguished the skyscraper from its neighbors, as did the distinctive **4** symbol upon its roof.

That trademarked logo had the Human Torch worried now. The telltale **4** drew Annihilus to the Fantastic Four's penthouse headquarters like a bull's-eye. The Torch watched in alarm as the ageless mass murderer swooped downward toward the landing pad atop the Baxter Building, intent on some serious home invasion. In theory, with the Thing and Mr. Fantastic away in the Negative Zone, Sue was the building's sole defender at the moment.

Not if I have anything to say about it, Johnny resolved. Achieving supersonic speed, he jetted north toward home, determined to get there before Annihilus. A ribbon of fire streaked across the sky behind him as he flew above the intervening rooftops, passing both the Empire State Building and the New York Public Library. Annihilus was less than sixty feet above the Baxter Building when the Human Torch rushed between the flying monster and the landing pad. His flame was burning hotter by the moment.

"Back off!" he challenged Annihilus. "I don't know what you're after in there, but if you think you're just going to waltz right into my home, think again!" A wall of flame vouched for his determination. "The Baxter Building is strictly off-limits to scum like you!"

Annihilus flapped in the air above the Torch. "Brainless mammal!" he chittered. "What else would I desire within your domicile except the gateway to my own universe? Even now my allies wait to pour into your world in unstoppable numbers—once I seize control of Reed Richards's Negative Zone portal!"

Allies? What's he talking about? Johnny was confused by Annihilus's typically egotistical rant. Why did the homicidal alien need Reed's Nega-Portal if he had already found a way to make it to Earth? *One thing's for sure. That "unstoppable numbers" business can't be good.*

"Over my dead body!" the Torch declared, tempting fate somewhat. If Annihilus wanted the Nega-Portal, then Johnny didn't intend to let him anywhere near it. "You're not getting past me without a fight!"

This time he was going to pull out all the stops. As a rule, he tried to avoid unleashing his nova-flame burst in densely populated areas, but it looked as if nothing less was going to stop Annihilus this time around. *All right,* he thought fervidly. *You asked for this!*

Throwing out both his arms in front of him, the Human

Torch tapped into the volcanic fury growing within him. Every cell of his cosmically irradiated body went into overdrive, producing a high-intensity conflagration comparable to the heat pulse of a low-grade nuclear warhead, which he hurled upward at Annihilus with an exuberant whoop. Thermometers climbed for blocks in every direction, while pedestrians below blinked and averted their eyes from the sudden inferno. Computers, TV sets, and radios blacked out within a three-block radius. Blasts of superheated air scorched the sky. Hundreds of panicked citizens dialed 911, mistakenly reporting an atomic strike on midtown. Commuters and tourists emerging from Grand Central Terminal, less than a block away, turned around and raced back into the station, frantic to catch the next train out of the city.

For a few minutes, the nightmarish form of Annihilus was lost within the seething mushroom cloud rising above the Baxter Building. Johnny held his breath, waiting to see whether Annihilus had survived the blast. His heart pounded and he felt as though he had just run a marathon. His flaming sheath flickered weakly, and it was all he could do to keep himself aloft. Sweat boiled off him.

That had better have done the trick, he thought. After fighting a Borer, a medusa, and now Annihilus himself, all in one afternoon, he could barely stand, let alone fly. *I can't remember the last time I felt this wiped out.*

Then a figure emerged from the roiling fireball, its daunting wingspan silhouetted against the billowing smoke and flames like that of a demonic angel. The Torch's heart sank like a stone.

"Idiotic stripling!" Annihilus taunted him. To Johnny's dismay, the invader's wings and carapace didn't even look singed. "My Cosmic Control Rod draws on the primal energies of reality itself. What are your paltry flames compared to that?"

Johnny recalled the cosmic power he had briefly enjoyed as an unwilling herald of Galactus—what he wouldn't give to have just a fraction of that power back right now.

"I have wasted enough time with your puerile tactics!" Annihilus said disdainfully. The golden cylinder beneath his throat began to glow with coruscating yellow energy. "Now shall you taste my power!"

Before the Torch could even try to get away, a wave of destructive energy shot forth from the Cosmic Control Rod, hitting Johnny with the force of a hurricane. The blast snuffed out his flames in an instant and sent his battered body tumbling through the air beyond the edge of the rooftop below. No longer afire, he looked like any other helpless mortal. Gravity seized him and he felt himself falling toward the deadly pavement dozens of stories beneath him. Dazed and groggy, he tried to flame back on, but it was no use. All he could muster were a few feeble sparks.

I'm sorry, Sue! Even worse than his own impending death was the realization that he had let his sister down. *I tried to keep him away from you. . . .*

In the monitor room on the thirty-fifth floor of the Baxter Building, the Invisible Woman watched her brother confront Annihilus in the sky above the roof of the building. Part of her still couldn't accept that what she saw was really happening. One of the Fantastic Four's worst nightmares had finally come true: Annihilus was loose on Earth—and at the height of his powers, no less.

The last time Annihilus had successfully invaded the Baxter Building, he had been dying due to the temporary loss of his Cosmic Control Rod; even still, the murderous alien had nearly destroyed two universes using Reed's technology—and sent both Franklin and Alicia to the hospital. Now, judging from the gleaming cylinder visible upon the monster's chest, he was as lethal as he'd ever been. For the first time that she could remember, Annihilus prowled the positive universe at full strength.

Be careful, Johnny! she thought urgently. *Don't underestimate him!*

Her brother's voice blared from the monitor directly in front of her. Additional screens filled the walls surrounding her, presenting real-time images from dozens of potential trouble spots, earthly and otherwise. Dinosaurs stampeded through the Savage Land and the lost jungles of Wakanda. Moloids and cave monsters labored in Subterranea. The spires of Attilan, home of the uncanny Inhumans, rose from the Blue Area of the Moon, not far from the lunar citadel of the Watcher. Sea serpents guarded the undersea kingdom of Atlantis. Yet more screens kept watch over assorted parallel universes and micro-realms. Even the all-consuming Vortex within the Negative Zone warranted its own permanent monitor.

Sue ignored the exotic alien vistas, intent only on the life-or-death conflict taking place umpteen feet above her head. "Over my dead body!" the Torch exclaimed. His sister winced at his choice of words. "You're not getting past me without a fight!"

An incandescent flash lit up the rooftop monitor, hurting her eyes before the brightness settings adjusted themselves automatically, and she realized that the Torch must have resorted to his nova-flame burst. The rest of the screens flickered and threatened to go blank, but Reed's emergency backups kicked in, restoring everything to working order. On the central screen, however, she could still see nothing but billowing flames.

Would the nova-blast be enough to stop Annihilus? Sue couldn't just sit still, waiting to find out. Taking a second to ensure that the building's automatic defenses were up and running, she dashed out of the monitor room and into the express elevator leading to the landing pad. As the building's owners, the Fantastic Four had exclusive use of this particular elevator, so the passenger compartment was ready and waiting for her. "The roof . . . now!" she instructed the voice-activated controls.

The maglev compartment swiftly carried her past the intervening three floors to the roof directly above them. Sue impatiently counted them off as the elevator zipped upward.

Thirty-sixth floor. Private suites, bedrooms, and nursery.

Thirty-seventh floor. Family areas. Living room, kitchen, dining area, gymnasium, et cetera.

Thirty-eighth floor. Vehicle hangar.

Roof and landing pad. *Finally!*

A gust of hot air (left over from Johnny's nova-burst?) hit her the instant she stepped out onto the landing pad, but the unseasonable heat barely registered on her. The elevator doors sealed shut behind her, and as a precaution, she concentrated just long enough to psionically bend the sunlight around her body, rendering her completely transparent.

Now living up to her name, the Invisible Woman scanned the sky to see whether the Human Torch had defeated Annihilus. To her dismay, she saw the unscathed insectoid lash out at her brother with a devastating blast from his Cosmic Control Rod. "Johnny, watch out!" she cried, but it was already too late. The cosmic energy struck at the speed of light, dowsing the Torch's flames in a heartbeat. Unable to keep himself aloft, he plummeted toward Madison Avenue, over a thousand feet below.

No! Reacting quickly, Sue formed an invisible force-slide underneath his falling body. The slide broke his fall and guided him safely down onto the roof, depositing him directly at her feet. He sprawled limply on the cold enamel tiles, stunned from Annihilus's devastating attack. His durable blue uniform was torn in places and his hair was a mess. A purple bruise marred his face, and one eye was slightly swollen. Hot blood streamed from his nose. Perspiration steamed off him.

"Hey, Sis," he said weakly, spitting out a mouthful of blood. He tried to stand, but his legs gave out beneath him. "And here I thought we had the easy job. . . ."

Sue couldn't bear to see Johnny like this, but there was no time to tend to his injuries. She cast a field of invisibility over both of them, hopefully hiding them from Annihilus's view, and hastily helped him to his feet. His shredded uniform was still hot to the touch, but her own gloves kept her from being burned. She slung an arm under his shoulders, supporting his weight, and half-carried, half-dragged him toward the waiting elevator. "We have to hurry!" she whispered.

Circling in the air above them, Annihilus acknowledged the Invisible Woman's presence. "You cannot deceive me, Susan Richards!" His inhuman voice sent a chill down her spine. "I know your handiwork!"

Force bolts slammed into rooftop as he sought to obliterate his unseen targets. A moving force field protected them from the brunt of the barrage, but Sue experienced a jolt of psychic feedback every time one of the blasts grazed her see-through shield. Pain stabbed at her head from the inside out. The floor of the landing pad shuddered beneath her feet, nearly throwing them both off-balance. The decorative **4** symbol adorning the pad was quickly reduced to an incomprehensible ruin. Fragments of shattered enamel bounced off her force field.

The elevator's sealed doorway beckoned to her, only a few more steps away. The solenoid activator in her belt buckle shot out an high-frequency beam to the elevator's sensors, and the heavy steel doors slid open in front of her, automatically recognizing her security clearance. "Almost there!" she gasped, as much to herself as to Johnny. "We're going to make it!"

But Annihilus must have spotted the entrance as well. "You shall not elude me!" he threatened, wheeling about in the sky. He blithely plunged through what remained of the Torch's firewall.

Annihilus dived for the open doorway, only to slam face-first into a sudden force field. The transparent barrier blocked him long enough for the Invisible Woman to get herself and Johnny all the way into the elevator. "Seal doors!" she shouted. "Emergency lockdown!"

The doors slammed shut at a potentially hazardous speed. A heartbeat later, the entire elevator assembly sank into the rooftop. Heavy blast doors, made of solid titanium, slid loudly into place above them, blocking access to the elevator shaft.

Still holding on to Johnny, Sue let out a sigh of relief. That had been close, but they'd timed it just right. Annihilus was locked out of the building, at least for the moment. She dispelled her invisibility field, giving her overworked brain cells a rest. She could feel a headache coming on, but that was the least of her worries.

What are we going to do about Annihilus? We can't just tran-

quilize him and throw him in the holding cells with the Borer and the Scavenger. He's far too powerful—and cunning—for that.

As if in proof of this, pounding blows suddenly struck the blast doors overhead. The elevator wobbled alarmingly. Annihilus was obviously trying to force his way into the building, and he wasn't taking no for an answer.

"Control room," she instructed the elevator. "Thirty-fifth floor."

Although they owned the entire building, the Fantastic Four occupied only the top five floors of the skyscraper, with the rest of the building given over to various tenants and business offices. A heavily shielded buffer zone between the thirty-fourth and thirty-third floors provided civilians with a degree of protection from supervillain attacks, interdimensional accidents, and other rigors of daily life around the Fantastic Four, but sometimes it was still necessary to evacuate the lower floors for safety's sake.

This was definitely one of those times.

"Commence general evacuation," she said aloud, counting on the Baxter Building's sophisticated programming to take care of the rest. Somewhere below her, emergency alarms began to sound and escape slides opened to allow for quicker exits. Underground tunnels beneath the adjacent blocks would allow the tenants and their visitors to depart the skyscraper without risking the exposed streets. "Crisis Level Delta-Four."

The elevator beeped to a stop and the doors slid open. She helped Johnny out of the compartment and was relieved to discover that he seemed to be feeling a little stronger. He limped beside her, only occasionally leaning his weight against her. He wiped his bloody nose on the tattered sleeve of his uniform.

The thirty-fifth floor held the Fantastic Four's com-

mand center, complete with reception area, conference
rooms, monitor room, launch control, communications
center, infirmary, and other vital function spaces. Sue was
tempted to take Johnny straight to the infirmary, but went
to the building's internal defense center instead. Johnny's
injuries, as ugly as they were, did not appear to be life-
threatening.

Annihilus was.

Like the monitor room, the defense center was filled
with visi-screens. But these screens were all focused in and
around the Baxter Building itself, allowing them to track
the progress of any invader from this single location. The
holographic control panels were infinitely versatile and
could be slaved to direct just about every defense system
from any one of four identical consoles. Manual controls
and overrides provided a degree of redundancy if the voice
or VR controls shut down. Subdued lighting made the images on the screens even more vivid, cutting down on reflective glare. Ergonomic seats could be adjusted to
accommodate either the Thing or his less bulky associates.
All controls were biometrically configured to respond only
to the Fantastic Four and a few select friends and allies.
Discrete sensors scanned visitors for evidence of mind control or shape-shifting.

I hate this place, Sue thought. Even though she knew
that it was vital to the safety of her entire family, not to
mention the rest of the world, she couldn't help resenting
that her home required what was essentially a war room.
What does that say about our lives?

As Johnny sank gratefully into one of the auxiliary seats,
Sue sat down at the main control panel. She quickly confirmed that all thirty-three of the lower floors had successfully been evacuated. She then double-checked to make

sure the top five floors were completely sealed off from the outside world. The Baxter Building was equipped with its own environmental controls and life-support capability and was even capable of providing a breathable atmosphere in the event that the entire skyscraper was abruptly transported into outer space (as had been known to happen). Recyclable water sources and a substantial stockpile of concentrated nutrition packets meant that, in theory, they could last out any siege.

Provided, of course, that the attacker didn't make it past their defenses. *That's a big if,* Sue realized. *If anyone can force their way into the building, it's Annihilus.*

She transferred the images from the rooftop monitor to the screen in front of her. Through anxious eyes, she saw that Annihilus was still trying to blast his way through the titanium doors blocking the elevator shaft. Primal energy blazed from his Cosmic Control Rod, pounding against the barrier with unimaginable force. A flashing red light on her console warned her that the blast doors were already in danger of buckling.

"My God," she commented. "He's really determined to get to us."

Johnny shook his head. "It's not us he's after," he corrected her. "At least not yet. He wants to open the Nega-Portal, to let through some kind of invading army."

This is getting worse by the moment, Sue thought. Random incursions from the Negative Zone were bad enough, but now they were talking about a full-scale invasion? She felt as if she were trapping inside a never-ending nightmare. *Franklin. Valeria.* Her children's faces flashed through her mind. Even though they were not in any immediate danger, nowhere in the city would be safe if Annihilus had his way.

Maybe no place on the planet.

"We have to stop him," she said forcefully. "We can't let him get to the portal."

The Negative Zone access chamber was one story below them, among Reed's laboratories on the thirty-fourth floor. Nestled between the command center above it and buffer zone below, the labs were safely insulated from the FF's personal quarters on the thirty-sixth and thirty-seventh floors. Along with the Time Platform, the Negative Zone Chamber was one of the most securely guarded areas of the building. The defenses there weren't merely state-of-the-art, they were decades ahead of their time. Adamantium vault doors were the least of the security measures.

But would even that be enough to deter Annihilus?

9

HETHAEL TURNED OUT TO BE AN ICY moon, orbiting a radiant gas giant somewhere deep within the Negative Zone. Mr. Fantastic could see the frozen globe through a porthole in the imperial shuttle as the compact spacecraft carried them down to the planetoid. Behind them, *Burstaar's Revenge* cruised in orbit above Hethael. The rest of Blastaar's fleet was nowhere in sight, having apparently remained behind to patrol the area around the Vortex.

"Hah!" Blastaar laughed maliciously. He occupied a seat of his own in the center row of the shuttle cabin. Reed himself, trapped inside an intact adhesion suit, sat at the rear of the passenger compartment, flanked by two unsmiling guards. Commander Vatriin sat up front, next to the pilot. "Behold your future home!" Blastaar taunted Reed. "The perfect prison for such as you. Even you if manage to slip free of your bonds, and the installation below, there will be no place for you to escape to . . . except a frozen wasteland where a lesser being like yourself cannot possibly survive!"

After spending at least a day or so in a detention cell aboard Blastaar's flagship, Reed was glad just to be arriving anywhere. He refused to let the warlord's gibes break his spirit. The Fantastic Four had turned the tables on Blastaar before, not to mention any number of equally smug adversaries. *There's always hope,* he thought, *while life endures.* He had yet to encounter a challenge he couldn't outsmart. *As long as I have my brain, I am never out of options.*

He couldn't help wondering what Blastaar had planned for him. Why exactly had the merciless tyrant chosen to let Reed live? As far as Reed knew, Blastaar lived only for conquest and revenge. He would not have kept an old enemy alive without a reason.

The shuttle descended toward the moon's surface. Hethael appeared to have no atmosphere of its own, only the universal ether that permeated the Negative Zone. Nevertheless, heavy turbulence rocked the shuttle as it entered the moon's gravity well. Through a porthole, Reed gazed down upon a desolate arctic landscape. Vast sheets of snow-covered ice extended from pole to pole. *Frozen methane and nitrogen,* he wondered, *or some combination of elements known only to the Negaverse?*

"Transmitting approach codes to station security," the pilot reported from the helm. Reed wondered what sort of defenses the remote facility possessed. "Codes accepted and approved. We are cleared to land."

At first, Reed couldn't see any form of installation at all. Then, as the shuttle drew closer to the surface, he spotted a solitary landing pad embedded in the waste. A hangar-shaped structure occupied one end of the pad. With its frost-covered curved roof, at first glance it resembled an enormous snowdrift. Underground heating units presumably kept the landing area free of ice, but Reed was surprised at just how small the installation was; from the look of it, the lonely hangar would barely hold the shuttle, let alone any sort of detention facilities.

Is that all there is?

Then he recalled that the Baluurians preferred to build their homes and cities downward, into the interior of their worlds, rather than upward from the surface. Indeed, Blastaar had been greatly taken aback by the sight of New York's towering skyscrapers on his first uninvited visit to Earth. "I take it the rest of the installation is underground," Reed said aloud. "Beneath the permafrost?"

"Silence, human!" Vatriin glared at Reed over the back of his seat. He seemed not to have forgiven Mr. Fantastic for stealing his rifle during that melee in the throne room. "You have not been given leave to speak."

Blastaar was in a more loquacious mood. "You shall see soon enough, Richards." Once again, he obviously enjoyed withholding information from the inquisitive Earthman. "Rest assured, you will have time enough to become *very* familiar with our ultimate destination . . . before it becomes your final resting place."

I've heard that before, Reed thought, *and from greater monsters than you.* He warned himself not to get overconfident, however; it was not by chance that the formidable Blastaar had carved out an interstellar empire.

With a jarring bump, the shuttle touched down upon the landing pad. Powerful fusion engines fell silent. Reed heard the high-pitched howling of an icy wind outside the vessel. The endless keening of an eternal winter.

"Landing complete," the pilot reported. "Beginning docking procedure."

The nose of the shuttle faced the hangar ahead. The hangar door retracted into the tarmac and Reed glimpsed a spacious interior. He expected the shuttle to taxi forward, but instead the landing pad turned into a giant conveyor belt, carrying the spacecraft into the waiting hangar.

Bright overhead lights revealed a single docking bay along with various pieces of maintenance equipment. Reed looked in vain for evidence for any other vessel. Was Blastaar's shuttle the only way off the planetoid?

Small wonder he considered Hethael escape-proof.

The hangar door rose back into place, shielding them from the adverse conditions outside, and the party exited the shuttle. Despite the thick steel walls surrounding them, the temperature in the hangar was several degrees colder than aboard the shuttle. Reed could still hear the whisper of the winds, and he found himself momentarily grateful for the thick insulation of the cumbersome adhesion suit. The soldiers' breaths frosted the air in front of them, and Reed's own breath fogged the interior of the clear faceplate in his hood, making it difficult to see. Only Blastaar seemed unaffected by the bitter cold, despite his bare arms and legs.

"Invigorating weather, is it not?" he addressed Vatriin. "Pleasingly brisk."

"A-as you s-say, sire," the officer agreed through chattering fangs. "M-most r-r-refreshing."

Despite his avowals, Vatriin wasted no time keying another a set of codes into a touch pad mounted at the rear of the docking bay. An elevator opened before them and they entered the compartment. The armed guards kept watch over Reed as the elevator descended for what felt like several minutes; wherever Blastaar was taking him, it was clearly deep beneath the moon's surface. The temperature within the elevator grew warmer as they left the frigid hangar behind.

"Impressive," Reed commented. His faceplate gradually defogged, allowing him a clearer view of his surroundings. "This installation must have required considerable effort to excavate."

Vatriin shot him a dirty look, but his monarch did not

object to Reed's inquiry. "Not with enslaved Borers at your command," Blastaar boasted. "You will find this facility fully equipped with all the necessities: living quarters, security, laboratories, geothermal generators, even a menagerie of live test subjects. Everything you will need for the duration of your existence."

"Doing what?" Reed asked suspiciously. The reference to test subjects worried him. Annihilus had once confined him, Ben, and Johnny to a bizarre alien zoo, to test their superhuman abilities. Did Blastaar have something similar in mind? *That seems out of character. Blastaar prefers brute force to scientific research.*

"Soon all your questions will be answered," the tyrant promised with an imperious smirk. "Although I cannot guarantee that those answers will meet with your approval."

A succession of colored lights, mounted in the ceiling of the lift, charted the elevator's descent. They passed the first three levels before coming to a stop only one level before the bottom of the shaft. A wall slid open and they stepped into an antechamber facing a massive steel air lock. The closed doorway was guarded by an armed Baluurian sentry on one side—and a scaly, purple Scavenger on the other.

Reed blinked in surprise. What was the bat-winged creature doing here? The Scavengers were Annihilus's loyal servitors, whom he had evolved for his own convenience by means of a gene transmitter salvaged from a crashed alien spaceship. Although barely sentient, they possessed enough intelligence to operate simple machinery and follow Annihilus's commands, but not enough to pose a threat to their insectoid master. The Scavengers had literally been engineered to obey Annihilus's every whim; it was hard to imagine any Scavenger choosing to serve Blastaar instead.

Moreover, unlike the crippled Scavenger on display in

Blastaar's throne room, this specimen appeared to be no mere trophy or prisoner. It clutched a charged electrolance in its talons and watched the approach of the newcomers intently. Its leathery purple wings were draped over its shoulders.

Reed recalled the messenger's reference to "the Death-Bringer" back aboard *Burstaar's Revenge*. More and more, he feared that the nameless technician had been alluding to Annihilus, the Living Death Who Walks. The Scavenger's presence, alongside one of Blastaar's own Baluurian soldiers, only heightened Reed's growing suspicion that Blastaar and Annihilus were working in concert once more.

"Hail, Blastaar!" the Baluurian sentry barked, raising his rifle in salute. The Scavenger emitted an inarticulate squawk.

Blastaar acknowledged the guard's homage with a nod. "Admit us," he instructed. "I would have words with your charge."

"Yes, sire!"

The guard hastily entered a coded sequence into a touch pad by the door, and the ponderous air lock door swung open. He eyed Reed warily as Vatriin and his men escorted Reed through the air lock into a large and remarkably sophisticated laboratory. Computer banks and cluttered steel counters lined the walls. Flashing lights and gauges reported on the equipment's functions. A hum of electronic activity pervaded the scene. The temperature and gravity were tolerable by human standards. The sterile atmosphere smelled only faintly of Baluurian musk.

"Welcome to Science Station Omega-17," Blastaar said expansively.

Despite his captivity, Mr. Fantastic could not resist gawking in curiosity. The alien laboratory was positively crammed with intriguing-looking apparatuses. Most were unfamiliar to him, although he could make some educated guesses as to their functions. *That looks like a fifth-dimensional resonance detector, while that device over there is quite possibly a subatomic gravity wave inducer.* Inside his heavy gloves, his fingers yearned to tinker with all this advanced experimental equipment. *As prisons go, I could do worse.*

But what did Blastaar have in mind for him?

Before he could open his mouth to ask, a vault at the opposite end of the lab opened. A husky voice greeted them from across the room.

"Emperor Blastaar. You wasted no time getting here, I see. How . . . fortunate . . . for us."

The speaker belonged to a species Reed had never before encountered. Dark magenta plates appeared to cover her body, not unlike the Thing, but her natural armor was smooth and glossy, not rough and uneven like Ben's. A widow's peak of iridescent copper scales adorned her scalp in lieu of hair. A rumpled lab coat was belted around her waist, beneath which she wore a simple one-piece tunic. Exotic tools were stuck to the exterior of the coat in a haphazard fashion. Reed thought he spotted a pair of micro-calipers and a pen-sized laser projector.

"Permit me to introduce Magister Samra Qury," Blastaar declared. His deep voice contained a mocking tone. "Magister Qury, Reed Richards of Earth, as promised."

Her shoes rapped briskly against the floor as she joined the landing party. She was nearly as tall as Blastaar himself, and of roughly She-Hulkian proportions. Shimmering bronze eyes, alive with wit and intelligence, regarded Reed with fascination. "It's an honor to meet you, Dr. Richards. Your work has been an inspiration to me. Forgive me for staring, but I confess I've never met a being from the positive universe before."

"There's no need to apologize," he assured her. "Scientific curiosity is something I understand very well." Nevertheless, a certain tension crept into his voice. "But what did you mean, my work has inspired you?"

Before she could answer, Blastaar interrupted, stepping between Reed and the female scientist. "Magister Qury is a remarkable creature," he stated. "Imagine your brain in the Thing's body!"

"I'll take that as a compliment," she said drily. "I think."

Reed got the distinct impression that there was no love lost between Blastaar and Qury. *Interesting,* he mused. Perhaps the other scientist could be made into an ally? "Are you in charge of this science station?" he asked her.

"I'm the sole researcher," she replied, carefully qualifying her answer. She glanced disdainfully at the armed Baluurian soldiers. "Whether that puts me in charge is another matter."

What does that mean? Reed pondered. He considered the possibility that Qury was being forced to work for Blastaar against her will. Certainly, it wouldn't be the first time a well-intentioned scientist was suborned into the service of a tyrannical regime. Nearly a generation of Latverian scientists had been forced to labor under the total domination of Victor Von Doom.

"Hah!" Blastaar chortled at Qury's implied reproach. "The magister is too modest. Without her genius, none of this would have been possible." He gestured toward the doorway at the far end of lab. "Come, let us show our visitor exactly what your brilliance has accomplished."

Qury flinched involuntarily at the sight of the warlord's explosive fingers raised amidst all her delicate equipment. A portion of her independent spirit seemed to seep out of her as she nodded in compliance. "Very well, as you command."

She led Mr. Fantastic and the others into an adjacent control room, where Reed experienced an unexpected moment of déjà vu. Beyond the control room, on the other side of a thick transparent wall, was something that bore an unmistakable resemblance to the early versions of his own Negative Zone access chamber. Instead of a vertical shaft sinking into the floor, however, an enormous wall-sized portal dominated the chamber. Coruscating flashes of blue energy crackled around the edges of the gigantic screen, providing evidence of an artificial force field sealing off the gateway. Banks of space-time distorters lined the adjoining walls, while a pair of empty steel manacles were built into the floor of the chamber, directly in front of the portal, the better to hold unwilling test subjects in place.

But it was the portal that captured Reed's full attention. About the size of one of the smaller screens at a multiplex, the portal was like a window looking out onto another universe. His universe. On the circular screen, Mr. Fantastic was dismayed to see the Baxter Building looking much as he had just left it. The familiar skyscraper gleamed beneath the light of a clear blue sky. *She's done it,* he realized, torn between dread and admiration. *Opened her own gateway to the positive universe.*

"Good Lord!" he gasped out loud.

Blastaar grinned evilly. "I thought you would be impressed. No longer is yours the only route to the benighted dimension you call home. Now at last, my legions can establish a beachhead on Earth itself!"

A beachhead? Reed shuddered at Blastaar's ominous choice of words. *Merely a military metaphor, or something more literal?*

Reed forced himself to look away from the portal. "Congratulations," he wished Qury, his voice strained. "You are clearly as ingenious as Blastaar says."

Was it just his imagination, or was that a flicker of guilt

upon her armored features? "Thank you," she said in a hushed tone. Her bronze eyes took in his adhesion suit. "I only wish we could have met under somewhat altered circumstances."

Blastaar ignored her contrite attitude. "Truth be told," he admitted, "there is still progress yet to be made. The Posi-Portal, as the magister has christened her device, requires absurd quantities of energy simply to open the portal for mere seconds at a time. Hardly long enough to mount an invasion," he added, as though that was the only thing that mattered.

Mr. Fantastic was relieved to hear as much. Yet he feared that there was still more to the story. *I'm getting an uncomfortable feeling I know why Blastaar brought me here.*

"This is true," Qury confirmed. "At present, even the slightest fluctuation in the power stream causes the interface to destabilize. The rift lasts only long enough to send a single test subject through."

Reed had no reason to doubt her. What she and Blastaar were saying was in line with what he had observed back on Earth. "Like the Borer and the Scavenger," he said.

"And Annihilus," she divulged.

"What?!" Reed exclaimed. Annihilus was on Earth already? This was even worse than he had feared. He stepped forward and grabbed Qury's shoulders with the padded gloves of his adhesion suit. "You can't be serious. Tell me you're lying, that you didn't set that monster loose on my planet!"

His outburst alarmed Vatriin's men, who raised their rifles and took aim at the agitated human. "Hold your fire!" Blastaar commanded, waving at them with his hand. All pretense at congeniality evaporated as he basked in his enemy's distress. "Show him," he brusquely instructed Qury.

The female scientist gently disengaged herself from Reed's grip and went to the control console, where she deftly increased the magnification of the image on the screen. Reed's heart sank as he saw Annihilus, in all his malevolent might, laying siege to the Baxter Building. The roof of the skyscraper looked like a war zone, with the 4 insignia on the landing pad blasted into rubble. Annihilus himself flapped just above the roof, obviously trying to get inside. His Cosmic Control Rod fired with devastating power at a pair of blast doors whose deployment implied that the entire high-rise had been locked down.

Sue! he thought anxiously. *Johnny!* He derived scant comfort from the knowledge that Franklin and Valeria were most likely still down in SoHo with Alicia. How safe were his children—how safe was anyone—with Annihilus free to attack mankind at will? Unlike Blastaar, Annihilus would not be content to merely conquer Earth. The fearsome insectoid lived only to destroy.

"I'm sorry," Qury insisted with what sounded like genuine regret in her voice. Her mournful eyes sought out his. "I had no choice."

But Blastaar did. Mr. Fantastic turned on the heartless tyrant angrily. "How could you do this?" he demanded. Only the unyielding fabric of the adhesion suit kept him from springing at Blastaar like a striking cobra. "What can this possibly gain you?"

"A beachhead, as I said." Blastaar glanced up at the portal, where even now Annihilus was hurling another barrage of destructive energy against the recalcitrant blast doors. "Once Annihilus has gained control of your headquarters, he will open your own portal into the Negative Zone, where my fleet stands ready to pour into your universe, overwhelming Earth's pitiful defenses!"

With horror, Reed recalled the Baluurian armada that had attacked the *Explorer* shortly after he and Ben had arrived in the Negaverse. *Small wonder they detected our presence so quickly,* he realized. *They're staking out the area around the Debris Belt, just waiting for the access tunnel to open.*

He had no doubt that, once in control of the Nega-Portal, Annihilus had the intellect to expand the portal until it was large enough to accommodate Blastaar's battle cruisers. Unlike his bombastic rival, the insectoid had demonstrated considerable scientific expertise over the years. Indeed, he had once attempted to use the Nega-Portal to destroy all life in both universes. On that occasion, he had been dying—and was determined to take all of existence with him. The insectoid had since restored his health, by means of his Cosmic Control Rod, but no doubt he remained determined to exterminate any life-form that potentially posed a threat to his precious immortality.

"But . . . Annihilus?" Reed challenged Blastaar, horrified at the thought of the inhuman monster's genocidal agenda. "How could you possibly ally yourself with Annihilus again, after all the times you've betrayed each other? Good Lord, he killed Nyglar, your own mate. It's only a matter of time before he tries to destroy you, too. What could be worth taking that risk?"

"Vengeance," Blastaar said darkly. His heavy brows knitted in smoldering fury. "Not just for all the times you and your miserable breed have bested me, but for Burstaar as well!"

As in Burstaar's Revenge? Reed thought. "Who?"

"My son!" Blastaar snarled. "Slain by a so-called hero from your wretched dimension, the one who calls himself Captain Marvel." Blastaar's deadly fingers flexed at his sides, eager to blow the offending mortal to atoms. "He broke my son's neck with his bare hands, but he will pay for his crime even if I have to conquer your entire cosmos to do so.

There is nothing I will not do to find my son's murderer, even ally myself with that treacherous insect once more."

Reed assumed that Blastaar was referring to the current Captain Marvel, the son of the original Mar-Vell. "I am truly sorry to learn of your son's death. As a father myself, I can empathize with your loss." Reed prayed Blastaar could hear his sincerity. "But revenge will not bring your son back. Do not let your grief blind you to the danger posed by Annihilus. If Captain Marvel is indeed guilty of wrongdoing, I give you my word that the Fantastic Four will see that he stands trial for his crime."

"Keep your sympathy," Blastaar spat indignantly. "I have no use for either your pity or your word. The only reason you are still alive is that I need a backup plan in the unlikely event that Annihilus is defeated by your fellow humans." He glanced at the portal before them. "You will remain here to assist Qury in perfecting her device, so that it can be kept open indefinitely. If Annihilus fails, *you* will provide me with the means to invade your universe . . . and avenge my son!"

"Why should I help you?" Mr. Fantastic argued. His fists were clenched impotently inside the adhesion suit. "You must be insane to think I would assist you in conquering my own planet!"

Blastaar began to raise his hands in anger, then hesitated. Apparently he was not about to fall for the same trick twice. Instead of blasting another hole in Reed's adhesion suit, he stomped forward and delivered a backhanded blow that sent Mr. Fantastic flying across the room. "The subspace inverter!" Qury cried out in alarm as Reed slammed into a bank of blinking machinery, then collapsed in a heap onto the floor. Even trapped inside the suit, however, his malleable body absorbed the brunt of the impact. The image within the portal flickered momentarily, then restored itself.

"Listen to me, mortal!" Blastaar ranted. "One way or another, tomorrow or the day after, your pathetic world will fall beneath my legions. If you cooperate, perhaps I will spare your mewling offspring. If you do not . . . well, I have other scientists in my service, many of whom would no doubt be delighted to dissect your freakish anatomy." He smiled cruelly. "Perhaps we will see precisely how far you can be stretched before you snap!"

Shaking his head to clear his mind, Reed climbed unsteadily to his feet and staggered away from the equipment behind. Samra Qury rushed over to inspect the apparatus, which appeared to be undamaged. "Thank the Sacred Spores!" she gasped in relief, before glaring angrily at Blastaar. Clearly, she did not appreciate having the volatile warlord storming through her laboratories.

"Enough," Blastaar grunted impatiently, not at all bothered by Qury's resentful gaze. He wiped his hands of the feel of the adhesion suit. "I have wasted too much time here. I am anxious to return to the fleet." He turned toward Vatriin. "You and your men will remain here, to keep watch over the prisoner."

"But, sire!" the officer protested. Shock and dismay were written all over his weathered features. "I had hoped to take part in your glorious invasion of the other realm. Surely, there are already enough guards stationed here."

Blastaar scowled. "To guard one female academic, perhaps. But Richards requires greater care. You must watch him carefully, to ensure that he does not attempt to return to his world via the Posi-Portal." He glowered at Reed balefully, as if half-expecting Mr. Fantastic to make a break for the portal at any minute. "You must also maintain a vigilant watch for the Earthman's remaining comrades. It may be that the Human Torch and the Invisible Woman have troubles of their own to contend with." On the screen, the blast doors were visibly buckling beneath Annihilus's unremitting assault. "But you must be ready should they attempt to rescue their leader."

For himself, Reed hoped Sue and Johnny would not be so reckless as to venture into the Negative Zone while Annihilus remained at large in Manhattan. Defeating the genocidal invader was their top priority, even above Reed's own safety. *Just as my own priority has to be to destroy the Posi-Portal,* he realized, *and persuade Qury not to construct another one. No matter how much I want to rush home to defend my family.*

Vatriin knew better than to argue further with the volatile tyrant. Swallowing his disappointment, he stiffened his spine and assumed an erect military posture. "You may rely on me, sire. I shall not shirk my duty."

"See that you don't," Blastaar snapped. He cast a menacing gaze at Mr. Fantastic. "And the same applies to you, Richards. I will be monitoring your progress. If you are wise, you will not disappoint me." Blastaar's lips peeled back, exposing the fangs of a born predator. "As my subjects can tell you, I have never been known for my patience."

That much I had figured out for myself, Reed thought bitterly.

Without further adieu, Blastaar stalked out of the Positive Zone access chamber, leaving Reed and Samra Qury behind. Commander Vatriin glared at Mr. Fantastic venomously, no doubt blaming the human for this unsought reassignment. "What are you waiting for?" he growled at the two scientists. "Get to work."

10

THE BAXTER BUILDING WAS UNDER SIEGE.

But unlike a medieval fortress, the Fantastic Four's penthouse headquarters had more than a moat or drawbridge to defend it.

Plasma cannons rose from the ravaged rooftop, targeting the winged demon assailing the skyscraper. Streams of energized particles bombarded Annihilus, as he relentlessly pounded at the blast doors over the sealed elevator shaft with destructive bursts from his Cosmic Control Rod. Flashes of prismatic sparks detonated wherever the plasma beams clashed with the insectoid's cosmic energy blasts. Loud buzzes and hisses filled the air, but failed to drown out Annihilus's vainglorious ranting.

"This shall not deter me!" he proclaimed. His flapping wings held him in place above the rooftop. "I am Annihilus. I am invincible!"

In the command center, over four stories below, Sue feared that Annihilus was all too correct in his assessment of the situation. The plasma cannons, which she had raised to their highest settings, only seemed to be making him angry. *At this intensity, those beams would already have knocked out any lesser entity.*

Yet Annihilus merely chittered in annoyance. Momentarily distracted from his assault on the blast doors, he swept the roof with his cosmic broadsides, obliterating the automated plasma cannons, which had seemed nothing more than petty vexations to him. "There!" he declared. "Nothing shall hinder me from my goal!"

Satisfied that cannons were no more, he touched down on the battle-scarred remains of the Fantastic Four's private landing pad. All that remained of the brilliant blue 4 at the center of the pad was a cracked and discolored carpet of broken enamel tiles. He strode across the rooftop until he reached the impregnable blast doors lying flat against the floor of the roof. He gazed down at the obstinate barrier at his feet. The reinforced titanium had already started to buckle inward, the six-inch-wide metal crumpling like cheap aluminum. One more blast might be enough to knock the doors off their hinges.

A hellish glow crackled around the invader's Cosmic Control Rod. Pure, primal energy lashed out, and the ruptured doors collapsed at last, plunging down into the depths of the empty elevator shaft. In the command center, four floors down, Sue heard the mangled metal fortifications crash against the top of the elevator compartment resting several yards away.

He's done it, she realized in horror. *He's in!*

She stared at the monitor, where Annihilus stood upon the brink of the exposed shaft, peering down in the murky abyss. "What's he waiting for?" she asked aloud.

"Just playing it safe," Johnny guessed. Her brother sat a few feet away, in his own contoured seat. His color was looking better, even though his face and costume still looked as if they'd been kicked from one end of Latveria to another. "Don't forget, Sis, he's as paranoid as he is nasty. He didn't get to be over a thousand years old, or so he claims, by not looking before he leaped."

This is true, Sue thought. Over the years, she'd had less contact with Annihilus than the rest of her family, but what Johnny had suggested matched everything she knew about the ruthless alien conqueror. Her slender fingers were poised over the controls of the building's internal defense network. *Let's hope we can give him something to be paranoid about.*

After a moment's surveillance, Annihilus's desire to reach the Negative Zone Chamber won out over his eternal suspicion. Folding his wings against his back, he began crawling headfirst down the walls of the elevator shaft—just as Sue had hoped he would.

She had already slaved the elevator controls to the console in front of her. "Going up," she said darkly, and stabbed the button beneath her finger.

In response, the elevator went surging up the shaft at a ridiculously unsafe speed. With any luck, the rocketing steel box would squash Annihilus like the bug he was.

"Cool," Johnny remarked, impressed by Sue's improvised assault on the insectoid. He lurched from his seat to stare over her shoulder at the graphics charting the elevator's ascent. "Remind me not to get you mad at me."

"Nobody invades my home," she informed him. "Especially not a cockroach with delusions of grandeur."

The image on her monitor had switched from the rooftop to the interior of shaft. On the screen, the speeding elevator collided with the creeping insectoid at nearly one hundred miles an hour. Cosmic energy flashed around

Annihilus a split second before the elevator hit. The jarring sound of tearing metal echoed down the shaft, penetrating the command center itself. Red-hot sparks cascaded from the site of the collision.

In truth, Sue wasn't nearly as confident as she sounded. Annihilus had already survived a nova-burst and plasma cannons; was a runaway elevator really going to do him in? *Who knows?* she thought, crossing her fingers. *Sometimes you just need to hit something hard enough.*

She suspected Ben would agree.

A mass of pulverized steel now blocked the shaft just below the roof. Sue clicked hurriedly from camera to camera, hoping to determine Annihilus's fate. She caught a view of the elevator's undercarriage, then caught her breath as a pair of nacreous purple gauntlets ripped the floor of the elevator asunder, creating a gap through which Annihilus could crawl back out into the shaft.

"Oh, hell," Johnny blurted. "What's it going to take to stop this guy?"

I don't know, Sue thought despairingly. Swallowing her disappointment over the failure of her elevator stunt, she realized that she had to drive Annihilus out of the elevator shaft somehow. *That's a quick route down to the lab area. I can't make it that easy for him.*

A thought occurred to her and she activated the fire suppression system. Thousands of gallons of flame-retardant foam poured into the shaft, filling it up in seconds. The thick, opaque froth was unlikely to suffocate Annihilus, as it might a more vulnerable entity, but it would certainly interfere with his vision and perhaps discourage him from continuing down through the cloying spume. *And as if that's not enough, let's make that route even less appealing.*

An instant later, a lattice of sizzling photonic beams

formed all along the length of the shaft. The crisscrossing ruby rays were so tightly woven that even Mr. Fantastic would have had trouble contorting himself through them, plus the heat of the beams caused the foam to seethe and steam almost immediately. Scalding fumes rose from the simmering gook.

" 'Double, double toil and trouble.' " Sue was no witch, but she could whip up a pretty noxious cauldron if she had to. "Go ahead, Annihilus. Be my guest, dive right in!"

The crawling insectoid buzzed angrily. Perhaps too conscious of his dignity to crawl headfirst into the boiling foam, he rejected the polluted shaft in favor of the nearest exit. A pair of sliding doors blocked the entrance to the top floor of the building, but Annihilus dug his armored fingers into the airtight crack between the doors and tore them apart. Sue tracked his progress on her monitor as he stormed into . . .

The hangar on the thirty-eighth floor.

A variety of space-age vehicles resided within the spacious hangar, along with a vintage hot rod Johnny was restoring. The latest model of the Fantasticar occupied a position of honor upon a hydraulic lift platform in the center of the vast chamber. Spare modules for the car, each capable of independent flight, were stowed in convenient niches, in various states of repair and renovation. A rack of gravity-defying Skycycles ran along the southern wall of the hangar, while Johnny's latest toy—a 1957 Ford Thunderbird with a cherry-red paint job and a pearly-white top—was up on jacks, looking slightly out of place among the various futuristic vehicles. An air lock led to the cockpit of the Pogo Plane, which rested in the five-story rocket silo attached to the building's exterior. An aircraft R&D lab, machine shop, and air-traffic control station also shared the garage.

Annihilus glanced around the hangar in disdain, seeing no sign of the Negative Zone Chamber. "This is not what I seek!"

How well does Annihilus know his way around here? Sue wondered. The Baxter Building had been completely destroyed and rebuilt since the last time Annihilus had invaded the Fantastic Four's home, and even then, according to Alicia, he had barely ventured beyond Reed's laboratories. Plus, the actual layout of the labs and the command center, along with the rest of the headquarters, often shifted in response to Reed's never-ending improvements and inspirations. Indeed, her brilliant husband had occasionally been known to teleport entire rooms from floor to floor, depending on the needs of his current project. *With luck, Annihilus doesn't know exactly where to find the Nega-Portal.*

"Hang on, Sis!" Johnny said. "I have an idea." He sat down at the adjacent console and vigorously worked the controls. Waves of heat rippled off him in his enthusiasm. "All our rides can be remote-controlled, providing you know the right passwords, so . . . ."

In the hangar, the Fantasticar rose noiselessly off the lift platform and turned toward Annihilus. High-intensity xenon headlights caught the invader in their glare, and violet tractor beams grabbed hold of Annihilus, locking him in place. "What fresh impertinence is this?" he demanded. A golden aura crackled around him, and with a convulsive motion, he broke loose from the stasis beams. "No mere mechanism can hold me!"

Feverishly operating the controls, Johnny fired up the Fantasticar and sent it barreling at Annihilus. The four-thousand-pound vehicle accelerated from zero to a hundred in less than a second. "That's it!" Johnny said. "You're going to be a smear on our windshield!"

But the immortal monster threw up his hands and halted the oncoming vehicle with nothing more than the preternatural strength of his own two arms. Powerful thrusters strained against Annihilus's might, but the insectoid didn't budge. The stalled vehicle revved loudly in frustration.

Let's call in some reinforcements, Sue thought. Following Johnny's lead, she activated the Skycycles resting against the wall. Five shining chrome cycles, including a smaller version equipped with training wheels and a parachute, came to life at once and lifted off from their berths. The lean, stripped-down vehicles resembled conventional bikes, except that the antigrav repellers took the place of wheels. Not quite as versatile as the Fantasticar, which was the flying equivalent of an SUV, the Skycycles were more maneuverable—and much easier to park.

Right now, though, they were useful only as missiles. At Sue's command, they launched themselves at Annihilus one after another. The kamikaze cycles smashed to pieces against the insectoid's wings and shell-like exoskeleton, hitting him at over one-hundred-and-fifty miles per hour, even as he continued to hold back the surging Fantasticar.

"Enough!" he raged. Lifting the Fantasticar above his head, he hurled it across the length of the hangar, right toward the cherry-red T-bird.

"Oh, no!" Johnny gasped. "Not again!" The customized sports car had already been trashed months ago, during an all-out brawl between the Thing and Wolverine. "I just got the transmission working again!"

Twenty-first-century engineering met classic automotive design as the diverted Fantasticar slammed into the Thunderbird, merging together in a violent marriage of past and present modes of transportation. A whitewall tire spun uselessly above the wreckage. A modular segment broke off from the rear of the Fantasticar, landing upside down on the floor of the garage. Oil and liquid deuterium spread out from beneath the demolished vehicles, like blood from a corpse.

Johnny whimpered as though being tortured. "Oh, man . . ."

Unlike her brother, the Invisible Woman barely reacted to the widespread destruction within the hangar. Cars and cycles could be rebuilt; what mattered now was keeping Annihilus from the Nega-Portal for as long as possible.

But why did he need the portal in the first place? Hadn't Reed theorized that someone in the Negative Zone had already found another way through to the positive universe? Annihilus's very presence here on Earth would seem to bear that theory out, and to provide fairly damning evidence as to who was responsible for the recent incursions. So why would Annihilus want Reed's portal as well?

Unless, she speculated, the gateway in the Zone had certain limitations that interfered with Annihilus's professed goal of bringing an entire army through the cosmic barrier dividing the two universes. Hadn't Reed said something about each of today's rifts only lasting for seconds at a time, just long enough to admit a single lifeform?

That must be it, she concluded. *Our portal is the only one that can hold the gateway open long enough to bring through his troops. That's what Annihilus is after.*

She shuddered at the realization that only she and Johnny stood between Earth and a full-scale invasion from the Negative Zone.

There was still time to destroy the Nega-Portal, of course, before Annihilus could reach it. But that might leave Reed and Ben with no way to return to Earth. Reed may have hypothesized the existence of another portal, somewhere within the Negative Zone itself, but Sue couldn't be sure that Reed and Ben would find the other portal, or even that it truly existed. *No,* Sue thought. *I can't destroy the Nega-Portal, not until the rest of my family returns.*

"Worthless humans!" Annihilus wiped the residue of the Skycycles from his carapace as he glared at them over the monitor. "I know you must be observing me from somewhere in this wretched den. Know that none of your delaying tactics will keep me from my destiny. The day of humanity's extinction is at hand!"

"You know," Johnny said, scowling, "just once I'd like to fight someone who wasn't in love with the sound of his own voice."

"Count your blessings," Sue replied. "How else are we supposed to figure out what our enemies are up to if they aren't constantly boasting about their powers and master plans?" She paused. "We can't let him get to the Nega-Portal."

"I know," her brother intoned. She could tell from his voice that he realized the awesome responsibility that had been laid upon them—and what was at stake if they failed. "Dammit, why did Reed have to keep messing with the Negative Zone anyway? Why couldn't he just leave well enough alone?"

Sue came to her husband's defense. "Johnny Storm! Don't you dare blame Reed for any of this. You know that everything he does is for the betterment of mankind."

"Sure he means well," Johnny shot back, "but you and I both know that sometimes his curiosity gets the better of him. We wouldn't be in this mess if Reed had just shut down the Nega-Portal years ago!"

"Reed's genius has saved this planet many times over," she reminded him sharply. Deep down inside, though, she knew that Johnny wasn't completely wrong. In fact, Reed had occasionally talked about closing the portal to the Negative Zone forever, but he had never actually gone through with it. Perhaps because the lure of an entire alien universe was just too much of a temptation to his scientific instincts? "You need to have faith in Reed," she insisted, as much to herself as to her brother. "Just like I do."

Something in her tone must have alerted Johnny that he might have gone too far. "Sorry, Sis," he said, backing down. "This whole situation just sucks, you know?" He let out a worried sigh. "Man, I wish the Avengers weren't out of town."

On the screen, Annihilus had given up looking for the best way out of the hangar. Choosing to forge his own path to the lower levels of the Baxter Building, he directed an earth-shattering cosmic blast at the floor in front of him. Blastproof steel tiles melted before the onslaught. Four stories down, Sue and Johnny felt their headquarters tremble.

"So what now?" he asked her.

Sue's face mirrored her resolve. "We hold the line, until Reed and Ben get back."

She only hoped the rest of the Fantastic Four were faring better than they were.

11

BLASTAAR HAD DEPARTED, TAKING his shuttle and flagship with him. Now there was no way off Hethael, except perhaps through the Posi-Portal itself. Commander Vatriin's men zealously guarded the entrance to the portal, however, depriving Mr. Fantastic of that recourse, even if he had been ready to return to the Earth, which he wasn't.

Not yet.

"Your work is truly impressive, Magister Qury," Reed commented as he reviewed the female scientist's notes on a monitor in the main laboratory. Abstruse calculations and graphs flashed across the screen. The gloves of his adhesion suit made operating the attached control pad difficult, but Vatriin had been adamant about the Earthman remaining in the suit, only occasionally opening the garment so that Reed could feed or relieve himself. It felt as though several hours had passed, but Reed knew how subjective that could be within the Negative Zone. "Some of the approaches you've taken to finessing the space-time differential are quite creative."

"Thank you, Dr. Richards," Qury said. "That's high praise coming from a scientist of your stature." She seemed more relaxed now that Blastaar was not striding through her lab like a bull in a china ship, or whatever the Negaverse equivalent of that would be. She worked at stainless-steel counter nearby, assembling a complicated apparatus from diagrams provided by Mr. Fantastic. Her laser welder fused two crystalline diodes together. "And, please, call me Samra."

Vatriin scowled at their easy collegiality. The Baluurian officer watched them like a hawk from the rear of the lab. Two armed soldiers stood by, ready to enforce their commander's edicts. They looked more than a little bored.

"And you can call me Reed," he insisted. Conscious of Vatriin's baleful scrutiny, he made a point of turning the conversation back to the task at hand. "It looks like you've made substantial progress regarding the targeting mechanism."

"Don't remind me!" she said, sighing at the memory. "That was a nightmare. It wasn't enough that I open up a gateway to an entirely different universe. I was under orders to find a path that led, more or less, to your own headquarters in your own city on your own homeworld! It took me months just to find the correct planet, let alone the right continent. I confess, before I managed to zero in on the island of New York Manhattan, several of my earliest test animals ended up lost in space, or in some inhospitable desert or ocean."

Reed couldn't help wondering what exotic life-forms from the Negative Zone might have managed to survive in the remote corners of the Earth. *That might explain some of the more recent "monster sightings" reported in the tabloid press,* he theorized. Apparently the most recent wave of incursions was hardly the first. *I should probably attempt to track some of those other specimens down—if and when I ever return to Earth.*

He recalled the colossal jellyfish that had invaded Times Square shortly before his departure. "That reminds me," he said, hoping that Johnny had managed to contain the misplaced creature before Annihilus had appeared on the scene. "How on Earth did you manage to get that gigantic invertebrate through your portal? The entrance hardly seemed large enough."

"Gigantic?" For a moment, she appeared puzzled by his query. Then comprehension dawned in her eyes. "That's easily enough explained. Let me show you." Walking over from the work counter, she leaned over Reed's shoulder and typed a command into the touch pad. The equations on his monitor vanished instantly, to be replaced by transmitted images from a menagerie located on one of the upper levels of the underground science station. Dozens of exotic alien specimens—some familiar to Reed, some not—were kept confined by a variety of cages, tanks, and force fields. Mr. Fantastic felt a stab of sympathy for the captive creatures, remembering once again his own stint in Annihilus's personal menagerie.

Qury adjusted the controls, and the picture zeroed in on a translucent jellyfish floating in water-filled tank. It looked identical to the one Reed had seen oozing down Seventh Avenue, but only a fraction as large.

"The icthyplasms live in the depths of the Southern Vashomian Ocean, under extremely high pressure. Taken out of that pressure, into the open air, they expanded to several times their original size." She looked inward, searching her memory. "I recall now that I had reservations about sending that one icthyplasmoid to those particular coordinates, but Annihilus overruled me. I think he wanted to cause a disruption on your homeworld, perhaps to distract you and your teammates from his larger agenda."

That sounds like Annihilus, Reed thought. The diabolical insectoid was as cunning as he was powerful. "I take it the tank on the screen is artificially pressurized to approximate the conditions of its native environment?"

"Naturally," Qury replied. She held her three-fingered hands only a few feet apart. "Believe me, the specimen was only this large when it went through the Portal. But Annihilus had loosened the seal on its tank, so that the container would come apart during its passage through the Distortion Area."

"I see," Reed said, his curiosity satisfied on this one nagging detail. "And I suppose Annihilus insisted on numerous test runs before venturing into your portal himself?"

Qury laughed bitterly. "Risk his sacred immortality on an untried device? Not likely! I half-expected him to push me through the portal first." She glanced around at the confining walls of the underground laboratory. "Which would have been one way to get away from this place, I guess."

Vatriin cleared his throat ominously.

Taking the hint, Reed tapped on the touch pad and restored Qury's notes to the monitor. "In any event, I think I see a way to further fine-tune the targeting mechanism, if we expand the coordinate field to the subatomic level."

"Of course!" she exclaimed, her husky voice alive with excitement. She peered over his shoulder as Reed keyed a few crucial changes to the relevant equations. "I think I see where you're going. But won't that throw off the quantum probabilities?"

"Not if we divide the spin coefficient by the square root of infinity," he pointed out. As it happened, he had dealt with many of the same issues while developing the new cross-temporal search engine he had been testing right before this entire crisis had erupted. "Then the eighth-dimensional phase variable will cancel out the prime uncertainty factor."

Query slapped the smooth red plates upon her forehead. "Why didn't I think of that!" A cascade of new ideas flashed behind her eyes. "Now if we can just find a way to reduce the energy expenditure by a several degrees of magnitude ..."

Careful, Mr. Fantastic cautioned himself. He didn't want get so caught up in the thrill of scientific accomplishment that he lost sight of what really mattered, namely saving the Earth from a full-scale invasion from the Negative Zone. The last thing he wanted to do was emulate the Alec Guinness character in the movie *The Bridge on the River Kwai,* who became so engrossed in the monumental challenge of constructing the titular bridge that he completely forgot that he was building it for his Japanese captors. *Ultimately, I'm here to shut down Qury's portal, not perfect it.*

Which meant he needed to change the subject.

"Tell me about yourself and your people," he said, turning his seat around to face her. "I don't believe I've ever met your species before."

She stepped back from the control panel, apparently willing to take a break. "Well, I confess I'd never even heard of you or Earth before, until Annihilus found me."

"Annihilus?" Reed sat up straight, instantly wanting to know more. What was the connection between Qury and Annihilus?

Her voice took on a forlorn quality. "My people are called the H'Zarri. We come from a constellation not far from here, where we lived in peace until our existence came to the attention of Annihilus. He and his Scavengers devastated our world, killing thousands. He would have exterminated us all, except our leaders offered him our greatest minds in exchange for the preservation of our species."

"Including you," Reed guessed.

She nodded grimly. "As it is, he destroyed our industrial base and technology, reducing us to a barely subsistence living." A silver tear leaked down the glossy planes of her face. The metallic secretion resembled liquid mercury. "We had an advanced technological civilization once, with a rich and vibrant culture, but now my fellow H'Zarri are little more than starving cave dwellers. That's the only way Annihilus could be certain that we would no longer pose a threat to him—as if we ever did!"

A high price to pay for survival, Reed thought. The wanton destruction of the H'Zarri's culture appalled him. All those centuries of striving and intellectual progress wiped away, just to satisfy Annihilus's obsessive need for absolute security. *Humanity will suffer the same fate, or worse, unless I can find some way to foil his current scheme.*

"I'm very sorry," he told Qury sincerely. His heart went out to the oppressed scientist and her unfortunate people. "What happened to your people was a tragedy of catastrophic proportions."

"Thank you." She wiped the glistening tear from her cheeks and tried to regain her composure. "Anyway, when Annihilus discovered that my speciality was the physics of multiversal reality, he immediately put me to work on devising some way for him to cross over into the positive universe. He told me of you and how you had breached the barrier in the past, shared with me everything he had gleaned of your technology from his various encounters with you, and forced to me to find a way to adapt your discoveries to the physical laws of our own plane." She looked away from Reed, unable to meet his eyes. "I regret to say that I found the challenge quite stimulating."

I don't blame you, he thought. He knew only too well how intoxicating the pursuit of knowledge could be. He had been known to lock himself in his labs for days at a time, doing without sleep or relaxation, while hot on the trail of some earthshaking new discovery. *If I hadn't opened the door to the Negative Zone in the first place, neither Blastaar or Annihilus would even know Earth existed.*

Yet, despite the grievous consequences of that particular discovery, part of him still couldn't bring himself to regret pursuing that, or any other, line of inquiry. To believe otherwise went against one of his core values: that, in the long run, the pursuit of knowledge was worth any risk. No true scientist could turn his back on the truth. *I have to believe that,* he realized, *or my life's work is meaningless.*

"But I don't understand," he said. "How did Blastaar get involved? If this was all Annihilus's doing, why did he even need to join forces with Blastaar again?"

Qury's gaze darted toward Vatriin and his men. "The region of space around the Vortex is currently controlled by the Baluurians. Since that's where your own portal leads to, Annihilus would have had to wage a costly war against Blastaar and his empire before he could have even begun to implement his scheme to conquer your planet. It was easier to make a temporary alliance with Blastaar now than try to seize and hold that region with his own forces, especially while he was otherwise occupied in your own universe."

Mr. Fantastic nodded thoughtfully. What Qury was saying made sense. Annihilus's plot would proceed more smoothly with an accomplice who could remain behind in the Negative Zone while the insectoid attempted to seize control of the Baxter Building. No doubt Annihilus intended to dispose of the Baluurians at some later date. *I wouldn't be surprised if he considers Earth a greater threat.*

And Blastaar's need to avenge his son's death had made

the barbaric warlord all too willing to enter into yet another deal with the Negative Zone's resident devil.

"But what about you?" he said softly to Qury. "How could you help Annihilus invade my world? Surely, after what happened to the H'Zarri, you must know what he has in store for my people. How could you be a party to such a heinous atrocity?"

He hated to be so hard on his fellow scientist, who had already endured so much heartbreak. Heaven knew he bore his own share of responsibility for the present crisis. But there was no way around it, not if he wanted to succeed in his mission. Before he even attempted to escape the Negative Zone, he had to be certain that Samra Qury would not build another Posi-Portal for his enemies. *If that means I have to jab at her conscience, so be it. The future of everything I care for is at stake.*

She recoiled from Reed's harsh words, staggering backward from the control panel. "I had no choice!" she sobbed. "They have my family. My parents and my brother. They're holding them hostage on some Spore-forsaken prison planet. They said they'd kill them all if I didn't complete the portal!"

Reed suddenly felt like a monster. "I didn't know," he began. *What would I do,* he thought, *if someone threatened Sue or the kids? Especially if I had already lost everything else in my life?* "I didn't realize—"

"That's enough," Commander Vatriin barked. Reed guessed that he had kept quiet up until now because he had also been interested in what Qury had to say about Annihilus and his motives. Perhaps Vatriin had his own secret doubts about the wisdom of his monarch's current alliance. The plight of Qury's family, on the other hand, meant nothing to him. "Get back to work, both of you!"

Qury retreated to her workbench, probably grateful to escape Mr. Fantastic's painful accusations. Reed turned back to his equations, torn between guilt and frustration. Qury's fears for her family's safety reminded him of the danger his own wife and children were facing at this very moment. Were Sue and Johnny still fighting back against Annihilus, or had the cosmically powered insectoid already defeated them, perhaps even killed them? What if even now Annihilus was opening the Nega-Portal for Blastaar's fleet? He had to resist the temptation to run to the Posi-Portal to find out what was happening back home.

Had the conquest of Earth already begun?

Beeeep!

An incoming transmission hijacked his monitor and Blastaar's bestial visage appeared upon the screen. "I grow impatient," he stated without preamble. Behind Blastaar's head and shoulders could be seen a glimpse of the tyrant's throne room upon *Burstaar's Revenge.* "What progress have you made?"

This was not the first time Blastaar had intrusively checked on them. Reed took this as a good sign, as it meant that Annihilus had not yet activated the portal in the Baxter Building. Once Blastaar had an open gateway to Earth, he would no longer need Samra Qury's more problematic Posi-Portal. *Good for you, Sue, Johnny,* he thought gratefully. *Don't let Annihilus get through to my portal!*

"I'm working on it," Reed insisted, "but you mustn't underestimate the difficulties involved. The Negative Zone operates under an entirely different set of physical laws than my own universe. That's why Magister Qury's device demands so much energy to function." He shook his head, as though intimidated by the daunting task before him. "It's not just a matter of reversing my own equations."

He was only partly lying. The Negaverse *did* function differently from the positive universe, as demonstrated by such paradoxical phenomena as the universal atmosphere and the Annihilation Vortex, but, in truth, Mr. Fantastic did have some promising ideas on how to reduce the power drain on Qury's space-time distorters. From what he could tell, just bypassing the temporal singularities along the sixth multiversal axis should cut several terajoules of energy out of the process.

Still, there's no reason Blastaar needs to know that.

"It's true, Emperor," Qury confirmed, joining Reed by the monitor. She stuck her tools back onto her lab coat. "But we are making progress. We were just discussing ways to improve the targeting mechanism." She glanced over her shoulder at their Baluurian guards. "Commander Vatriin can vouch for that."

Blastaar scowled. "Not good enough! The targeting is already accurate enough for my purposes. What I need is a portal that will stay open long enough to transport troops through." He glowered at the two scientists from light-years away. "Perhaps you need more incentive, Richards! Vatriin, I think the Earthman would like to take a walk outside. The subzero temperature might stimulate his brain—if he doesn't die of frostbite first!"

"As you command, sire!" Vatriin responded crisply. He gestured at his men, who stepped forward and seized Mr. Fantastic by the arms. Reed could feel their viselike grip even through the heavily insulated adhesion suit. "To the surface with him!"

"Wait!" Reed shouted at the monitor. "I have something else to offer! Something that should be of great interest to you!"

Vatriin held up his hand to halt his men. He looked to Blastaar for instruction.

"What is it, human?" the warlord asked. His black eyes narrowed suspiciously. "You had best not be toying with me."

"A weapon," Reed volunteered. He nodded at Qury, who fetched the apparatus she had been working on. "A weapon you can use against Annihilus—when the time comes."

Interest showed on Blastaar's bestial features. Qury held up the partially-assembled device in front of the monitor, and the tyrant scratched his beard thoughtfully. "Tell me more," he instructed.

"I can do better than that." Reed tapped at the control panel. "Let me send you the specs."

Blastaar glanced down at the complicated diagrams, which had presumably appeared at the bottom of his own screen. "Bah! These mean nothing to me," he snarled after a moment. "I'm interested in results, not technical details. Tell me what this so-called weapon does."

"Well, in brief," Reed began, "I call it the Distortion Ray." He dragged out the explanation for as long as he could, stalling for time. Every moment he kept Blastaar listening was another moment he could avoid working on the Posi-Portal. "In short," he concluded, "not even Annihilus will be able to resist the effect of the ray. His utter destruction is all but assured."

Blastaar eyed Mr. Fantastic warily, as though what the human was saying was too good to be true. "One thing puzzles me, Richards. Why should you offer me the means to vanquish my ally of the moment? What stake do you have in our rivalry?"

"That's simple," Reed answered without hesitation. "You're a brute and a barbarian, Blastaar. An arrogant conqueror without scruples or honor. But at least you're sane, to a degree. Under you, Earth would suffer only the oppression of a ruthless tyrant. Annihilus, on the other hand, is an insane killing machine who will not rest until the entire human race is rendered extinct. Given a choice, you're definitely the lesser of two evils."

Not that I intend to let either of you get your bloodthirsty hands on my world, he added silently. *Not if I can help it.*

Still, his cogent analysis of the situation had the virtue of being true and seemed satisfactory to Blastaar. "Excellent," he pronounced. "Have your guards release the prisoner, Vatriin. It seems Richards has more important things to do than visit the surface of Hethael." On the screen, an aide approached Blastaar and whispered something inaudible into the monarch's ear. "I must attend to affairs of state. You may continue your work." His hirsute mane bristled. "But be warned: the next time I deign to contact you, I expect a working Distortion Ray *and* an improved portal for my legions. Do not disappoint me!"

The transmission ended abruptly, restoring Reed's equations to the screen. The guards released his arms and resumed their positions at the rear of the lab. "You heard the Emperor," Vatriin informed Reed and Qury sourly. "Resume your labors."

Qury took the piece of the Distortion Ray back to her counter. Reed heard the hiss of intricate components being welded together.

That went well enough, he decided. But how much longer could he stall before Blastaar demanded results? The erratic passage of time within the Zone only made it harder for Reed to determine just how long he had been held captive. *Everything is going as planned,* he reminded himself. *I just have to wait a little longer. . . .*

12

IN CONTRAST TO THE FUTURISTIC DECOR preva-
lent throughout much of the Fantastic Four's headquarters,
the Richards family kitchen and dining area on the thirty-
seventh floor was markedly conventional. Homey even.
Instead of sterile steel walls and air locks, faux-wood cabi-
nets and imitation linoleum were the order of the day.
Crayoned drawings and finger paintings were magnetized
to the family-sized refrigerator, alongside shopping lists and
PTA schedules. A fruit bowl, brimming over with fresh ap-
ples and oranges, served as a centerpiece atop the stained-
wood kitchen island. An old-fashioned paper calendar was
pinned to the wall next to the telephone, with important
dates and meetings scribbled in pencil. Valeria's high chair
was rolled against the kitchen table, while dirty cups and
dishes were piled in the sink, just waiting for robotic drones
to attend to them. Perfectly ordinary microwave and toaster
ovens, purchased downtown at Macy's, rested upon the
kitchen counter. A CHUCK E. CHEESE mug held spare change
and paper clips.

Sue had insisted on the relative normalcy, in an effort to
maintain some distinction between their professional and

personal lives. "We're not just the Fantastic Four," she had often reminded Reed, whenever he felt an urge to replace the "obsolete" technology in the kitchen with something more efficient. "We're the Richards family, too, and I don't want our children to ever forget that." She could only guess how much it cost her husband not to tinker with the coffeemaker, or add nanotechnology to the blender, but it was a testament to the strength of their marriage that the kitchen was as retro as it was. (Aside from the robotic cleanup crew that is; she wasn't completely unreasonable.)

All of which explains why Sue's heart broke a little when, upon the screen in the command center, she saw Annihilus smash through the ceiling into their breakfast nook. *This isn't just our headquarters,* she thought, fighting back tears. *This is our home.*

Debris rained down from the hangar deck above as the ageless invader dropped down onto the kitchen floor. His wings flared out behind him, knocking over the baby's high chair and overturning the fruit bowl. Cold green eyes searched the area, the cozy domestic atmosphere Sue had worked so hard to foster completely lost on them. Did Annihilus even eat or drink as mortals did, or was the eldritch energy of his Cosmic Control Rod all he needed to sustain him?

"Monster!" Sue spat. Sentiment gave way to an icy rage as she watched the intruder violate the sanctity of her home. How dare Annihilus defile this precious space? Only hours ago, she had served her children breakfast mere inches away from where this . . . creature . . . now stood.

"It'll be okay, Sis," Johnny said. Sitting beside her, he gave her hand a comforting squeeze. Their squabble over Reed's responsibility for the crisis had been put behind them. "We'll get this creep, one way or another."

Unluckily for Annihilus, the kitchen's harmless appearance was deceptive. Not only was every fabric and surface completely fireproof, as only made sense in a household whose residents included the Human Torch, and reinforced to stand up to the punishing weight of the Thing, but the homey facade also hid a multitude of advanced security measures—as the immortal insectoid was about to find out.

A solid titanium/spent-uranium capture cage sprang upward from the linoleum floor, trapping Annihilus behind thick steel bars. He instinctively grabbed on to the bars to pull them apart, only to be jolted by twenty-five volts of electricity, the maximum amount allowed by the safety protocols. All the containment devices in the building were designed to be nonlethal, with the degree of force automatically calculated based on various parameters Reed had programmed into the system, including the ability to recognize any and all of the Fantastic Four's recurring foes. Sue trusted her husband to have long ago entered Annihilus into the computer's database.

"Filthy mammals!" he protested. "Is there no end to these primitive booby traps?" Bracing himself for the shock this time, he again took hold of the spent-uranium bars and wrenched them from their slots. The cramped dimensions of the cage forced him to fold his wings tightly against him as he squeezed out of the cell through the gap he had created. Once free, he angrily threw the twisted bars aside, shattering both a mug rack and cookie jar. "You but delay the inevitable. No power on this world or any other can stand against me!"

He stalked out of the dining area into the adjacent living room. A large plasma television screen dominated the far end of the room, above a combined DVD/VHS/VR player. Plush armchairs and sofas faced the screen, including a jumbo-sized easy chair designed specifically for Ben. A half-finished "Captain America" jigsaw puzzle took up the better part of a low mahogany coffee table, while this morning's edition of *The Daily Bugle,* open to the Saturday crossword, rested on the end table next to Ben's chair, beside an unusually large and stubby pencil. Framed photos, including one of Sue's late father, Dr. Franklin Storm, were displayed on the mantel above the fireplace. A holographic fire blazed in the hearth. Stuffed animals and model race cars littered the carpet.

Annihilus eyed the TV screen with interest. Perhaps he thought it might offer a window into the Negative Zone? In his paranoid imagination, he no doubt assumed that the Fantastic Four spent their every waking hour plotting to depose him and steal his Cosmic Control Rod.

The TV remote, sitting upon the coffee table amidst the scattered pieces of the jigsaw puzzle, caught his eye, and he snatched it up and started jabbing the buttons experimentally. The TV screen lit up and music blared from the speakers. On the eighty-four-inch screen, a human female wearing a skintight, silver outfit zipped about a dance floor on roller skates while singing her heart out. Glittering bracelets and bangles adorned the young woman's slender arms. Turquoise face paint added an exotic touch to her graceful features. Strawberry-blond hair tumbled over her bare shoulders. Brightly colored starbursts flared all around her, strobing in time to the music.

"You're watching VH1," a male announcer's voice interrupted the woman's song. "Behind the Music . . . Dazzler!"

"Human inanity!" Annihilus pronounced. He hurled the remote into the screen, which exploded in a shower of sparks. Watching on her own monitor, Sue didn't know whether to laugh or cry.

"So much for watching TV tonight," Johnny quipped. "We're going to need an 'Extreme Makeover' of our own, assuming we come out of this okay."

Concealed gas jets protruded from the ceiling and began spraying the living room with powerful narcotic fumes. As before, the nature of the knockout gas had been determined by the building's automated defense system, depending on the identity of the intruder. Sue wondered if this gas was a variant on the tranquilizer Reed had used on both the Borer and the Scavenger earlier this afternoon.

Has it really been only a few hours? she marveled. It felt as if ages had passed since she and Alicia had taken the kids out for brunch. She felt a lump in her throat as she considered just how quickly that idyllic Saturday morning had been torn away from her. They were supposed to be having a picnic now, but instead her entire family was apart and in danger. She didn't even know where Reed and Ben were right now. *How long have they been away?*

If the gas was indeed based on the same drug as before, it seemed to have less effect on Annihilus than on his inhuman servitors. He coughed irritably upon inhaling the acrid fumes, but did not fall. Instead he extended his demonic wings to their full span, then flapped them energetically, generating a gale-force wind that overturned furniture and sent all three-hundred-and-fifty pieces of the "Captain America" puzzle blowing in the air like red-white-and-blue confetti. Ben's crossword and pencil went flying as well, and the photos upon the mantel toppled over. Sue winced as the frame containing her father's photo crashed on the hearth, cracking in two.

Johnny growled heatedly, incensed by the wanton vandalism. The temperature within the defense center rose by a degree. "I'd like to toast him over a slow fire!"

Sue knew just how he felt.

The sudden wind dispelled the gas within seconds, crushing her hopes once more, and leaving Annihilus free to explore the rest of the floor at will. His heavy green boots trampled over Valeria's favorite stuffed bunny as he swept out of the desecrated living room. A miniature Spider-Mobile crunched beneath his heel.

"Tremble in fear, humans!" he taunted Sue and Johnny, adding insult to injury. He crashed through a pair of locked double doors into the narrow hallway that divided the kitchen and living room from the family's recreational facilities. "Soon your universe will fall before me. Soon I shall be safe from your kind at last!"

Bypassing the men's and women's locker rooms, he charged into the Fantastic Four's private gymnasium. Weights, treadmills, mats, balance beams, and other exercise equipment filled the soundproofed chamber, which must have looked strange and inexplicable to the insectoid's alien eyes. The Thing had his own designated workout section, safely partitioned from the rest, where the weights were measured in tons, not pounds. A ten-ton, titanium medicine ball was numbered among Ben's training gear, along with a punching bag stuffed with shredded iron. Vibranium panels on the walls and floor of the gym were capable of absorbing literally earthshaking bumps and jolts.

Now one of those same panels slid open to release another variety of anti-intrusion measures. A pair of metallic disks, about the size of Frisbees, flew from the walls and attached themselves to the front and back of Annihilus's shell-covered thorax. Humming loudly, the disks set the startled invader spinning above the floor at incredible speed. Centrifugal force sucked the air from his insectile lungs, while hopefully keeping Annihilus too disoriented to free himself before the ever-increasing acceleration rendered him unconscious.

The gravi-polarizers, Sue thought, recognizing the magnetic disks. She recalled how the same devices had once immobilized the Thing, not long after Reed had first invented them. Mr. Fantastic had only improved on the technology since then. *But will that be enough?*

The Baxter Building's automated defense system was trying every trick it had against Annihilus, adapting and adjusting its strategies in response to its ongoing analysis of the intruder's reactions and capabilities. That the countermeasures were growing steadily more advanced and sophisticated was a distressing indication of the escalating nature of the emergency.

"Wow," Johnny murmured, watching the gravi-polarizers in action. "Those things make me dizzy just looking at them. They ought to come complete with barf bags."

By now, Annihilus was rotating too fast to be seen clearly. All Sue could make out on the monitor was a whirling green-and-purple blur. Then an unholy radiance emanated from the twirling figure so that he resembled an enormous pinwheel. Sue glanced down at her control panel, but knew already that the unearthly glow was not being generated by the gravi-polarizers. This was Annihilus's doing.

Heat from Annihilus's Cosmic Control Rod melted the metal disks to slag. Molten steel, and bits of charred crystal circuitry, went flying in all directions, spraying the walls, floor, and ceiling of the gymnasium. With the devices destroyed, Annihilus quickly slowed to a stop. His boots touched down on a slag-splattered exercise mat.

Only a few minute traces of the gravi-polarizers still clung to the monster's purple carapace. He didn't even look dizzy, let alone nauseated.

"Still you persist with such diversions?" Annihilus accused Sue and Johnny. He sounded annoyed and impatient with their stubborn inability to grasp the hopelessness of their efforts. "How much longer will you continue your futile attempts to hinder me?"

As long as it takes, Sue thought vehemently. *Guess we're just slow learners.* She was tempted to reply to Annihilus over the building's public address system, but what was the point? *He's beyond reasoning with.*

Departing the gym, Annihilus ventured back into the hallway outside. "I have seen enough of this level," he declared. "What I seek is not to be found here." Once more, he turned the awesome potency of his precious Rod against the floor at the tiles at his feet, blasting his way through to the floor below.

Dammit! Sue swore silently. Annihilus was only one floor above them now, and just two stories away from Reed's laboratories, including the Negative Zone Chamber. *We're losing ground. . . .*

The thirty-sixth floor held the various family members's personal quarters. Here, too, Sue had tried for a cozy, contemporary feel, while also allowing the individuals to personalize their own rooms according to their tastes. Her and Reed's bedroom had been tastefully furnished with genuine wood paneling, a four-poster bed, various antique drawers and dressers, and a Persian rug imported from the Middle Eastern kingdom of Aquira. An Amy Tan novel resided on a end table next to Sue's side of the bed, while abstruse scientific journals were stacked next to Reed's. Laptops and computer terminals were banned from the bedroom by Sue's decree, though a combination baby monitor and hotline was mounted on the wall over Sue's bedside table (where Reed's elastic arms could easily reach it as well). A walk-in closet contained Sue's extensive wardrobe, neatly divided between garments made from stable and unstable molecules. The bed was neatly made.

An intense sense of personal violation struck Sue as Annihilus invaded her bedchamber. Her jaw tightened and she imagined invisible pincers cracking open Annihilus's shell. This wasn't the first time an enemy had callously rampaged through her home, but that didn't make her any less angry.

Get out of my house, vermin.

The heartless insectoid dismissed the elegant bedroom with a scornful glance. Did he ever sleep himself, or was that just another mortal frailty he had long ago evolved beyond? As far as Sue knew, he had no mate as well. Why concern yourself with reproduction when you intend to live forever? Annihilus was a species unto himself. He neither needed nor desired companionship.

He moved to exit the suite, but another entity entered the room first, blocking his path. "Attention, intruder!" an electronic voice addressed him. "Your presence at this location is unauthorized. You are instructed to surrender to our custody at once."

H.E.R.B.I.E. (short for Humanoid Experimental Robot B-Type Integrated Electronics) had been designed by Reed to assist him in the lab and to add an additional degree of security for the Baxter Building. This model had a round, metallic torso, supported by built-in antigrav units, surmounted by a toaster-sized head above a pivoting neck column. A lit display screen served as its face. Bright red sensors mimicked eyes, while a horizontal wave function suggested the appearance of a mouth. The robot's rather cartoony countenance had been intended to put first Franklin's, then little Valeria's, minds at ease, while also hinting at a whimsical side Reed showed all too rarely.

Annihilus found nothing at all cute about the new arrival. "Out of my way, automaton!"

"Warning!" H.E.R.B.I.E. hovered in midair, at eye level with the intruder. "Force is authorized in the event of resistance. Please allow me to escort you to a comfortable detention cell. Thank you for your cooperation."

The robot's good manners were lost on Annihilus. "I need not waste my cosmic energy on the likes of you!" He reached out and seized H.E.R.B.I.E. with both hands. The robot attempted to defend itself with a neural disruptor blast, but Annihilus merely buzzed irritably before ripping H.E.R.B.I.E.'s head off. Sparks erupted from the severed neck column. Lubricant dripped from the broken gap at the base of the robot's steel-plated skull. Agitated servos whirred within its stainless steel casing.

"Malfunction!" Bursts of static distorted H.E.R.B.I.E.'s voice. Warning lights flashed upon its chest. "Unit in need of immediate repair. Primary systems fading . . ."

The robot's voice faded away. The face upon its display screen flickered once, then went black.

A harsh, unfeeling laugh escaped Annihilus's throat. "That was so pitiful it was almost amusing," he gloated. "If that is all that remains of your defenses, your plight is desperate indeed!"

We'll see about that, Sue thought.

Casting the pieces of the decapitated robot aside, Annihilus strode imperiously out of the bedroom into the hallway beyond—where more than two dozen identical robots awaited him.

"Attention, intruder!" they said in unison. They filled the hall from one end to another, trapping Annihilus between them. They bobbed in the air like rubber ducks in a bathtub. "Use of force is duly authorized."

Neural disruptors fired from the robots' chest units, catching the surprised insectoid in an scathing cross fire. Designed to shock the nervous systems of biological beings, the cadmium rays had no effect on the cybernetic ganglia of the H.E.R.B.I.E.'s themselves, allowing them to fire freely without fear of injuring each other. Multiple disruptor blasts strafed the hallway. Annihilus recoiled behind his wings, taken aback by the emphatic attack of the robotic reinforcements.

"Awesome!" Johnny cheered the H.E.R.B.I.E.'s on. "And to think I used to find those things annoying!"

"You were just afraid they were going to replace you," Sue reminded him. "As if that were possible." She didn't mourn the robot whom Annihilus had torn apart in the bedroom. Not truly alive, H.E.R.B.I.E.'s were thoroughly expendable and easy to replace. *I'd sacrifice a hundred robots,* she thought, if it meant keeping Annihilus away from the Nega-Portal for just a little while longer. *The very future of Earth is at stake.*

Recovering from the initial salvo, Annihilus let out a furious screech. "Mere pinpricks!" he said, dismissing the robots' assault. "And hardly enough to dissuade me. Annihilus does not fear pain, only death!" Provoked beyond reason, he charged into the mass of robots and started ripping them to pieces with his armored hands. His knuckles slammed into one robot's face screen, then pulled back clutching a fistful of smoking wires and circuits. Another

H.E.R.B.I.E. came too close to Annihilus's spiked shoulder-plates and the insectoid flapped upward, impaling the luckless robot on the sharpened points. Disruptor bursts sparked against the invader's time-hardened carapace, but they only served to enrage Annihilus further. "A wasted effort! Do you think I have never battled cybernetic life-forms before? Over the ages, I have destroyed entire worlds of sentient machines!"

Dead and dying robots soon littered the hallway, but the surviving H.E.R.B.I.E.s kept up their assault. Retreat and surrender were not in their programming. Even as Annihilus advanced down the corridor, laying waste to their identical siblings right and left, the remaining robots chased after him. "Halt, intruder!" they called out in sync, amplifying their voices to be heard over the discordant clanging of robots being massacred. "Warning! Continued resistance will authorize use of potentially lethal force. Please desist aggressive action. This will be your last warning."

But Annihilus kept on going, smashing through the robots and their rays like an unstoppable force of nature. The battle carried its participants into the children's wing at the end of the hall. As Franklin had recently insisted that he was too old to keep sharing a room with his baby sister, a sizable playroom now divided his bedroom from Valeria's nursery. Preschool-appropriate wallpaper, featuring teddy bears and baby elephants, covered Valeria's half of the playroom, while posters of jet planes and professional baseball players were taped to the walls on Franklin's side. Little League trophies and souvenirs from outer space were proudly displayed on the eight-year-old's shelves, alongside albums containing his prized stamp, coin, and trading-card collections. A toy monorail set ran over much of the floor. Action figures, many of them based on his family and their friends and foes, were strewn across the carpet like battlefield casualties. Some of them, like those of the Avengers or Fantastic Four, were officially authorized by their inspirations. Many of the others, including those of the villains and X-Men, were not. A redheaded Invisible Woman that bore little or no resemblance to Sue Richards was obviously a cheap knockoff manufactured overseas for the black market.

Across the room, Valeria's playpen was filled with plush animals and other toddler-friendly toys. A stuffed black panther, a birthday gift from the king of Wakanda, shared the enclosed pen with a large toy bulldog that appeared to have a tuning fork glued to its forehead. A blue-skinned baby doll that was either Kree or Atlantean was lovingly swaddled in soft woolen blankets. A pacifier had fallen between the bars of the playpen and now lay on the carpet next to an empty juice bottle.

Sue winced as Annihilus lunged into the playroom, driving maybe a third of the surviving H.E.R.B.I.E.'s before him. A sweep of his arm sent an overwhelmed robot flying into Franklin's shelves. Trophies and stamp albums went crashing to the floor. Sue let out an involuntary whimper as she saw Franklin's MVP Award, from last season's Little League championship, break into pieces.

"Easy, Sue," Johnny comforted her. "It will be all right."

No, it won't, she thought bitterly. How could it ever be all right when Annihilus could just trample over her family's treasured keepsakes like this? She kept spare copies of family photos and videos in a lockbox on the moon, but she couldn't keep their entire lives in storage, which left them vulnerable to heartless vandals like Annihilus. *How am I ever going to explain to Franklin about his trophy?*

On one level, she knew it was silly to be worrying about her son's awards and stamp collection while humanity's very existence was in jeopardy. But how was she supposed to watch Annihilus run roughshod over her home without feeling something? *He's in my children's room, damn him!*

"Come at me if you dare, automatons!" Annihilus's gauntlets held one H.E.R.B.I.E. apiece, his fists wrapped around their neck columns. Their heads spun in 360-degree circles, trying to break free of his grip. He slammed the two robots together, flattening them both to cymbals, then threw the pancaked metal fragments to floor, where they knocked over Franklin's train set. Having disposed of all the robots before him, Annihilus spun around to face the last of the stragglers as they came levitating into the playroom after him. "Your numbers matter nothing to me!"

Sue counted six, maybe seven, H.E.R.B.I.E.'s left. Her control panel confirmed that the rest of the robots had gone off-line, permanently. *They don't stand a chance,* she thought. She had pretty much given up on the idea of stopping Annihilus in his tracks. Now her only goal was to delay him for as long as humanly possible. But were the building's defenses even weakening him at all? From where she was sitting, it was hard to tell.

Please, H.E.R.B.I.E.'s. Don't let me down.

"Use of lethal force authorized," the last robotic defenders reported. Having determined that the neural disruptors were ineffective against this intruder, they were now programmed to escalate to more formidable weaponry. They spread out around the playroom, forming a circle around Annihilus. "Deploying atom-igniter beams."

The deadly rays, which disintegrated matter by causing its atomic nuclei to explode spontaneously, forced Annihilus to call upon the defensive power of his Cosmic Control Rod once more. The golden cylinder burned brightly upon his chest, and an impervious force field protected him from harm. But that was only the beginning; he paused for a moment at the center of the storm, as the atom-igniter beams converged on his shielded form like the spokes of a wheel, then willed the force field to expand outward with the force of a tidal wave. The swelling bubble smashed the last few H.E.R.B.I.E.'s into the walls of the playroom, which were made of enhanced titanium beneath the colorful posters and wallpaper. Simultaneously, the final robots were crushed flat.

Annihilus retracted the field and nodded in satisfaction as the crumpled metal ruins dropped lifelessly onto the floor, where they joined the fallen action figures and derailed train set. One of the wrecks smashed down into Valeria's playpen, fracturing the porcelain head of the blue-skinned baby. Another landed only a few inches away from an eight-inch plastic duplicate of Mr. Fantastic.

Spotting the latter, the triumphant insectoid stretched out his hand above the toy. The Cosmic Control Rod shimmered briefly and the action figure rose from the carpet and into Annihilus's waiting grip. A dry, insectile chuckle emerged from his chitinous green mask.

"Have your fellow mortals made an idol of you, Richards?" he asked mockingly. "If so, I fear their faith is sadly misplaced."

He squeezed his fist, crushing Mr. Fantastic into powder.

Watching on her monitor, only one floor away, Sue could only pray that the real Reed Richards had not met an equally dire fate.

Where are you, Reed? What's happening to you?

13

"DONE!" SAMRA QURY DECLARED, stepping back from her workbench. On the gleaming steel counter, now littered with scraps of exotic materials, the Distortion Ray projector rested. The completed weapon vaguely resembled the Ultimate Nullifier the Human Torch had once stolen from Galactus, being a steel-plated cartridge equipped with a trigger grip and telescoping lens. "I must admit I haven't the foggiest idea how this device can do what you say it can. I followed your diagrams and instructions to the letter, but how it actually works is beyond me."

"Trust me," Mr. Fantastic said hastily. He cast a furtive glance at Vatriin and his two guards. "I know what I'm doing."

His terse reply took Qury somewhat aback. "Of course. I didn't mean to challenge your work. It's just that I can't see—"

A strident warning Klaxon cut her off in midsentence, much to Reed's relief. Commander Vatriin looked up in alarm and immediately activated a communications device on the wrist of his gauntlet. "What is it?" he demanded. "What's happening?"

"Long-range scans detect a vessel approaching Hethael at high speed," a voice reported from elsewhere in the science station. "It's not one of ours."

Reed concealed his excitement at the news. *Could it be?* He discreetly tapped a preprogrammed command code into the control panel before him. His finger hesitated over the final keystroke. *It must be him! It's the only explanation.*

"Who in Purgatorium?" Vatriin swore. He slammed an armored fist into his own palm. "If that treacherous arthropod has betrayed us already . . . !" He turned and glared at Mr. Fantastic. "Or is this your doing, outzoner? The emperor warned that your kinsmen might try to rescue you!"

"I don't know what you're talking about," Reed said innocently.

Samra Qury, unsure whether to be relieved or dismayed, instinctively hefted the Distortion Ray for protection. A Baluurian guard saw her seize the weapon and turned his own energy rifle on the bewildered H'Zarri scientist. "Put that down *now!*" he ordered.

She reluctantly complied.

"Unknown vessel coming within visual range," the voice from the comm link reported. "Entering firing range in seven-point-six kilometers."

"On-screen!" Vatriin barked.

An image appeared on every monitor in the laboratory. Reed's heart surged as he saw his own Negative Zone Explorer zooming toward the icy moon. The once pristine spacecraft was distinctly the worse for wear—dents and scorch marks marred its formerly sleek hull—but the silver module was still very much spaceworthy. The glow of its photonic thrusters lit up the screen.

Right on time, he thought proudly.

"The Earth vessel!" Vatriin gasped, recognizing the

Explorer as well. His black eyes blinked in confusion. "But I thought it was destroyed in the Debris Belt."

That's what you were supposed to think. Reed keyed the final command into the control panel, then waited for the countdown to begin. He remembered the titanic fireball that had supposedly signaled the Explorer's destruction. *Nothing but an ejected matter-antimatter charge.*

Smoke and mirrors . . .

"Intruder approximately one hundred meters away from landing pad," Vatriin's gauntlet reported. "Entering firing range."

"What are you waiting for?" the commander raged. "Blow that Vortex-sucking ship out of the sky!"

Mr. Fantastic held his breath as high-intensity ionic beams blasted from the surface of the moon, targeting the Explorer. But the module easily dodged the crimson beams, pitching, yawing, rolling, and banking in a breathtaking display of aeronautic artistry. Knowing who was piloting the Explorer, Reed expected nothing less. His brain silently ticked off the seconds in the countdown. *Any minute now,* he thought.

"What's the matter with you?" Vatriin bellowed at the unseen gunners. His shaggy gray face flushed nearly purple. "Shoot down that ship!"

As if on cue, the ionic beams disappeared from the screen. The Explorer straightened out its flight path and flew on unobstructed. Many meters beneath the ice, Reed wondered if one could see or hear the Explorer from the surface yet.

"What in Stygor's Shade?" Vatriin exclaimed. Spittle flew from his lips as he shouted into his wrist communicator, "Where are my mane-shedding ion cannons? Fire, curse you all! *Fire!*"

"We can't!" a frantic voice reported. Agitated shouting, and alien profanities, could be heard in the background. "Our entire defense grid has shut down! The controls aren't responding!"

A hint of a smile played upon Reed's lips. He congratulated himself on a job well done; it had been child's play to hack into the station's weapons system while pretending to work on the portal. *I've done my part,* he thought. *The rest is up to my partner in crime.*

Qury caught his pleased expression and gave him a quizzical look. Reed smiled back to assure her that everything was under control.

At least in theory.

On his monitor, the battered Explorer came swooping down through Hethael's turbulent winds. Vatriin was near apoplectic at the sight of the module touching down on the landing pad above. Everyone in the lab looked up at the ceiling, as if they could hear the Explorer landing.

It was nighttime on this region of Hethael, and the station's landing lights had apparently succumbed to the same ingenious computer virus that had shut down the weapons grid. Darkness cloaked the icy terrain, so that Reed and the others could barely glimpse the Explorer capsule as it blossomed open, like an enormous night-blooming flower. With the radiance of the nearby gas giant currently shining on the other side of the moon, the inhabitants of the lab had to strain their eyes to see a hulking, dimly lit figure emerge from cockpit and march decisively toward the nearby hanger. Heavy footsteps sounded from the monitor.

"Increase magnification!" Vatriin ordered. The view from the monitor swiveled to keep the intruder in sight. "Go to infrared sensors!"

The new arrival must have heard the surface scanner

moving, because it suddenly crouched at the edge of the landing pad and scooped up a boulder-sized ball of snow and ice. Packing the snowball tightly with what looked like two enormous hands, the shadowy figure turned and hurled the frigid projectile right at the scanner. Vatriin instinctively recoiled from the monitor as the snowball filled the screen right before image blacked out entirely.

"Surface cam inoperative," the disembodied voice reported redundantly. "We've lost visual contact with the intruder."

"I can see that, you brainless incompetent!" Vatriin snarled. He savagely jabbed the controls on his comm link. "Attention, all station personnel! This is Commander Vatriin. We are under attack. Mobilize all forces to stop and destroy the intruder. Shoot to kill!" His mane bristled aggressively. "This facility and its prisoners are of vital importance to the Baluurian war effort. Defend the lower laboratories with your lives. In Blastaar's name!"

The battle was swiftly engaged. Grunts, smashes, gunfire, and groans blared from Vatriin's gauntlet. Judging from the noise, stopping the intruder was proving easier said than done. The tumult went on for several minutes, much to Vatriin's agitation. How hard could it be to stop a single invader? The officer looked as though his entire mane was likely to turn white at any minute.

Reed was not at all surprised by what he heard. *Our plan worked perfectly,* he mused. Even before they had departed Earth in the Explorer, Reed's sensors back in the Baxter Building had detected the sizable Baluurian military presence around the Debris Belt. Guessing that massed fleet had something to do with the recent incursions, he had decided then that getting captured by Blastaar's forces was probably the best way to locate the source of the rifts. *Which is exactly what had happened.*

The trickiest part had been putting up just enough resistance to make his capture and ongoing captivity believable. Even his failed escape attempt aboard *Burstaar's Revenge* had primarily been intended to allay any suspicions on Blastaar's part. The crafty warlord would have expected Mr. Fantastic to fight back somehow. . . .

By now, the sounds of strife emerging from Vatriin's comm link had largely fallen silent. All that could be heard were muffled groans, static, and the occasional clang of heavy equipment hitting the floor. Dust rained down from the ceiling of the lab, shaken loose by the heated conflict above.

"Report!" Vatriin shouted into his gauntlet. "Security forces, what is your status?" He stabbed at the wrist controls, trying to raise somebody, anybody. "Level Three, Level One . . . Report at once!"

Almost in answer, a tremendous din suddenly arose outside the sealed air lock guarding the lab. Tortured metal screamed in protest as the elevator doors were audibly torn asunder. An energy rifle zapped loudly and a Scavenger screeched in anger as the guards in the antechamber defended the entrance to the lab. Reed heard the Baluurian sentry shout out a belligerent warning: "Stay back, ogre, or—!"

The defense was short-lived. One after another, limp bodies hit the floor outside. A grinding sound, of steel scraping against steel, reverberated from the air lock. Wrenched free from its hinges, the outer door clattered onto the floor of the antechamber.

"It's not possible!" Vatriin gasped. He gazed at the groaning air lock. Pounding blows caused the reinforced inner door to bulge inward, revealing the impression of blocky knuckles. "That door would test Blastaar himself!"

Never underestimate old-fashioned Yancy Street cussedness, Mr. Fantastic thought, not believing for a moment that the barrier was a match against the irresistible force smashing its way in. Within his seamless hood, his malleable ears folded over to protect his hearing from the deafening blows. Lacking his flexibility, Samra Qury clapped her hands over her own ears. If Reed hadn't known better, he would have sworn that a battering ram was repeatedly slamming against the inner door. *I knew I could count on you, old friend.*

"To the door!" Vatriin ordered his two men. They hurried to take up defensive positions in front of the trembling air lock. Their ionic rifles targeted the door. "We must hold the line here," their commander exhorted them, "for the glory of the Empire!"

One final seismic shudder shook the air lock. The forty-ton door toppled forward, forcing the two soldiers to jump backward to avoid being flattened. The mangled metal hit the floor with a resounding boom. A rocky, orange figure appeared in doorway.

"Knock, knock!" the Thing exclaimed, alive and kicking. Blue eyes peered from beneath petrified brows. Smoky fumes rose from various cracks and blemishes in his craggy hide, where the station's security forces had apparently taken shots at him. A yeti-sized foot booted a broken hinge aside. "Anybody seen a walkin', talkin' rubber band?"

"Ben!" Mr. Fantastic called out, not at all shocked to see his comrade still in one piece. The Thing's explosive "death" within the Debris Belt had been carefully staged, and with full awareness that their seemingly frantic transmissions were being monitored by Blastaar and his fleet. "Right here, partner!"

Commander Vatriin was considerably less pleased by the Thing's tumultuous entrance. "Slay the outzoner freak!"

Ionic beams streaked from the muzzles of the soldier's guns. The crimson rays chipped away at the Thing's brick-encrusted form, but that barely slowed him down. "Hey, whatya tryin' ta do, spoil my good looks?" He charged forward like the quarterback he once was, right into the Baluurians' line of fire. Two colossal mitts, the size of anvils, grabbed each guard, effortlessly lifting them off their feet. The Thing slammed their shaggy heads together, then tossed their unconscious bodies over his shoulder. "Some people got no sense of hospitality!"

"By the Spores!" Qury breathed, her bronze eyes rapt in wonder. She caught her breath. "He's magnificent!"

The Thing's boots stomped across the fallen door, which clanked noisily beneath his weight. He glanced around at the futuristic computer banks and apparatus. "Shoulda known I'd find ya playin' mad scientist in some crazy lab."

"You'll come no further, monster!" Vatriin declared. He drew a service pistol from his hip and opened fire on the advancing Thing, but the pistol's beams had even less effect than his men's useless rifles.

Still, Ben scowled as a crimson blast glanced off his wounded shoulder. "Ouch. That smarts." He reached for a blinking piece of machinery to shield himself with.

"Ben, wait!" Reed shouted. "Be careful of the equipment!" They might well need a working Posi-Portal to return to Earth, with or without Samra Qury. "It's of vital importance!"

"Sheesh!" the Thing said in exasperation. He stooped and picked up the toppled door instead. "You and yer nutty gizmos!"

Using the air lock door as a shield, he marched toward

Vatriin and his two prisoners. Ray blasts struck impotently against the heavy steel barrier. Discarding the useless pistol, Vatriin looked about frantically for another weapon. His gaze fell upon the completed Distortion Ray.

"Give me that!" he snarled, lunging for the workbench. His greedy hands reached for the one-of-a-kind device.

But instead of getting out of the way, Qury placed her Amazonian bulk between the irate officer and the Distortion Ray. A glossy red fist smashed into Vatriin's face, knocking him backward with surprising force. Caught off-guard, he landed flat on his back, practically at the Thing's feet. His face betrayed his confusion, as if he couldn't comprehend what had just happened. Oily black blood dripped from his nose.

Qury seemed equally taken aback. She stared at her own fist in astonishment. "I can't believe I just did that!" she exclaimed. "I'm H'Zarri . . . and a scientist!"

The Thing whistled in admiration. "Nice work, sister!" He chucked his improvised shield to one side and glared down at the sprawled form of the Baluurian commander. He raised a stony fist above his head. "Awright, buster," he rumbled menacingly. "It's clobber—"

"I surrender!" Vatriin blurted.

"Aw shucks!" Ben said, deflated. "Ain't nobody gonna let me finish sayin' that anymore?" His fist dropped to his side and he stared at the downed officer in disappointment. "Don't tell me ya got all the fight knocked out of ya already?"

"The outzoner Richards is correct," Vatriin offered by way of explanation. "I cannot risk damaging the portal in a useless show of resistance." He glared at the Thing with hate-filled eyes. "But rest assured that the mighty Blastaar will avenge my defeat when he learns what has transpired here!"

"Let him try," Ben said gruffly. Grabbing on to the collar of Vatriin's armor, he lifted the commander off the floor and carted him over to where the two guards' energy rifles lay upon the floor. He picked up one of the rifles and wrapped it like a pretzel around Vatriin's wrists, binding his hands together. Then he used the second rifle to shackle the Baluurian's ankles. "Now sit tight while I find out what sorta no-good business your mangy boss is up to this time."

Leaving Vatriin helpless upon the floor, the Thing joined Reed and Qury by the control panel. To Reed's amusement, the female scientist couldn't take her eyes off his friend.

"Good to see you, Ben!" Mr. Fantastic said, slapping the Thing on the back. "You're a sight for sore eyes."

"Wish I could say the same, pal." Ben nodded at Reed's bulky adhesion suit. "What's with the wacky pj's? You joinin' A.I.M. or somethin'?"

"Not exactly," Reed said. Come to think of it, the all-enclosing garment *did* somewhat resemble the uniforms worn by the unscrupulous scientists of Advanced Idea Mechanics, a criminal organization that the Fantastic Four had contended with in the past. "More of a precautionary measure on Blastaar's part." He turned toward Qury. "If you'd please do the honors?"

"Gladly," she replied. Retrieving her pen-sized laser from the workbench, she deftly sliced open a gap large enough for Mr. Fantastic to slide out of. He emitted a grateful sigh of relief; after being cooped up in the suit for so many subjective hours, it was a pleasure to be able to *stretch* again. Just to work the kinks out, he extended his arms the entire length of the lab before retracting them back to standard human proportions. Qury gaped in amazement at his feat. "I had heard of your abilities, but to see them with my own eyes . . . !"

"Hey, Stretch," Ben said, "ain't ya forgettin' somethin'?" He glanced at Qury. "Who's yer friend?"

"My apologies," Reed said. "Ben, meet Magister Samra Qury." About the same height, the Thing and the H'Zarri scientist could easily look each other in the eyes. "Samra, this is my oldest friend and comrade, Benjamin Grimm."

Her admiring gaze swept over the Thing's rugged form. "I've heard of you as well, but I never realized how heroic you were in person. Why do Blastaar and Annihilus and their minions all refer to you as the Thing? It seems an incongruous label for such a handsome specimen." She shrugged at Mr. Fantastic apologetically. "Please don't take offense, Reed. I truly admire your mind, but I'm afraid that, to H'Zarri eyes, your physical form is somewhat off-putting."

Ben's jaw literally dropped like a stone.

"No offense taken," Reed assured Qury. He couldn't resist smiling at Ben's dumbfounded expression. It wasn't often the Thing found himself in this position. "I'm quite accustomed to being overshadowed by Ben's manly physique."

Reed wasn't sure whether to be glad or disappointed that Johnny wasn't here to witness this role reversal. He wondered how his girl-crazy brother-in-law would cope with being the homely one for once. *Might be an interesting psychological experiment . . .*

"Forgive me for speaking so boldly," Qury said, giving Ben a coy smile. The iridescent scales upon her head sparkled beneath the overhead lights. "I suppose it has been a long time since I've seen any male who resembled my own kind. I hope I am not embarrassing you."

A pink blush showed through the irregular fissures in Ben's face. His eyes took in the polished contours of Samra's face and figure. "Well, this ain't exactly a re-voltin' development," he admitted.

"Ahem," Reed said. "As much as I hate to interrupt, time is running out." He quickly brought Ben up to speed on Blastaar's plans, as well as on his unholy alliance with Annihilus. "Even as we speak, Sue and Johnny are most likely battling to keep Annihilus away from the Nega-Portal."

"Annihilus, too, ya say." Ben's voice and expression darkened. "That crawfish-faced creep's been nothin' but trouble since day one." He clenched his mammoth fists, perhaps remembering the time Annihilus had put both Alicia and Franklin in the hospital. "Now I wish I coulda got here sooner. Sorry to keep ya waitin'. It wuzn't easy dodgin' Blastaar's patrol ships. Plus, I hadda stop and make some pretty necessary repairs ta the Explorer when nobody wuz lookin'."

"I'm just glad you made it," Reed told him. "I wouldn't have trusted anyone else to weave the module through the Debris Belt the way you must have done. No wonder Blastaar and his troops assumed that the Explorer had been destroyed."

"Yeah," Ben recalled. "That wuz fun an' a half."

"But I don't understand," Qury said. "How did you find us in the first place. This installation is top secret!"

"Cosmic energy," Reed explained. "There's a homing device in my chest insignia, but I couldn't take the chance that Blastaar might find or disable it somehow. But every cell of my body is imbued with the same cosmic energy that gave my friends and I our special abilities. That energy is unique in this universe, even after being translated into antimatter by the Distortion Effect, so it can be detected by a very sensitive tracking device back on our Explorer vehicle."

"Plus," Ben added, "I just kept an eye on where that big battle cruiser of his wuz headin'." He looked at Reed. "So what's our next move, big brain? We headin' for home yet? I don't like the idea of Suzie an' the punk fightin' the big A all on their lonesome."

"Neither do I, Ben. Believe me." Mr. Fantastic knew just how the Thing felt. Every minute Reed was away from the besieged Baxter Building was a torment to him. He longed to be battling at his family's side. *But first,* he knew, *we have a mission to complete.*

"Samra," he addressed his fellow scientist urgently. "Come with us. I think I've figured out a way to keep your Posi-Portal open long enough for all three of us to pass through to Earth. We can rig the portal to self-destruct a few minutes later. You'll be free of Blastaar and Annihilus—and no one else will ever be able to use your technology to endanger another innocent world."

She backed away from him uncertainly. "But my family!" she protested. "Blastaar still has my family locked up somewhere. Who knows what he'd do to them if I disappeared." She wrestled visibly with her conscience, her agonized emotions contorting her shiny magenta features. Tears of liquid silver leaked from her eyes. "I can't do it," she said finally. "I can't leave without my family."

Reed couldn't blame her for her decision. How could he, after all she had already suffered? The loss of her entire civilization? She had made the only choice she could.

"Then I guess we gotta go get 'em," Ben said.

14

UNTOLD AGES AGO, DEEP IN THE NETHER reaches of what would someday be known as the Negative Zone, a starship crashed on a lifeless, dark, volcanic planet. The inhabitants of that ship belonged to a highly advanced race who called themselves the Tyannans, who believed that it was their manifest destiny to spread the seeds of life throughout their cosmos. To this end, they had engineered special, highly adaptive spores that their far-ranging spacecraft then carried across the universe, planting them on whatever worlds were deemed capable of supporting life. From these spores, the Baluurians evolved, as did the myriad other races and species of the Negative Zone.

But the Tyannans whose ship crashed upon that desolate rock never returned to their fabled homeworld, which in time receded into myth and legend. Those ill-fated castaways released their cache of experimental spores into the barren environment, but soon perished themselves, leaving behind only the ruins of their crashed starship—and the possibility of a new future for this world, which would eventually achieve infamy as the planet Arthros.

Eons passed, and, as elsewhere, a profusion of primitive

life-forms evolved on Arthros. Among these was a weak, defenseless insectoid that nonetheless possessed the beginnings of a rudimentary intelligence. Day and night it was pursued by the planet's many predators, but its crude intellect managed to keep it alive—until one day, while searching blindly for shelter from both its enemies and the elements, the lowly arthropod stumbled onto the remains of the doomed Tyannan starship, whose vast technology had lain dormant for many millions of generations.

Through chance, the insectoid was altered by a helmet it discovered amidst the ruins. The helmet filled the creature's simple brain with all the lost knowledge of Tyanna, so that its mind evolved many eons in mere moments. Thus transformed, the insectoid soon mastered the arcane technology he discovered within the ship—and turned that unparalleled science to his own purposes. From the spacecraft's mighty star-drive, which drew upon the fundamental forces of creation for its power, he fashioned a tool that would both preserve his life indefinitely and also allow him to strike back at all the mindless predators that had ever menaced him. This tool he called the Cosmic Control Rod, and his implacable campaign to *annihilate* his enemies soon earned him an appropriate title as well. . . .

Over a thousand years had passed since the fateful day his earlier self had first set foot in that ruined starship, but Annihilus had never forgotten that epochal event. Nor had he ever forgotten what his existence had been like before he became Annihilus, the endless hours spent fleeing from one predator or another, constantly in fear of his life. The ever-present threat of death.

Never again!

Now, as he stalked the benighted corridors of the

Baxter Building, Annihilus vowed once more to eliminate all who endangered his hard-won immortality, even if that had meant crossing over from one plane of reality to another. *Little did I know, as I spent a millennium purging the Negative Zone of potentially hostile life-forms, that the greatest threat would come from an entirely different universe.*

The facts could not be denied, however. Ever since Reed Richards and his accursed brood had first ventured into the Negative Zone, Annihilus had suffered one challenge to his power after another. First the Fantastic Four, then the Avengers, the mighty Thor, Doctor Doom, Captain Marvel, and others had dared to defile his realm, bringing with them the obscene prospect of an end to his undying existence and power. More than once, he had been brought near to the brink of absolute destruction by such interlopers, whose intolerable exploits had even encouraged barbarians such as Blastaar to contemplate his demise. For the first time in centuries, Annihilus had felt death closing in on him once again.

No more!

Soon the positive universe would no longer pose a threat to him. All of Earth would pay the price for Reed Richards's transgressions, until the hated human race was no more than a memory, and this very planet nothing more than a lifeless cinder. Unlike the foolish Tyannans of antiquity, Annihilus did not intend to spread life throughout this strange new cosmos. Instead he would do the opposite, cleansing the alien galaxies of life until only he remained to endure, forever and forever. Even if it took him another eternity, he would bring universal death to every last corner of this universe.

The only question was whether he would slay Blastaar and his Baluurian forces before or after the total conquest of Richards's reality. *I have need of him and his armada now, but that will not always be the case.* Fleshless lips sneered in anticipation. *The day will come when Blastaar will perish like the rest!*

But first I must open the Nega-Portal to his ravening troops. . . .

Now that those bothersome robots troubled him no more, Annihilus quickly determined that this level of the Baxter Building did not contain the apparatus he sought. To his disgust, the entire tier seemed devoted to nothing more than the base creature comforts of Richards and his abominable spawn. He recalled the Negative Zone Chamber from his previous invasion of the Baxter Building. That had been some years ago, and the structure had obviously been reconfigured since, but he knew that he would find the portal in the heart of Mr. Fantastic's admirably well-equipped laboratories, not surrounded by the fragile ephemera of his domestic life.

Tossing aside a broken crib, whose very existence suggested that Richards and his mate had produced yet another offspring since the last time he had taken possession of the Fantastic Four's headquarters, Annihilus left the children's warren behind and strode out into the hallway beyond. Junked robots littered the floor, so that he had to kick his way through the motionless metal corpses. Cold fury revisited him as he thought of the painful blasts the irksome robots had inflicted on him before he had destroyed them all. The machines had been the first victims of his latest campaign.

They would not be the last.

He was about to blast through the floor when he spotted an open doorway up ahead. An exit sign, which he did not remember noticing before, glowed above the threshold. Approaching cautiously, he discovered that the doorway opened onto a stairwell leading down to the floor below. His antennae detected the hum of powerful machinery rising up from downstairs.

Promising, he thought. *Perhaps too promising?*

Wary of a trap, he peered through the doorway, but saw nothing overtly menacing. Drawing his wings about him like a verdant cloak, he entered the stairwell and descended the steps. He remained suspicious, but none too worried; had he not already demonstrated that the building's paltry defenses lacked the power to deter him? His Cosmic Control Rod would protect him from any lurking treachery, as it had since time immemorial.

Of course, he reminded himself, the Human Torch, the Invisible Woman, and perhaps the rest of the Fantastic Four were still hiding somewhere within the skyscraper, no doubt plotting yet more mischief against him. He liked to think that they were cowering in fear in some nook, too petrified even to contemplate raising a finger against him, but he knew them better than that. Their naive human obstinacy would surely compel them to defend the Nega-Portal to their last breaths, no matter how incontrovertibly hopeless the endeavor. Regardless of where they had retreated to for the present, he knew they would once more meet in battle before today's momentous business was concluded.

He looked forward to crushing the lives from their bodies.

To his slight surprise, no trifling snares or ambushes accosted him as he navigated the stairs, which led him to what appeared to be some manner of carpeted reception area. Mock-leather chairs and a sofa, now mercifully devoid of human rabble, were situated around the room. Low tables, stacked with inane human periodicals, added to the furnishings. Framed photographs, magazine covers, and newspaper headlines, all commemorating the petty triumphs of

Richards and his clan, adorned the walls. One headline in particular caught his gaze:

FF AVERT "ANNIHILATION"
Alien Monster Blamed for Panic

Below the blaring type, a crude artist's rendition of Annihilus offended the insectoid's eyes. He relished the thought that the talentless mammal responsible for the insulting caricature would soon join the rest of his species in oblivion.

Let your people extol your accomplishments all they desire, Annihilus thought spitefully of the Fantastic Four. *It will not be enough to save them.*

A high steel desk guarded the portal to the chambers beyond. A human female sat behind the desk, beneath a large, three-dimensional **4**. With her blond hair and trim figure, she vaguely resembled Susan Richards, especially to Annihilus, to whom all humans except the Thing looked much the same. Glasses and business attire gave her an impeccably professional look.

"Welcome to the thirty-fifth floor," she said cheerfully, apparently undisturbed by the insectoid's fearsome appearance. "My name is Roberta. Please state your business with the Fantastic Four."

He was briefly bewildered by the receptionist's unruffled demeanor. Was it possible she was blind, like that other mortal female he had once encountered in this building? Then he looked more closely and the truth became clear to him: this "Roberta" was merely another robot, albeit more human in appearance than the ones he had obliterated only minutes ago. Richards obviously had fondness for manufacturing such childish mechanisms.

"Take me to the Negative Zone Chamber!" he

demanded. Perhaps this mannequin was programmed to be more cooperative than the security drones? He stalked toward the open portal, his wings fluttering impatiently. The humming noise he had heard earlier appeared to emanate from farther down a hallway beyond the reception desk. "I will not be delayed!"

"No!" Roberta protested. She wheeled out from behind her desk, and Annihilus saw that her human semblance existed only from the waist up. Beneath her neatly pressed blouse and vest, the robotic receptionist merged with her chair, which rolled across the carpet on motorized wheels until she sat between Annihilus and the remainder of the thirty-fifth floor. "Access to the Nega-Portal is strictly forbidden to unauthorized personnel and visitors!"

He chittered irritably. "Out of my way, mannequin!" He stepped forward to sweep her aside, but Roberta rolled backward down the corridor behind her, finally coming to rest directly in front of a sealed metal door.

"Access to the Nega-Portal is restricted!" she repeated. Twin weapon barrels projected from the armrests of her chair. Stun beams of some nature blasted Annihilus's exoskeleton. "Thank you for visiting the Baxter Building."

The vermilion beams pelted his carapace uselessly; he had endured worse during a moderate shardstorm on Ocanalos VII. The damage to his temper was more grievous than any bodily effects. Would these insufferable displays of defiance never cease?

"Begone, simulacrum!" A blast from his Cosmic Control Rod turned back her own feeble assaults, like a hurricane against a gentle breeze. A wave of primordial power blew Roberta into a thousand components while simultaneously smashing open the door behind her. Annihilus advanced implacably toward the breached entrance, crushing bits and pieces of the receptionist beneath his boots. "No mere mortal, counterfeit or otherwise, will stand between me and my goal!"

The Negative Zone Chamber looked much as he remembered it, even after so many years. Dense steel baffles guarded the access pit in the center of the room. The wall-sized monitor offered a generous view of the exploding area around the Vortex. Drifting asteroids, caught in the galactic eddy at the center of his universe, crashed against each in the Debris Belt. In theory, Blastaar's fleet cruised just beyond the reach of Richards's sensors, waiting for Annihilus to lay the positive universe bare before them. All he need do was open the portal wide.

He immediately noticed the absence of the podlike vehicle Richards used to trespass into his realm. Did that mean that one or more of the Fantastic Four had already absconded into the Negative Zone, perhaps in response to the arrival of him and the earlier test subjects? Annihilus had noted that neither Mr. Fantastic nor the Thing had shown themselves upon the rooftops earlier as had the Human Torch and (apparently) the Invisible Woman. Had Susan Richards used her devious abilities to conceal the rest of her team as well, or had her husband and his brutish associate left her and her incendiary sibling behind while the two men searched the Negative Zone for answers? It was also possible, he conceded, that the entire Fantastic Four had departed the building, leaving naught but automated security systems to defend the skyscraper in their absence.

No matter, he resolved. Blastaar was waiting for whoever entered the Zone, while his own power was more than enough to overcome whatever percentage of the Fantastic Four remained to oppose him. *I have nothing to fear from any or all of them.*

He scanned the room suspiciously, rather surprised, in

fact, that neither the Human Torch nor any of his team-mates had yet appeared to attempt to drive him from his goal. He would not have expected the unruly humans to let him get this far without a fight. Surely, they would not place the defense of their universe solely in the hands of a robot receptionist?

"Where are you?" he asked aloud. He stood perfectly still, listening for any muffled breathing or footsteps that might betray the presence of one or more invisible humans. He sniffed the air with his olfactory organs, but the noisome stench of mortal meat did not assail his senses. He extended his wings to the fullness of their magnificent span, but his armored pinions did not come into contact with any transparent lurkers. He appeared to be quite alone in the spacious chamber. "Why have you not come to battle for your species?"

Something is wrong here, he surmised. *But what?*

For a moment, he feared that Blastaar had betrayed him already, before Annihilus could betray the warlord first. Yet that made no sense; Blastaar was a universe away. Moreover, the upstart tyrant had no reason to deviate from their shared strategy so soon. His own feral dreams of conquest and revenge depended on Annihilus's mission.

Perhaps the Fantastic Four had truly fled this continuum entirely?

If so, he would not waste this enticing opportunity. Striding to the command console between the monitor and the access tube, he took a minute to refamiliarize himself with the controls. To one of his superior intellect, mastering the apparatus was the work of a moment. An impertinent program demanded a password of him, but he easily bypassed Mr. Fantastic's niggling security routines and gained control of the console. *Yes,* he thought, buzzing with satisfaction. *Just so.*

Hidden servos activated around the portal. Dense steel baffles slid aside to permit access to the tunnel below. An emerald radiance flooded the chamber. Annihilus braced himself behind the control panel, lest a sudden suction transport him back through the barrier. The phosphorescent green glow gave way to the erratic hues and shadows of the Distortion Area.

Annihilus waited for the first of Blastaar's soldiers to ride a jet-harness through the tunnel. According to the plan, a single scout would make the transition first, to confirm that the way was clear and the coordinates correct. Only then would Annihilus expand the gateway until it swallowed the whole of the Baxter Building and much of city outside, so that the rest of Blastaar's vast armada could come pouring through the burgeoning portal into this unsuspecting universe. Annihilus himself would watch the fleet's arrival from some lofty perch nearby, safely distant from the titanic military maneuvers.

But first he had to greet Blastaar's hapless scout. What in the name of lost Tyanna was keeping the doltish specimen? He circled around the console to face the towering monitor behind him, searching for some clue as to what might have caused the delay. *If Blastaar has failed me somehow,* he thought, *I will consign his entire loathsome species to nothingness even earlier than I had intended!*

Manipulating the controls before him, he flashed through view after view of the Negative Zone. The sight of his own home universe filled him with neither nostalgia nor any other sentiment, only a mounting sense of anxiety as he scoured the screen for evidence of the Baluurian armada that should have been converging on the open gateway at this very moment.

What has gone wrong? he fretted. His mandibles clacked

together restlessly. Frustration seethed within his veins. *This is Richards's doing, I know it!*

At last, he found Blastaar's fleet, but the massed warships were still cruising slowly in the region outside the Debris Belt, as though they had not yet detected the opening of the portal. What was wrong with them? The appearance of the rift should have triggered sensors throughout the entire armada. Had the whole of the Baluurian navy fallen asleep?

A high-pitched squawk came from behind him, and he turned to see one of his own Scavengers fly out of the access tube into the chamber. More Scavengers followed, clutching energy rifles and negato-guns in their bony talons, until the room was nearly packed to the rafters with winged humanoids. They screeched and flapped their wings exuberantly.

Annihilus did not understand. What was this horde of Scavengers doing here? This was not part of the plan. He had ultimately intended to deploy his own servitors in the positive universe, but only after Blastaar and his shock troops had done the hard work of pacifying Earth and its scores of superpowered defenders. And the Scavengers lacked the initiative to join the invasion of their own accord.

"Speak!" he commanded them. "What brings you here?" He had personally created their species, using a gene transmitter he had found aboard the wrecked Tyannan starship to evolve the Scavengers from a primitive nocturnal rodent that had once existed on Arthros. He alone understood their obscure articulations. "Who sent you? Blastaar?"

Various Scavengers squawked back at him, but their high-pitched squeaks were utterly unintelligible. The shrill chattering was just noise. It didn't even sound like the

Scavenger's protolanguage at all, just an incomprehensible jumble of sounds that would only fool someone who lacked any true understanding of their tongue—or was trying, unsuccessfully, to imitate the same.

Could it be . . . ? His earlier suspicions returned to him, and understanding lifted the veil of confusion. An icy certainty came over him and he turned his back upon the flocking Scavengers. His Cosmic Control Rod lashed out, and a bolt of supernaturally destructive energy struck the monitor of the "Negative Zone Chamber."

Instead of shattering, the immense screen wavered like a faulty transmission, then blinked out of existence altogether. Where once the supposed monitor had filled the view, a wall of shattered lenses greeted his eyes. Row after row of sophisticated projector units sparked and flickered. A Scavenger flew in front of the broken lenses and instantly disappeared from view, as though it had never existed.

Which indeed it hadn't.

An illusion, Annihilus realized. He wasn't in the Negative Zone Chamber at all; the access tunnel and everything around it were nothing more than a holographic projection. He had been deceived—but not for long. *I knew that something was wrong, that this was all far too easy.*

"Very clever, mortals!" he called out to whoever was surely watching him. Venting some of his displeasure at being tricked, he swept the room with his cosmic blasts, destroying the devious technology sustaining the illusion. Within seconds, the Scavengers, the access tube, and even the control console had vanished as surely as his adversaries' hopes of detaining him indefinitely. Annihilus found himself alone in an empty chamber, surrounded by warped and sundered walls. A scorched placard read:

Holographic Simulation Room #1
Not for Recreational Use
(This means you, Johnny.)

"Your trickery has earned you a few more moments of survival," Annihilus congratulated his foes. "Use them wisely, and make your peace with whatever gods you pray to. Your end is at hand, mammals. Prepare yourself for extinction!"

"Aw, man!" Johnny blurted, smacking his fist down on the control panel in front of him. Fortunately, the instrumentation had been designed to stand up to the pounding fingers of the Thing. "I didn't think he was going to figure it out so quickly."

"Annihilus is no fool," Sue reminded him. She was disappointed as well, but not surprised. "We never expected to fool him for long. It was only a matter of time before he saw through our scheme, especially after the Nega-Portal failed to bring him the victory he expected."

"But the illusion was perfect," Johnny insisted, not willing to give up on the trick so soon. "Even the images on the phony monitor were being lifted from the real monitor downstairs."

Including that massed Baluurian fleet, Sue thought grimly. The same one that Reed and Ben had spotted even before they'd left in the Explorer. Had Blastaar "captured" Reed just as they had planned? Was her husband the brutal warlord's prisoner at this very moment? Or had Ben already rescued Reed by now? *Please,* she prayed, *let them be on their way home. Let them get here before Annihilus reaches the Nega-Portal for real.*

"I just wish I knew what tipped him off!" Johnny

fumed, not quite literally. "You think it was something with the Scavengers?"

"We may never know," Sue told him. "Just be thankful that we managed to lure him into the holo-chamber in the first place, even if it meant sacrificing Roberta to make our trail of bread crumbs look convincing." She assumed Reed would able to rebuild Roberta if he ever got the chance; this wasn't the first time their mechanical receptionist had been wiped out by an overzealous intruder.

Sue set the security systems back on automatic, then rose from her seat. "Now then, we have to get out of here." She heard Annihilus march out of the holo-chamber, a few doors away, and lowered her voice. "We need to get down to the real Negative Zone Chamber before he does."

An emergency teleportation booth at the end of the hall would transport them down to a matching booth in Reed's laboratories, only one floor below. Thankfully, Annihilus was seemingly unaware of this option, not that he could easily overcome the system's encrypted passwords and biometric sensors. In theory, of course, she and Johnny could use the booth to escape the building altogether. Hell, they could escape the planet if they wanted to; Sue often used the teleporter to transport Franklin and Valeria up to their babysitter on the moon. But that would mean leaving the Nega-Portal undefended.

Not going to happen, Sue vowed. *One way or another, we're in this to the end.*

Johnny got up as well, wincing as he did so. Sue turned them both invisible for safety's sake. "And then?" he prompted her.

"I'm not sure." Abandoning the command center, they crept out into the hall—where Annihilus waited.

Even though she had known he would be there, the

Invisible Woman still clutched her heart at the sight of the monstrous insectoid standing in the hallway only a few yards away. It was one thing to watch Annihilus on a monitor, or to briefly glimpse him soaring through the sky; sharing a hall with him was something else altogether.

Sue had seldom felt so glad to be invisible. *Thank goodness he's not between us and the booth,* she thought. *If we're lucky, he won't even know we were here.*

The teleportation booth was roughly fifteen feet to their left. Holding their breaths, they snuck toward the booth, grateful for the sound-absorbing vibranium soles of their boots. Johnny limped awkwardly, but bit down on his lower lip to keep from groaning out loud. It pained Sue to see her brother hurting, but she admired his courage. Glancing back over her shoulder, she felt a fresh flare-up of anger at Annihilus for injuring Johnny in the first place. The sooner they got away from the murderous insectoid, the better she would feel.

They had only taken a few steps, however, when Annihilus stiffened and turned his insectile mask in their direction. "I smell fear!" he rasped. "Human fear!"

Blast it! the Invisible Woman thought. Annihilus's inhuman senses were obviously more acute than she had counted on. *I should have expected this,* she scolded herself. *Don't insects communicate by smell?*

"Run!" she shouted at Johnny as the monster lunged at them, nearly taking flight in the roomy corridor. She dropped their cloak of invisibility, the better to concentrate on the force field she threw up between them and their foe. Annihilus slammed into the invisible wall like a missile. She felt the impact all through her nervous system. "Hurry! I'll hold him off!"

"Not for long, female!" Annihilus barked at her. Digging

in his heels, he pressed against her force field with super-human strength. Greenish saliva sprayed from his mandibles as he mocked her efforts. "Have you run out of robots and mechanical snares? Very well. It is past time that you face me on your own!"

Frankly, I could have waited a while longer, Sue thought. Gritting her teeth, she pushed back with her mind. It felt as if she were lifting a Jeep with her brain.

"C'mon, Sis!" Johnny urged. Despite his injuries, he dashed down the hall. The solenoid activator in his belt triggered the entrance to the teleporter booth, which slid open to admit him. He hastily keyed their destination into the control panel. "We're good to go!"

Sue hurried after him, while straining to maintain her force field the whole way. Under pressure from Annihilus's irresistible might, the invisible barrier gave way slowly, re-treating down the hallway as well, practically on her heels. By the time, she darted into the compartment herself, the edge of the force field was right outside the door.

"It seems you have trapped yourself!" Annihilus gloated. His armored fists pounded on the transparent wall hard enough to make Sue's head ring. His shell-like green face was only a few feet away from hers, with only a thin wall of psionic energy between them. The Cosmic Control Rod glowed like hellfire. "All the better for me. I can dispose of you both with a single blast!"

Roughly the size of an elevator car, the booth was large enough to hold the entire Fantastic Four, and even a few more people, depending on how tightly Reed compacted his malleable body. Johnny's adrenaline heated up the booth, so that it felt like a sauna. His finger was poised over the GO button. "Ready?" he asked her tensely. Flames crackled along his hairline.

"Almost," she grunted. This was going to take split-second timing; she needed to drop her shield at the exact moment that the teleporter activated. Too late and her force field would interfere with the transference. Too early and Annihilus's cosmic energy blast would vaporize them. "On my count. Three, two, one . . . now!"

The force field dissolved.

The Cosmic Control Rod flared.

And a familiar tingling sensation rushed over Sue and Johnny as the teleporter instantaneously converted them into information, zapping them from one floor to the next.

We made it! Sue realized as they materialized downstairs in Reed's laboratories. The sealed teleportation booth looked identical to the one they had just entered, but she could tell that the transfer had succeeded simply because they were still alive. *I'm guessing the upstairs booth is a total wreck right now, although I should probably disable the transporter controls just to be safe.*

"Wow," Johnny exclaimed. "That was a close one." The flames upon this brow died down as both of them took a moment to catch their breaths. He glanced up at the ceiling, aware that Annihilus was only one floor above them. "Any idea on what our next move is?"

"Not a clue," Sue admitted. She massaged her aching forehead, which felt as though Blastaar himself were trying to burst out of her skull. Did Reed keep any aspirin in his lab?

"Well, we'd better figure something out," Johnny said. Although he was invisible to rest of the world, she could still see his worried expression. " 'Cause Annihilus is not stopping until he gets to that portal . . . and he's almost there."

15

THE PRISON WAS LOCATED IN THE southern hemisphere of Xorfo, a remote planetoid located deep in a region of space claimed by Annihilus. High sandstone walls rose from the shifting dunes of a barren desert, whose acres of arid wasteland were relieved by only the occasional oasis. Armed Scavengers patrolled the parapets and watchtowers, sometimes flapping from one perch to another. The vertical construction of the fortress, so Reed explained, clearly marked it as non-Baluurian in origin. "Blastaar's people prefer to build downward into the earth," he reminded Ben.

"Whatever," the Thing muttered. His injured shoulder still itched where that blamed Borer had bit him, and he scratched irritably at the hardened mortar patching the wound. "We gonna get this show on the road or what?"

Reed's search of the computer database back on Hethael, along with the Thing's interrogation of some of the more easily cowed station personnel, had confirmed that Samra Qury's family were being held in the forbidding prison before them, along with any number of other poor souls whom Annihilus had judged worth keeping alive. Ben couldn't help wondering what the rest of the inmates had done to warrant such a fate. *Probably nothin' worth lockin' 'em up for,* he guessed. *Knowin' Annihilus, I'd be surprised if there wuz anybody really guilty in there.*

Certainly, Samra's family didn't deserve to be cooped up just because their daughter was some kind of bona fide genius. He couldn't blame the female scientist for wanting to get her folks out of this place.

"In just a minute, Ben," Reed promised him. A fan-shaped hand sheltered Reed's eyes from the sun. "Give me a few seconds to make some quick calculations."

The two men crouched behind the crest of a weathered stone ridge overlooking the prison. With no time to mount a major offensive on the prison's defenses, they had resorted to stealth instead, landing the Explorer some distance away after taking a circuitous approach to the planetoid itself. With luck, the guards at the prison had no idea they were anywhere nearby.

"Well, make it snappy," Ben said. The harsh glare of an emerald sun beat down upon them. Perspiration seeped from the cracks in his cobblestone hide. Occasional gusts of wind blew sand in his eyes. "We ain't gettin' any younger."

He knew he didn't need to remind Reed that Annihilus was waiting for them back on Earth. Chances were, Reed's every other thought was of the danger facing his family back home. *Good thing that high-powered noggin of his has got plenty of thoughts ta spare.*

"Point taken," Reed conceded. He lowered his hand and ducked beneath the top of the ridge. A few feet away, the Thing kept watch over the special supplies they had toted from the Explorer. "In any event, I believe I've correctly calculated the amount of elastic tension required to produce the desired trajectory." He grabbed on to the top of the ridge with both hands. "You're up, old friend."

" 'Bout time." Ben fetched the first item in their improvised armory: a pressurized aquarium containing a familiar-looking translucent jellyfish. Samra had provided the tank and its slimy occupant from her menagerie back on Hethael. "Got yer icky-whatsit right here."

"Icthyplasmoid," Reed supplied.

"Right, what I said." The Thing cradled the bucket-sized tank against Reed's chest, then took hold of Mr. Fantastic's shoulders and pulled back on his friend's rubbery form until the blue-clad scientist resembled a gigantic slingshot. "Okay, Stretcho. Here goes nothin'!"

He released Reed's shoulders and Mr. Fantastic's taut body snapped forward, propelling the tank with the jellyfish high into the air. Ben clambered up onto the top of the ridge in time to see the projectile soar over the walls of the fortress and crash to earth somewhere in the middle of the prison's exposed exercise yard. *Bingo!* he thought. *Right on target!*

Raising a hand to shield his baby blues from the eerie green light, he waited for what was coming next. Although Reed had warned him what to expect, his jaw still dropped as the glistening form of a ninety-foot jellyfish suddenly rose above the walls of the prison, provoking a panicky response from the startled Scavengers, many of whom took flight like wild geese surprised by an unexpected gunshot. Ben could hear the agitated screeches of the gargoyles from dozens of yards away, followed by the sounds of squashed buildings and shouting prisoners.

Gotta hand it ta Reed, the Thing admitted. *That's one heckuva distraction!*

"Good shot!" Mr. Fantastic said, joining Ben upon the crest. His ribbonlike body contracted back into human form. He gestured toward the second and last of their surprise packages, currently resting a few feet away from Ben. "Now's our chance!"

Taking advantage of the pandemonium they had just engendered within the prison, Reed ran down the sand-covered slope of the ridge toward the embattled fortress. Pausing just long enough to heft a snoring bundle of scales onto his shoulder, the Thing hurried after his leader. His heavy boots left deep footprints in the shifting sands at the bottom of the ridge.

Hello, alien Alcatraz! he thought as he raced across the desert with his slumbering burden. *Ready or not, here we come!*

No energy beams or cries of alarm greeted their approach to the prison, which suggested that the sentries were still plenty occupied with the rampaging icthy-plasmasaurus (or whatever). Still, Ben kept his head low and his voice lower as he joined Reed in the shadow of the nearest sandstone wall. *Too bad Suzie's not around,* Ben thought. *We could use a little extra invisibility right 'bout now.*

"Here ya go," he whispered to Reed, dropping his bundle at the other man's feet. It hit the sand with a muffled thud. "Time ta wake up Sleepin' Beauty here."

Oblivious to its surroundings, the tranquilized Borer slept even through the chaotic din emanating from the other side of the prison walls. One of Mr. Fantastic's handy-dandy knockout patches was affixed to the saurian's scaly green neck. Another unwilling conscript from Samra Qury's well-stocked menagerie on Hethael, the Borer was about to earn its keep.

"I quite agree," Reed said. He peeled the adhesive patch off the monster's throat, then stepped back cautiously.

"Careful," he warned Ben. "You don't want another nip taken out of you."

"Tell me about it." The Thing scratched again at the itchy plaster. There weren't many things that could take a chunk out of his granite hide, but a Borer's jaws were definitely on the list. *Once is enough,* he thought.

The creature stirred sluggishly at his feet. Ben prodded it awake with the toe of his boot, and a pair of reptilian eyes snapped open. With a foghornlike wail, the Borer lurched to its feet, aroused and upset by its new surroundings. Its hooked jaws snapped irritably. Ben suddenly wondered what was up with the displaced Borer they had left behind in New York. Was that critter still safely confined in its holding cell beneath the Baxter Building? *Guess we'll find out soon enough.*

Before the newly awakened Borer could turn on its liberators, the Thing gave it a kick in the right direction. The Borer yowled in protest, but took the hint; as the men had hoped, the dense sandstone wall in front of the omnivorous creature proved too tantalizing to resist. The Borer burrowed voraciously into the solid wall, swiftly digging out a tunnel into the interior of the prison. Ben and Reed hurried after the scaly eating machine until they reached a cramped corridor lined with detention cells. Alien beings, many of them entirely unfamiliar to the Thing, peered out from behind bars composed of coruscating blue energy. A cacophony of agitated voices reacted to the sudden intrusion of the Borer. The reek of countless nonhuman bodies assaulted Ben's nostrils.

The stench had no visible effect on the Borer's appetite. The hungry monster continued straight ahead, eating through the wall on other side of the hall, on its way to creating yet more havoc within the beset prison. Its enthusiastic gnashing was met with cries of alarm from deeper within the prison. The two Earthmen lingered behind in the corridor, quickly taking stock of their surroundings. *Bon appétit!* Ben thought as the Borer's chomping jaws receded into the distance. *Lunch is on me.*

The entire cellblock appeared to be in lockdown. More energy beams blocked both ends of the corridor. A high-pitched siren, perhaps attuned to the batlike ears of Annihilus's loyal Scavengers, testified to the crisis created by the gigantic jellyfish. Ben guessed that the Borer's hungry attack on the outer wall had probably triggered an alarm or two as well. Whoever—or whatever—was in charge of this place was definitely having a bad day.

My heart bleeds, Ben thought sarcastically. *Serves 'em right fer working for a bum like Annihilus.*

A solitary Scavenger, left to hold down the fort while his fellow guards coped with the monster jellyfish, burst from his station clutching an electrolance in his talons. Its beady black eyes bulged from their sockets at the sight of the departing Borer and, somewhat less so, at the appearance of the Thing and Mr. Fantastic. The Scavenger held up its high-voltage prod hesitantly, uncertain whether to stand its ground or flee. A blue-white electrical charge crackled around the head of the lance.

"Gimme that!" the Thing said, yanking the weapon out of the creature's grip. He snapped the lance over his knee and let the broken pieces fall harmlessly onto the floor. Then he grabbed the Scavenger's neck and lifted him off the floor. Leathery purple wings flapped wildly, but the Scavenger could not break free from Ben's stony fist. "Awright, ya ugly mook. Where ya keepin' the Qury family?"

An incoherent screech was the only answer he received. "It's no use," Reed explained. "Not even the automatic translator can make sense of their crude articulations. I doubt those squeaks even constitute a language per se."

"Figgers," Ben grumbled. "Come ta think of it, I guess I ain't ever heard one of these creeps do much gabbin'." He knocked the Scavenger unconscious with a flick of his finger, then dropped the bat-winged creature onto the floor. He looked up and down the crowded cellblock. "Don't tell me we gotta search this whole place from one end ta the other?"

"That may not be necessary." Reed extended his neck into the guard's station, a closet-sized compartment lined with monitors and control panels. "There appears to be a computer terminal here. I should be able to call up the Qurys' precise location in a matter of moments."

"Sounds good ta me." Ben stood watch outside the guard station. His foot drummed impatiently against the floor. From where he was standing, he could see into several of the adjacent cells. Confused and frightened prisoners stared back at him through the incandescent bars of their cages. Ben recognized a warty, green figure as a Kestoran, from that generation ship the FF had visited a few years back. A group of thin, auburn-haired humanoids with pale yellow skin were obviously from Ootah's planet, while a leonine creature with a bright red mane, who looked as if he shared a common ancestor with Blastaar and his buddies, resembled their old ally Gornkai. The other inmates looked less familiar, but none of them looked terribly happy to be where they were. Soiled rags barely covered their bodies, many of which displayed the marks of starvation and torture. They looked more like concentration camp victims than convicts.

Ben couldn't help remembering the very first time the FF had run into Annihilus. Trapped in a similar prison, they had watched in horror as Annihilus had callously disintegrated a dozen alien inmates right before their eyes. Were these captives intended for an equally brutal fate?

"Say, Stretch," Ben asked uncomfortably. "Whatya wanna do 'bout the rest a these poor saps?"

"I'm way ahead of you." Reed flicked a switch on a control panel, and the caustic beams trapping the prisoners in their cells evaporated. Within seconds, a full-scale prison break was in the works. The empty corridor was suddenly filled with fleeing inmates, heading off in every direction. A few grateful prisoners paused long enough to offer their heartfelt thanks to the Thing and Mr. Fantastic, but most were in too much of a hurry to seize this unanticipated opportunity for freedom. Jubilant cries, chirps, howls, gurgles, and hisses echoed throughout the cell block.

Happy Independence Day, Ben thought. He backed up against the nearest wall to let the flood of escaping prisoners rush past him. He had to snatch the snoozing Scavenger off the floor to keep the creature from being trampled to death by the heedless inmates. He tossed the Scavenger into a now empty cell, and positioned himself in the doorway just in case any of the more vengeful fugitives wanted to beat the unconscious guard into a pulp. More than a few prisoners gave the Scavenger murderous looks as they rushed by the cell. Ben felt sorry for the rest of the Scavengers. *Guess Annihilus's goons have really got their hands full now.*

Reed exited the guard station. "Sadly, this is as much as we can do for most of these unfortunates, but there are oases on this planetoid capable of supporting life, provided they can make a clean escape from the fortress." He watched the chaotic exodus empty out the cellblock. "Who knows? They may even be able to seize a spacecraft or two from elsewhere in the prison. In any event, at least we've given them a chance at liberty."

Ben silently wished the escapees luck. The way he figured it, nobody deserved to be in Annihilus's murderous clutches, no matter what he may or may not have done.

Well, mebbe I'd make an exception in Blastaar's case.

Thanks to the prisoners' mass evacuation, the two men soon had the whole cellblock to themselves. "I've successfully located the Qurys' cell," Reed announced, stretching to the right. "This way!"

They hurried through the now-deserted corridors, occasionally turning at various intersections within the sprawling prison. Assuming that Reed knew where he was going, Ben tagged after his elastic cohort. Often he heard heated shouts and fighting not far away, but they encountered little in the way of resistance. Amidst the hordes of alien prisoners making a break for it, he and Reed passed almost unnoticed. Row after row of empty detention cells confirmed that Reed had successfully released the prison's entire population. Torture chambers, reeking of bizarre alien secretions, and bone-filled crematories were also mercifully empty.

Not a bad day's work, Ben thought.

"We should be right about there," Reed stated as they rounded a corner into yet another cellblock. To their surprise, a sizzling beam of crimson energy zipped past their heads. A rifle-toting Baluurian soldier stepped into view, brandishing his weapon.

"Turn around!" the guard snarled, baring ivory fangs. Behind him, stuck behind an array of still-active azure beams, three inmates remained trapped in their cell. Dingy brown rags hung in tatters upon their bodies, but the magenta plates covering their hands and faces instantly proclaimed their kinship to Samra Qury. "These prisoners are claimed by His Excellency, Blastaar the Supreme!"

"So what else is new?" Ben shot back.

Mr. Fantastic's right arm snapped out like a whip, lassoing the barrel of the ionic rifle and yanking it out of the grip of the flabbergasted soldier. Now unarmed, the guard took one look at the great, rocky Thing advancing on him, mammoth fists raised high, and skedaddled in the opposite direction.

"Wuz it somethin' I said?" Ben quipped.

Reed discarded the captured rifle. Retracting his arm, he rushed over to the Qurys' cell. "I kept Samra's family locked up," he explained quickly to Ben, "to ensure that they stayed put until we could reach them." He pressed a button in the wall next to the cell and the energy beams disappeared. "It's all right," he assured the bewildered prisoners. "We're friends of Samra's. She sent us here to free you."

"Samra?"

The three H'Zarri stepped out into the corridor. Samra's parents, Rasam and Masra, proceeded cautiously, holding on to each other for reassurance, while a younger male, who was obviously Samra's kid brother, Armas, barely waited for Reed's greeting before dashing out of the cell. "Who the spongy Spores are you?" he challenged.

"Yer lucky stars," the Thing replied.

Upon closer inspection, subtle differences in texture and shading distinguished the three H'Zarri. The reddish purple plates encrusting the older pair were chipped and weathered compared to those of their offspring, the glossy sheen of the parents' plates somewhat faded with time. Ben couldn't also help noticing that the rocky segments of the two males were bumpier and more irregular than the smoothly polished armor of the females; in other words, the men looked more like him. *No wonder Samra wuz givin' me goo-goo eyes,* he thought.

The Thing still wasn't sure what to make of the female scientist's apparent infatuation. Although not at all human, Samra Qury was certainly easy on the eyes. Her lustrous magenta armor was molded to undeniably feminine contours, and she obviously found him attractive. *I could get used ta that,* he admitted, *but what kinda future could we have? She ain't even stepped foot on Earth before. And the Negative Zone's no place I wanna set up housekeeping.*

"Our Samra?" Masra repeated. Fear and anxiety suffused every syllable. "Is she safe? Well?"

"Yes," Reed assured the distraught mother. "And eager to see you again."

"You have a ship?" Rasam asked urgently. He had a grave, scholarly manner that reminded Ben of a rabbi he had known as a child. Rasam kept a protective arm draped over his wife's shoulder.

"Not far from here," Reed said. "But we have to hurry."

"You bet," Ben agreed. Obviously, now was not the time to ruminate on his romantic prospects, such as they were. The sooner they got Samra's family back to Hethael, the sooner he and Reed could head home to tangle with Annihilus. "After me, folks."

"Just a minute," Armas insisted. He scrambled to retrieve the fallen ionic rifle. He grinned as he took possession of the weapon. "Okay, *now* I'm ready!"

Ben eyed the teenager skeptically. "You sure you know to handle that thing, squirt?"

"Try me!" he dared the Thing. His cocky attitude was way too Torch-like for comfort.

Just what we needed, Ben groused. *Another smark-alecky kid.* "Awright, no more yakkin'." He hustled Armas back to where his parents were waiting. "Let's get a move on."

Reed led the way, with the Thing bringing up the rear. Retracing their steps, they made it back to the Borer's entry tunnel without incident. The sirens were still going strong, while the corridor lights had gone out entirely, forcing Reed and Ben to activate the searchlights in their belts. They rushed out of the murky cellblocks into the blinding green daylight outside. The Qurys gasped at the glare.

"Keep goin'!" Ben urged them, even as his own eyes watered. He wiped the tears from his eyes with the back of a petrified mitt and pressed the three H'Zarri forward, beyond the shadow of the high outer wall. There was a whooshing sound from overhead, and Samra's mother glanced back over her shoulder.

"Watch out!" she hollered. "Pulsar grenades!"

The Thing spun around and looked up to see two miniature missiles arcing through the sky toward them. Apparently a guard upon the wall had spotted their escape and wasn't about to let them get away in one piece. *What the heck is a pulsar grenade?* Ben thought as a projectile landed directly at his feet, less than a yard away from the other fugitives. *And do I really wanna know?*

Without thinking, he hurled himself on top of the grenade. And just in time; in a heartbeat, a tremendous paroxysm of force and heat erupted beneath the Thing, nearly lifting his armored body from the ground. The impact exploded against his chest, which felt as if the Hulk had just given him CPR. Every bone in his body vibrated like a gong.

But what about the second grenade? He lifted his aching head in time to see the other projectile come hurling down from the sky. Ben tried to scramble to his feet, but the first blast had taken too much out of him. He needed to catch his breath, but there wasn't any time. . . .

Fortunately, he wasn't alone. At the last minute, just before the grenade landed right in the midst of the escape party, Mr. Fantastic stretched over Ben and the others like an elastic blue canopy. Reed absorbed the grenade's kinetic energy as it slammed against the small of his back, then flexed his body to catapult the bomb back the way it had come. The expelled grenade sprang back through the air to land somewhere high atop the prison walls. A loud explosion sent chunks of shattered sandstone flying, only to rebound harmlessly off Mr. Fantastic many feet below. Distraught Scavengers, their wings torn and shredded, wheeled erratically in the sky above the smoking battlements. The glistening bulk of the monster jellyfish continued to loom above the battered walls.

That'll teach 'em to mess with us, the Thing thought as he staggered awkwardly to his feet. For an instant, the world seemed to spin dizzily around him, and he tottered unsteadily. Armas, his stolen rifle slung over his shoulder, reached out to steady him, and Ben felt his sense of balance returning. *Whoa there!*

"Ben!" Reed called to him. "Are you all right?"

"I guess so." The Thing did a quick inventory on his parts and found everything more or less intact. Chunks of colored glass, formed from the sand by the intense heat of the explosion, were fused to his chest, but he figured it was nothing a little sandblasting couldn't take care of eventually. They stung like the devil, though. *One more grudge ta hold against the Zone and its critters.* More glass lined the smoking crater at his feet. His multipurpose belt buckle was completely trashed.

"Let's go," he said.

The slope up the ridge was steeper and sandier than he recalled, but Mr. Fantastic grabbed on to the crest with both hands and stretched himself into a sturdy cable the Qury family could hang on to as they climbed to the top. Not wanting to put an even greater strain on Reed's rubbery spine, Ben made it up the ridge on his own. After the fetid atmosphere of the prison, the dry desert air came as a blessed relief.

Long months of captivity had left the elder Qurys short on strength, so their son had to help them along as the party traversed the barren wasteland as quickly as they were able. At last, they reached the cracked, sun-baked plain where Ben and Reed had left the Explorer. The Thing grunted in satisfaction as he spotted the dinged-up module waiting for them less than half a mile away. He experienced a moment of anxiety when he recalled that the Explorer only seated four, but then he remembered that Reed could easily squeeze himself into whatever extra room was available in the cockpit. *We're almost outta here,* Ben realized. *As jailbreaks go, this wuzn't so tough.*

He should have known better than to tempt fate. Before they could reach the Explorer, a sonic boom heralded the sudden arrival of another spacecraft, which came zooming down from the sky. Jagged fins and sharp angles betrayed its Baluurian origins. Landing rockets flared beneath the sleek one-man vessel, driving Ben and the others back, as the ship touched down between them and the Explorer. The Thing glimpsed a familiar, hirsute face through the windshield of the craft.

"Uh-oh," he muttered. "Figgers this joker would be showin' up right 'bout now."

His dubious expectations were confirmed when, moments later, the hatch of the other spacecraft banged open and Blastaar himself leaped onto the parched and lifeless ground. The savage warlord faced them single-handedly, his explosive digits poised and ready.

"Human fools!" he bellowed. "I knew I would find you here! As soon as I received an emergency transmission from Hethael, I guessed where you would be heading next, to steal my hostages from me." He reveled in his deductive prowess. "I had to commandeer my fastest interceptor to get here in time, but, as you can plainly see, my efforts were not in vain. Spotting your vessel from orbit posed no challenge at all."

"Well, hooray fer you!" the Thing hollered back. He stepped between Blastaar and the Qurys, shielding them with his impervious frame. "What ya want, a medal?"

Blastaar sneered at Ben. "So, you did not perish in the Debris Belt after all." Half a foot taller than the Thing, he appeared not all intimidated by the monstrous Earthman. "Perhaps it is just as well. Why should I be denied the pleasure of killing you myself?"

"Oh yeah?" Ben shot back. "Case ya haven't noticed, Simba, we got ya outnumbered!" He exchanged a glance with Reed, whom had positioned himself at the Thing's side. "Way I see it, jus' half of the Fantastic Four is enough ta whip you!"

"Arrogant mortals!" Blastaar cracked his knuckles ominously. "I need no reinforcements to vanquish the lot of you. My own legendary power will be more than sufficient to the task!"

"That why yer always teamin' up with Annihilus?" Ben taunted. "Cuz you're afraid of tacklin' us on yer own?"

"Annihilus is but a means to an end!" Blastaar insisted vociferously. "To be disposed of once he's served his purpose." Turning away from the Thing, he glowered at Mr.

Fantastic. "Where is the weapon you promised me, Richards? The Distortion Ray?"

Ben recalled the wacky-looking gizmo Reed had insisted they bring along in the Explorer. Last he'd seen the D-Ray projector, it was still resting safely in the module's cargo hold. *That must be why Blastaar ain't tried ta blow up our ship yet,* he figured. *He don't want ta wreck Reed's newfangled ray gun.*

"That Distortion Ray was designed to be used against Annihilus," Mr. Fantastic stated firmly. His humanoid form was ready to change shape at a moment's notice. "Which is precisely what I intend to do with it."

"Hah!" Blastaar laughed. "Do you expect me to trust you with a weapon like that?" He stalked toward the vulnerable Explorer. "Is the prize aboard your ship? You need not answer, as I mean to find out for myself!"

His greedy paws reached out for the Explorer's scorched and battered hull, no doubt intending to tear open the solid steel casing with his bare hands. The minute he touched the hull, however, a powerful electromagnetic shock flung him backward. "Tyanna's spawn!" he roared, reminding Ben of the Wicked Witch of the West when she tried to snatch Dorothy's ruby slippers. "What trickery is this?"

"Surely you didn't think that I would leave the Explorer undefended?" Reed said coolly. "Trust me, Blastaar, there's no way you're getting past my security measures without destroying the module entirely—and the Distortion Ray as well."

Blastaar snarled in frustration. "You will pay for your insolence, Richards!" He turned away from the Explorer, his huge hands glowing with pent-up energy. "I am Blastaar! I will not be denied!"

Ear-shattering booms rocked the arid plain as the Living Bomb-Burst unleashed his explosive fury on the escaping fugitives. The Thing braced himself, but Mr. Fantastic reacted even more quickly, stretching himself in front of Ben and the others like a long, horizontal wall. His ultraresilient form absorbed the impact of Blastaar's initial bombardment, but not without cost. Ben heard his partner grunt in pain. Not even Mr. Fantastic could take such punishment for long.

A stone outcropping several yards away offered cover of a sort. "Run for it!" Ben urged the Qurys. "Reed an' me will handle this loser."

Rasam and Masra sprinted for shelter, and Ben hoped Armas would do the same. Instead, Samra's brother lifted his rifle and fired repeatedly at Blastaar as the reckless teenager dashed toward the warlord's interceptor. Crimson beams struck Blastaar about his head and shoulders.

The indestructible tyrant reacted as though pelted with water balloons. "You dare?" he raged, turning the full force of his neutronic blasts at the fleeing youth. The desert floor exploded behind Armas's heels as Blastaar shot wildly at the teen, momentarily ignoring Ben and Reed. "Let death be your reward!"

Exhausted from the absorbing Blastaar's volcanic salvo, Mr. Fantastic collapsed back into human form. "Couldn't hold up any longer," he gasped. "The sheer concussive force is overwhelming!"

"Not ta worry," Ben told him. "Ya did yer part. Now lemme put the kibosh on this walkin' fireworks factory!"

The thunderous din of Blastaar's assault concealed Ben's pounding tread as he charged at Blastaar while the warlord's back was turned. The Thing tackled Blastaar from behind, throwing his granite arms around the Baluurian tyrant in an unbreakable bear hug and pinning Blastaar arms to his sides. "Gotcha!" Ben trumpeted. With his arms trapped, Blastaar could no longer target Armas and the others. "Ya leave that kid and his folks alone! They've gotten enough grief from you and your bug-faced partner!"

"Dolt!" Blastaar cursed. "Have you forgotten that my power allows me to defy gravity itself?"

His outstretched fingers fired straight down at the ground, causing him and the Thing to blast off like a Saturn V rocket. Ben held on to his enemy for dear life as he suddenly found himself rocketing upward at over twenty thousand miles per hour. A hot wind blew against his face, while the rushing air made it hard to hear even his heartbeat. Blastaar spun about in midair, trying to shake loose his unwanted (and unwilling) passenger, but the Thing refused to let go. They rose higher and higher, and Ben was suddenly grateful that the planetoid's breathable atmosphere extended all the way out into space. Glancing down, he saw the desert floor shrink away in the distance. *Yikes!* he thought. *Talk about a long way down!*

Without warning, Blastaar slammed the back of his shaggy head into Ben's face. The sudden jolt caused the Thing to loosen his grip and he lost his hold on the rocketing warlord. A deep-throated cry escaped Ben's throat as he plummeted toward the ground like a rocky, orange meteor.

His hands uselessly groped at the empty air, seeking purchase where none existed. Could he survive a fall from this height? Ben wasn't sure, but he wouldn't have wanted to bet on it. Alicia's face flashed his through mind, followed by Samra Qury's graceful features. *Too bad I gotta go out lookin' like a monster,* he thought, *'stead of the man I used ta be.*

The wind whipped past his ears as he accelerated toward the desert below. Gritting his teeth, he got ready for a rough landing. If he was lucky, maybe he'd only break every bone in his body.

But instead of hitting the earth like a stone, a large blue trampoline broke his fall. *Reed!* he realized, as he bounced harmlessly atop the distended form of his best friend. Mr. Fantastic's ductile anatomy readily absorbed the Thing's downward momentum, so that he emerged from his precipitous descent undamaged. *Good ole Stretcho,* Ben thought. *Shoulda known he wouldn't let me down!*

The "trampoline" tilted to one side, depositing the Thing gently onto the ground. "Oomph," Reed said. A certain amount of strain and fatigue showed on his distinguished face as he compacted his body back into shape. "Feels like you've gained a little weight, old friend. Thankfully, the gravity on Xorfo is a few degrees weaker than on Earth, reducing the impact somewhat."

"If ya say so." Ben shrugged his mountainous shoulders, while he wiped a trickle of blood from his nose. "Felt like there was more'n enough gravity fer me." Knowing that the fight was far from over, he searched the sky for their airborne foe. "Now where the heck is that no-good son of a Roman candle?"

"Over there," Reed said, pointing into the sunlight. Squinting against the glare, the Thing saw Blastaar zooming back toward them, propelled by his own explosive bursts. The blazing controlled blasts lowered Blastaar back down onto the ground. He looked refreshed and invigorated by his impromptu flight. "Is that the best you can do?" he challenged them. Another salvo of explosive discharges forced the Thing and Mr. Fantastic to dive away from each other to avoid taking the ferocious blasts head-on. "My power is inexhaustible! You do not stand a chance against me!"

"Izzat so?" Ben called back, shouting to be heard over the nonstop detonations. "Take a look behind you!"

Blastaar laughed in disbelief. "Do you expect me to fall for so transparent a ruse? Perhaps that ploy retains some freshness in the universe from which you hail, but here in the Negative Zone, that trick wouldn't fool a child!"

"Fair enough." Ben clambered to his feet and got ready to run. "But don't say I didn't warn ya!"

The thrum of mighty engines, growing in volume, caught Blastaar's attention. He spun around to see his own high-powered interceptor launching at him from across the plain. Ionic cannons pulsed from the nose of the spacecraft, targeting the tyrant with destructive red rays, even as powerful thrusters turned the interceptor itself into an enormous missile aimed straight at Blastaar. Behind the front windshield, a grinning H'Zarri youth could be seen at the helm.

Attaboy, kid! Ben thought. His boots pounded against the sunbaked earth as he dashed out of the way of the oncoming spacecraft. Out of the corner of his eye, he saw Reed doing the same. *Give that louse what-for!*

Guns blazing, the interceptor bore down on Blastaar, who threw up his hands, firing back at the ship with a volley of deadly bomb-bursts. Sizzling ionic beams clashed noisily with booming neutronic blasts. Armas ejected from the cockpit of the spacecraft a split second before the interceptor hit Blastaar head-on. Battle-hardened metal shrieked in agony and a stupendous crash rocked the desert. The interceptor flipped over on its nose, landing upside down on top of Blastaar. A violent shock wave hit the Thing across the back, all but knocking him off his feet. An immense fireball rose from a heap of mangled and smoking steel.

"Yow!" Ben exclaimed. He turned around to inspect the damage. He'd seen plenty of wrecks in his day, including the crash landing he'd made right after the cosmic ray accident that had created the Fantastic Four, but this one was a doozy. Nothing was left of the interceptor except a tangle of spare parts and scrap metal. *The kid done good,* he thought.

Looking upward, he was relieved to see Armas parachuting to safety. An elongated arm reached up to pull the young H'Zarri away from the flaming wreckage. Armas whooped and hollered triumphantly as he descended toward the ground, sounding more like Johnny every minute.

But what about Blastaar? The Thing approached the demolished spacecraft cautiously. The scorching heat from the wreck made the hot desert sun feel cool by comparison. Ben peered into the smoldering debris, looking for any sign of their enemy. Had being hit by a speeding spaceship put Blastaar down for the count?

Or was that too much to hope for?

A heavy chunk of fuselage shifted loudly, as though shoved roughly aside. A stentorian groan reached his ears and Ben saw a brawny figure rise from beneath the crumpled remains of the interceptor. Fragments of smoking debris tumbled from the figure's shoulders as he staggered out of the smoke and flames into the clear light of day. The Thing clenched his fists in anticipation.

Let's do this again, he thought.

Blastaar had seen better days. His proud gray mane was singed and disheveled. Multiple lacerations scarred his face, arms, and legs. One eye was swollen shut, and inky black blood dripped from a busted lip. His armored breastplate was blackened and dented. Sharpened toenails jutted from shredded boots. His arms hung limply at his sides and he winced with every breath.

"You ain't lookin' so good," the Thing observed. The reeling monarch reminded him of a punch-drunk prize-fighter who wasn't going to make it through another round. Ben *almost* felt sorry for him. "Wanna call it a day?"

"Never!" Blastaar snarled. He spit a broken fang and a mouthful of blood onto the parched soil. "Blastaar the Conqueror never surrenders." He struggled to raise his hands back into firing position. "You shall all suffer my terrible wrath!"

"Awright." Ben shrugged. "Have it yer way." A ruptured aileron had been thrown clear of the explosion, and the Thing snatched it up from the ground, hefting it like a club. The metal fin was toasty to the touch, but nothing compared to the hotfoots the Torch gave Ben all the time. "Hey, Blasty! Take a wild guess what time it is?"

Blastaar threw up his hands. His fingertips glowed like hellfire. "The end of your days, you grotesque monstrosity!"

"Wrong answer!" The Thing replied. He swung the heavy metal fin with all his prodigious strength. *"It's clobberin' time!"*

The aileron hit Blastaar in the head with the force of a stampeding elephant. The infernal radiance around the warlord's fingers went out—and so did the lights in his eyes. The unquestioned ruler of the Baluurian Empire crashed to the ground, where he lay still and unmoving. Only the steady rise and fall of his chest demonstrated that he was still among the living.

Finally! Ben thought. *I wuz startin' ta think that I wuz never goin' ta get a chance to say that.* He gazed down at Blastaar's unconscious form. "So what we goin' ta do with the Lion King here?" he asked Reed.

Mr. Fantastic joined Ben by the wreckage while Armas ran to check on his parents. "He's too dangerous to take with us, and we're hardly murderers." Reed contemplated the defeated tyrant. "Best to leave him here, stranded on Annihilus's prison planet without a ship. The rest is up to him."

"That's all?" Ben asked. "Sounds like he's gettin' off easy ta me."

"This isn't our universe," Reed reminded Ben. "I'm reluctant to interfere too much with affairs here." Reed symbolically wiped his hands of Blastaar's taint. "Let he and Annihilus deal with each other, assuming we can find a way to get that other monster back where he belongs."

Ya got a point there, Ben admitted. The heck with Blastaar; the big green bug was whom they needed to be worrying about now. He looked across the plain to where Amras was busy retrieving his folks. Ben could hear the excitement in the kid's voice as he relived his part in Blastaar's defeat. "Hey, where'd ya learn to steer a fighter like that?" Ben called out to the approaching teenager.

Amras shouted back, "I was the best junior pilot on our planet, back before Annihilus destroyed it!"

Ben was willing to believe it. "Let's get outta here," he told Reed. A smile cracked his rough-hewn face. "We got a family reunion ta arrange!"

16

FINALLY, IT HAD COME TO THIS.

Floor by floor, victory by victory, Annihilus had fought his way down to the most tightly guarded section of the Fantastic Four's penthouse apartment: Reed Richard's laboratories on the thirty-fourth floor.

Now, Johnny Storm stood alone just within the outer door of the lab, listening to the unstoppable insectoid blast away at the other side of the reinforced-steel air lock. With every blow, the ten-inch-thick barrier shuddered like a wobbly ladder. It felt and sounded as if an earthquake were right outside the door, demanding to be let in.

Johnny swallowed hard. "Oh my God," he said in a hushed tone. "He just keeps on coming. He's like the Terminator, if Arnold Schwarzenegger was a six-foot-tall cockroach."

"Or like Yul Brynner in *Westworld*," his sister supplied. Her voice emerged from the comm link in his fresh uniform, which he'd found a moment to change into once they'd reached the lab via the teleporter. Sue was locked inside the Negative Zone Chamber itself, as the Baxter Building's last line of defense.

The battered air lock door pealed rotundly, like the world's heaviest gong. He saw the topmost hinges snap apart and realized that the moment of truth was approaching. "Uh-oh. Here he comes."

They hadn't made it easy for Annihilus. After the trick in the holo-chamber had fizzled out, they had reactivated the security in the stairwells, forcing him to bulldoze his way through another round of lasers, knockout gas, and dense steel bulkheads. Unfortunately, he had proved all too willing to do so.

Just my luck, Johnny thought. *The darn bug's just as pig-headed as Ben.*

Without intending to, he jumped backward when the door of the air lock crashed onto the floor in front of him. A cloud of dust and debris momentarily obscured his view, then Annihilus stormed over the threshold into the lab. The nacreous sheen of his carapace was barely scuffed. The spikes upon his shoulders tapered as sharply as ever.

"At last!" he exulted. His inhuman voice held an unmistakable note of triumph. "This close, I can sense my home dimension calling to the Cosmic Control Rod. The Nega-Portal is nearby. I can feel it!"

Is he kidding? Johnny wondered. Probably not; he remembered that Reed had once theorized that Annihilus's good ole C.C.R. drew its power from the very core of the Vortex, the so-called Crossroads of Infinity. *I'm guessing it was the massive amounts of shielding surrounding Reed's labs that kept Bugface from locking onto the portal earlier.*

All that insulation was there for a reason. Mr. Fantastic's laboratories, the most advanced on the planet, held the most dangerous and revolutionary equipment in the entire Baxter Building, including the Nega-Portal, the gateway to the Microverse, and Doctor Doom's time machine. Johnny glanced at the latter chamber, whose own air-lock entrance had been left conveniently open. *It's showtime,* he thought.

Busy savoring his cosmic communion with the Nega-Portal, Annihilus had not yet noticed the slender human youth standing outside the time chamber. Johnny remedied that situation.

"Flame on!"

His respite in the command center, while the Baxter Building had done his fighting for him, had given Johnny a chance to recover some of his strength. He still felt like death warmed over, but he was back in the game again, just in time for the final inning.

The Human Torch burst into flame.

"Johnny Storm!" Annihilus turned toward the blazing figure. "I knew that we were not finished yet, you and I." His bulging green eyes scanned the interior of the lab. "Where is your sister, and the rest of your vile clan?"

The invader was standing in front of a transparent Plexiglas window that looked in on the Think Tank, a saline-filled sensory-deprivation tank Reed used for his most heavy-duty cogitating. Inside the liquid-filled environment, warmed to precisely 98.6 degrees Fahrenheit, Mr. Fantastic's thoughts and body were both free to assume any shape he could imagine.

The Torch threw out his arm and a white-hot ball of flame erupted from his palm. The crackling fireball missed Annihilus, but melted right through the window of the Think Tank, causing a scalding gout of steam to engulf the unsuspecting insectoid. Seconds later, hundreds of gallons of heated saline came pouring out of the tank. The sudden flood uprooted Annihilus, who fell backward into the wall of the tank, cracking the back of his head against the sturdy titanium.

The gushing water flowed across the floor toward him, but the Torch was in no danger of being dowsed by the saline. He just ratcheted up the heat a bit, and more steam filled the violated laboratory. In the instant mist, the shadowy outline of Annihilus looked more like a demon than ever.

"You have humiliated me for the last time, Johnny Storm!" he raged. Regaining his footing, he splashed across the steam-filled lab at the Torch. Water dripped from his soaked gauntlets. Beads of moisture clung to his carapace and mask. Droplets sprayed from his twitching wings. "You will meet your end before this mist clears!"

"Oh, yeah?" Johnny dared him. The Torch snapped his wrist and a flaming whip appeared in his hand. He cracked the whip at Annihilus, and a fifteen-foot-long strip of flame lashed the intruder across his face. "Come and get me!"

Johnny had no illusions that his pyrotechnic stunts could actually defeat Annihilus. Heck, the Living Death Who Walks had already stood up to the toughest weapon in the Human Torch's arsenal, his nova-flame burst. A little more fire wasn't going to stop him now.

But maybe, just maybe, it would make the immortal monster angry enough to step into a trap.

He gave Annihilus another crack of the whip, just to keep the insectoid's attention on him, then dashed inside the waiting time machine chamber. He ran right past the attached control room onto the innocuous-looking platform itself. "Like that? There's plenty more where that came from!"

With luck, Annihilus would follow him onto the Time Platform without pausing to consider the consequences.

At which point, Sue, who was monitoring the situation from the Negative Zone access chamber at the other end of the lab, would go into action. They had already slaved the time machine controls to the console in Nega-Chamber, so all she had to do was push the right button.

Sending Annihilus elsewhere in time was risky. The last thing they wanted to do was give the genocidal insectoid a chance to alter the timeline, and given how many times he had cheated certain death before, they couldn't count on any of history's known cataclysms and disasters to destroy him once and for all. Chances were, his blasted Cosmic Control Rod would allow him to survive even the eruption at Krakatoa or ground zero at Hiroshima. In the end, after a hasty discussion, they had decided to rely on the time machine's Observe mode, so that Annihilus would be transformed into an invisible, intangible phantom at the dawn of time. Not a permanent solution perhaps, but one that would keep the ageless destroyer trapped in limbo until Reed could come up with a better plan.

Ideally, Johnny would zip out of the time machine before Sue tripped the switch, relying on his speed and agility to get past Annihilus before the insectoid could figure out what was what, but if that didn't work and the Human Torch ended up stuck in immaterial mode also . . . well, Johnny figured he could bear that for as it long as it took for his family to figure out a way to rescue him. He wasn't looking forward to getting stuck in limbo with Annihilus of all people, but it would be worth it if it meant saving the entire planet—and maybe the whole darn universe—from Annihilus's insane agenda.

Now all we need is for Bugface to take the bait. Johnny held his breath as he watched the monster lunge through the swirling steam toward the threshold of the time chamber. The blurry white mist could only help conceal his intentions from Annihilus. *C'mon, you murdering scum. Just a few more steps . . . !*

He almost fell for it. Johnny marshaled his flame, poised to jet past Annihilus the minute the monster set both feet on the platform. Then his hopes crumbled as Annihilus paused right before the entrance.

"Wait," the insectoid declared. The steam began to thin and he could see more clearly into the seemingly empty chamber. "What craven trick is this?" He backed away from the threshold. "Do you think that I can be lured away from my goal a second time?"

His wings flared out majestically, blocking the exit entirely. "Small-minded creature. Your imagination is as limited as your future. I need not enter this compartment to destroy you utterly. My Cosmic Control Rod can extinguish you from where I stand!"

The cylinder beneath his chin glowed balefully. . . .

No! Sue thought.

From her vantage point within the Negative Zone Chamber, she watched the life-or-death drama unfolding outside. Having seen what Annihilus's Cosmic Control Rod could do to the Baxter Building's reinforced doors and air locks, she had no doubt that it could snuff out Johnny's life as well.

There was only one thing to do. Switching to their emergency backup plan, she activated the time machine—and sent her brother ten minutes into the future.

On the wall-sized screen facing her, Annihilus chittered in surprise as the luminous platform suddenly rose up and snatched his intended victim away from him. The Human

Torch vanished just as completely as the holographic Scavengers had earlier, albeit for a thoroughly different reason.

It was unclear if Annihilus grasped the distinction. "Deception!" he ranted, shaking his fist in anger. "Lies and illusions!" Turning away from the time chamber, he marched across the futuristic laboratory. By now, the scalding steam had evaporated and the flood of saline water had disappeared down precautionary drains in the floor, leaving only a few wet patches behind. Annihilus ignored the changing conditions. "Enough! Let me claim my prize and put an end to this tiresome charade."

Sue watched with growing apprehension as the obsessed insectoid neared the adamantium air lock guarding the Negative Zone chamber. If she had programmed the Time Platform correctly, events would catch up with her brother in less than ten minutes, but until then she was on her own.

I have to stand for the whole Fantastic Four right now.

Despite its solid adamantium construction, this final air lock fared no better than all the other bulkheads and barriers Annihilus had trashed during his relentless rampage through the Baxter Building. The Cosmic Control Rod unleashed its power once more, and the "unbreakable" steel door came crashing down. Only hours after he had first appeared above the Flatiron Building, nearly twenty blocks downtown, the dreaded scourge of the Negative Zone had overcome the last of the skyscraper's defenses.

Except the Invisible Woman.

Deep in her heart, she had always feared it would come down to this: her invisible force field against Annihilus's Cosmic Control Rod—with the entire positive universe at stake.

All right. Bring it on.

"Susan Richards," Annihilus addressed her. "Stand aside or be the first of your family to meet your doom."

"Watch your mouth," she told him. *"Doom* is a four-letter word around here."

Seen up close, he was even more chillingly inhuman than she remembered. Even the Skrulls and Shi'ar seemed less alien. Was that because reptiles and birds were closer to primates on the evolutionary scale than arthropods, or simply because the Skrulls, Shi'ar, and humans all belonged to the same universe, as opposed to Annihilus, who came from Somewhere Else? In any event, she had to resist the urge to turn invisible at the very sight of him.

But why bother? He knows I'm here.

"This is all so pointless," she lamented. "We don't even want your stupid Rod."

"Then you are either a liar or a fool."

He stepped toward the control panel, but Sue blocked his path with both her body and her strongest force field. The protective bubble surrounded her and the console, trapping Annihilus outside.

For now.

He pressed against the unseen barrier with his gauntlets, determining its boundaries and contours. Then he stepped backward, crossed his arms atop his chest, and let his Cosmic Control Rod speak for him.

Unspeakable power crashed against her shield, causing Sue's head to ring as though it had been struck with a crowbar, but the force bubble did not collapse. She gritted her teeth and held on, bracing her body against the console behind her. The onslaught did not abate, but she concentrated with all her might on keeping the field intact against the overwhelming force pressing against it. She thought back on the last few hours, called up all the anger and frustration she had felt as Annihilus had violated her home and used it to patch up the growing weaknesses in the bubble.

This is for Franklin's trophy, she thought, *and my father's photo, and my brother's blood. This is for our spoiled Saturday and the frightened screams of my babies as your monster ruined our afternoon together. This is for forcing my husband and my friend to risk their lives in a godforsaken universe they may never return from. . . .*

The outcome of the contest was never in doubt. But the Invisible Woman intended to keep on fighting for long as she was able.

This is for my family.

My planet.

My universe.

17

"SAMRA!"

The female scientist's joyous reunion with her family brought a smile to the Thing's craggy face. As he watched Samra Qury share a group hug with her parents and younger brother, it was almost enough to make Ben forget that Annihilus was waiting for them back on Earth. *Forget the bad guys fer a minute,* he thought. *This makes the whole blamed trip worthwhile.*

To their relief, they had returned to Hethael to find Qury still in control of the underground science station, with Commander Vatriin and his soldiers securely locked away in the station's escape-proof menagerie. Reed had restored the moon's defense grid just in case any of Blastaar's ships had come calling while he and Ben were away rescuing the Qurys, but Samra had not needed to repel any invading Baluurian troops.

At least not yet; according to the station's long-range sensors, an entire squadron of Baluurian warships was on its way to retake Hethael. In theory, they would be here in less than an hour.

Guess we'd better get a move on, Ben thought.

Still, only a soulless machine would have denied Samra and her family a moment to enjoy being together once more. The warmth of their heartfelt embrace stood in stark contrast to the cold, sterile environment of the laboratory. "Thank the Spores you're all safe!" Samra gushed, looking as if she never wanted to let them go again. "I was so afraid that we would be kept apart forever, or that something terrible would happen to you!"

"You should have seen it, Sister!" Armas told her. "I ran Blastaar's own spaceship right into him."

"Nothing more than he deserved!" she pronounced, while shaking her head at her sibling's headstrong recklessness, then turned to cast a grateful expression at Ben and Reed. "I don't know how to thank you for what you've done."

"Your help destroying the Posi-Portal will be more than enough," Mr. Fantastic assured her. The Distortion Ray was cradled against his chest. "As much as I hate to interrupt your reunion, we need to complete our business here." Lines of worry creased his brow; Ben knew Reed had to be fretting about Sue and Johnny, not to mention the safety of Earth in general. "Have you completed the modifications on the portal?"

Samra reluctantly tore herself away from her family. "Everything is in readiness," she reported. "I followed your instructions to the letter." She led them across the lab to the control room overlooking the Posi-Portal. "I've also destroyed all of my original notes on the portal and developed a computer virus that will systematically seek out and eliminate any backup copies I might have missed. There's no way anyone will be able to reconstruct my work after I've gone. Your universe will be safe once more, at least as far my technology is concerned."

"That's as much as we dare ask for," Reed said. Carefully placing the Distortion Ray aside, he sat down at the control panel to check over Qury's modifications one last time. Complex graphics and equations, all way above Ben's head, flashed over an attached monitor. "These improvements look satisfactory to me," he said after a few moments. "Now all that remains is to set the stage for your apparent demise."

The plan was to fake the Qurys' death in a matter-antimatter explosion that would also destroy all traces of her Posi-Portal. With luck, it would look as though Samra and her family had died while trying to use the portal to escape to Earth. In truth, however, the Qurys would flee Hethael in the Explorer, while Reed and Ben used her portal one last time to return to the Baxter Building.

And the sooner the better, Ben realized. According to Samra, no Baluurian fleets had been spotted invading the Big Apple yet, but he wouldn't entirely relax until he had confirmed that with his eyes. *And not just on some screwy alien monitor.*

"Almost ready," Samra announced. Using some sort of bizarre alien instrument, she extracted blood and DNA samples from herself and her relatives. Armas yelped indignantly as she deftly peeled away a couple of the smaller plates from his arm. "Oh, don't be a baby," she scolded him. "It's a small price to pay to ensure that nobody comes looking for us." She sprayed the exposed area with a topical anesthetic. "At your age, they'll grow back soon enough."

She placed the collected samples on a counter in the control room, where the eventual blast would disperse them in what she hoped would be a convincing manner. A tiny patch of raw blue skin showed upon her own arm before it slipped back into her rumpled lab coat. Rasam and Masra looked about the control room in wonder, then peered through the thick transparent wall at the portal itself. "By the Spores," the older woman whispered to her daughter. "Did you really build all this?"

"I'm afraid so," Samra said. "For better or for worse."

Ben wondered if she had any regrets about leaving the science station behind. In a way, the portal was the culmination of her life's work. *It can't be easy on her,* he guessed, *knowing we're gonna blow the whole shebang ta smithereens.* Lord knew Reed had never been able to bring himself to shut down his own portal for good.

"There," Samra said briskly, turning away from the portal. A small bundle of personal possessions rested by the soon-to-be mangled remains.

"Excellent," Reed stated. "I appreciate the sacrifice you're making. With the Explorer, though, you and your family will be able to find a new life far away from either Blastaar or Annihilus."

"Not too far," Armas asserted. He still had the ionic rifle he had claimed during the jailbreak. Ben had also given the kid a crash course on how to pilot the Explorer on their way back from Xorfo. Thankfully, the teen had proved a quick study—and just as much a natural at flying spacecraft as he had claimed. "Now that we're free, I'm going to organize an H'Zarri resistance movement. One way or another, we're going to take back our planet and rebuild our civilization!" He glanced over at his brilliant sister. "And you're going to help me, right, genius?"

Samra hesitated. "I'm not sure." While her family looked on in surprise, she joined the Thing and Mr. Fantastic by the control panel. She laid a gentle hand upon Ben's powerful arm. "To be honest, I'm tempted to go with you through the portal. What sort of scientist would I be if I wasn't intrigued by the prospect of exploring a whole new universe, especially after all my research into alternative planes of reality?" Although she spoke to both men, her shimmering bronze eyes were fixed on Ben. "Besides, I'm not sure I'm ready to say good-bye to you."

Jeez, Ben thought, thrown for a loop. *How 'bout that?*

For a moment or two, he allowed himself to fantasize about what it might be like to have Samra in his life. He and Alicia hadn't been an item for a while now, and he was sick and tired of being alone. Samra was smart and brave and actually thought he looked good. What more he could he ask for?

He shook his head. "That ain't a good idea, babe. You belong here, in yer own universe. Over here, you're a gal and a half, brains and beauty in one great package, but, back where I come from, you'd just be a Thing . . . like me." He gently removed her hand from his arm, wondering if maybe he was making the biggest mistake of his life. "Trust me, ya don't want that."

"But—" she started to protest.

He cut her off before she could change his mind. " 'Sides, yer family needs ya here, and ya don't want ta go draggin' them off ta anudder dimension, too. That wouldn't be fair to any of ya."

"You're right," she conceded, glancing over at the anxious faces of her family. Reality dawned sadly on her burnished features. "Then I suppose this will have to do."

Without warning, she stepped forward and placed her lips against his. Ben's heart skipped a beat and he surrendered to the kiss without hesitation. The delicate purple plates around her mouth were surprisingly warm. . . .

Far too soon, her lips pulled away, leaving him momentarily breathless. Regret showed in her moist, metallic eyes. "I'll never forget you," she promised huskily.

"Me, too," he told her. His heart was still pounding from her kiss. "And then some."

Blushing slightly through her glossy armor, she turned toward Reed. "It's been a pleasure meeting you as well," she said. "I only wish we could have worked together on a project with less dreadful applications."

"Perhaps someday our two universes will be able to share our knowledge without fear of each other," Reed prophesied. He rose from the control panel to offer Samra his hand in friendship, which she accepted gladly. "I certainly hope so."

"As do I," she said. Releasing Reed's hand, she cast a worried look at a chronometer on the instrument panel. "Blastaar's ships will be here soon." She quickly rejoined her family by the entrance to the control room. "We need to leave."

"So what's keeping us?" Armas chirped enthusiastically. "I can't wait to get behind the controls of that earthship!"

With a last lingering look at the portal and Ben, in that order, Samra Qury hurried out of the lab, taking her reunited family with her.

Just my luck, Ben thought, *I finally meet the perfect gal and she lives one whole universe away.*

Mr. Fantastic waited until the Explorer was clear of Hethael before firing up the Posi-Portal. Beyond the circular gateway, the Baxter Building gleamed in the sunlight.

Home sweet home, Ben thought. *And still in one piece, from the looks a it. But fer how much longer?*

Reed stepped away from the control panel and retrieved the Distortion Ray from where he'd laid it before. "I've rigged the portal to explode ten seconds after we pass through. All I needed to do was disable the dimensional translation protocols so that the positive and negative universes will briefly intersect on a subatomic level, without the benefit of an intermediary phase transition. The resulting matter-antimatter reaction should produce an exothermic energy discharge on the order of—"

"I'll take yer word fer it," the Thing interrupted. "Just so long as the whole place goes boom." A thought occurred to him and he looked up at the ceiling. "What about Blastaar's goons, plus all them other E.T.'s locked up in the dog pound?"

Reed dismissed Ben's concerns. "The laboratories and positive-universe access chamber are heavily shielded and insulated from the rest of the station. The explosion should pose no threat to the prisoners on the upper levels." Reed stretched his arms and legs, perhaps remembering the adhesion suit he had been confined in for so long. "I suspect that Commander Vatriin and his men will have some explaining to do when Blastaar's reinforcements arrive, but, frankly, that's the least of my concerns."

"Then what are we waitin' for?" Ben said. "We got our own family to look out for now."

Reed nodded grimly. "You took the words right out of my mouth."

Starting the final countdown, the two men exited the control room and entered the sealed chamber beyond. Crackling blue energies marked the boundaries of the force field sealing off the gateway, but not for long. At the count of five, the force field evaporated and a sudden, irresistible suction yanked the Thing and Mr. Fantastic toward the waiting portal. *Holy cow!* Ben thought. *This is just how Reed's first Nega-Portal worked, back in the old days!*

Ben wasn't sure he could have resisted the overwhelming suction even if he had wanted to. Even the air around him was rushing into the gateway ahead as though the chamber were undergoing some sort of interdimensional decompression. Glancing over at Reed, Ben saw his partner struggling to hold on to the D-Ray projector in his hands. Through the portal, they saw the Baxter Building growing closer and closer by the minute as Reed's new-and-improved navigation system zeroed in on their home. The exterior of the skyscraper gave way to the Negative Zone Chamber itself, where a fierce battle appeared to be under way. A bat-winged figure blasted away at a woman in a navy blue uniform, who seemed to be barely holding on by a thread. A cascade of eerie golden radiation engulfed an invisible bubble

Hang on, Suzie, Johnny! the Thing thought. *We're on our way!*

Side by side, they hurled themselves through the unearthly alien portal. . . .

18

SUE'S HEAD FELT AS IF IT WERE GOING to explode. Her temples throbbed and veins pounded upon her brow. Every heartbeat sent stabbing pains through her eyes. Pulsating waves of agony raced up and down the back of her neck. Her skull felt as though one of the Thing's ten-ton dumbbells was pressing down on top of it. Blood trickled from her nose. Her mouth felt as dry as the surface of the moon.

But she did not let her force field collapse.

"Surrender, Susan Richards!" Annihilus harshly urged her. She could barely see him through the blinding glare of the energy emanating from his Cosmic Control Rod. She could scarcely hear him over the concussed ringing in her ears. "Abandon this useless struggle. I promise that your death will be swifter than you deserve."

Forget it, she thought. Her family was depending on her. *I'll die before I let you get your vicious claws on these controls.*

But how much longer could she hold on? The destructive power of the Rod kept assailing her invisible force bubble, as relentless and unstoppable as its inhuman master.

Her legs felt as though they were being dissolved by one of Diablo's elemental potions, and she had to lock her knees straight to keep from tumbling over. How long had she been fighting back against Annihilus's merciless onslaught. Five minutes? Six?

A segment of her force field buckled inward, and she hastily concentrated on restoring the shield before Annihilus could notice and take advantage of the weakness. She could feel the burning heat of his blast even through the thinning bubble, like Johnny at his most excitable. Sweat bathed her skin, soaking through the unstable molecules of her uniform. Her blond bangs were plastered to her forehead. The whites of her eyes were streaked with red.

I can't keep this up, she realized. Adrenaline and anger had sustained her so far, but even they had their limits. She closed her eyes, the better to see the invisible barrier protecting her. Microscopic fissures and flaws spread throughout the field like an infection. It was like a balloon ready to pop, or a diamond that would crumble to pieces if struck at precisely the right angle. She wondered if she would even realize it when the field caved in, or would her first indication be the feel of the unchecked blast flaying the flesh from her bones?

"Your cause is hopeless, female," Annihilus crowed, perhaps sensing her weakness. "All who live, all who may someday covet my power, are my enemies and must perish accordingly . . . for only in the elimination of other life can I find true immortality!"

"Aw, shut yer big yap up and leave Suzie alone!"

What? The Invisible Woman couldn't believe her ears. Her eyes snapped open in time to see the ever-lovin', blue-eyed Thing deliver a haymaker that sent Annihilus flying. Behind him, Mr. Fantastic hurried toward her, clutching an unfamiliar weapon against his chest.

"Reed! Ben!" she called out to them from inside her fragile force bubble. "You made it! You're back!"

"Yeah, pretty good shot, Stretcho!" the Thing said. He stomped toward Annihilus with his colossal fists raised before him. Across the chamber, the stunned insectoid hit the floor and skidded across the smooth steel baffles covering the access pit before coming to a halt. "Ya got us right back where the action is!"

"All just a matter of getting the correct quantum mechanical coordinates aligned along the right axis," Reed insisted. He stretched across the room and looked anxiously into his wife's ashen face and blood-streaked eyes. "Sue, darling! Are you all right?"

I am now. She dropped her force field and let him wrap an arm around her three or four times. His other hand held on to the mysterious weapon. "Reed?" she asked anxiously. "Your mission? Did you find out how Annihilus got here?"

Before he could answer, a blazing figure came flying into the chamber, lighting up the reflective steel walls and raising the temperature. "Sue!" the Human Torch called to her, and she realized that ten minutes must have elapsed. "Are you okay? What's been happening?"

He paused in midair and did an unintentionally perfect double-take. "Reed? Benjy?" Confusion was written all over his incandescent face. "Er, what did I miss?"

" 'Bout time you joined the party, hot stuff!" Pausing in his pursuit of Annihilus, the Thing eyed the Torch dubiously. "You been slackin' off or what?"

"It wasn't my fault!" Johnny protested. He looked to his sister for support. "Sue, tell him about the time travel!"

Sue sagged against her husband's arm, letting his elastic coils hold her up while she caught her breath. *The Fantastic Four are back,* she thought jubilantly. *It's not just me anymore.*

"That's enough, both of you!" Mr. Fantastic said sternly. "We still have our unwelcome visitor to deal with." Holding on to his wife protectively, he regarded the insectoid warily. He held out the unusual weapon and aimed it directly at the intruder. "Don't make a move, Annihilus. This Distortion Ray was designed specifically with you in mind."

Annihilus rose from the floor on the other side of the Nega-Portal. Despite the wallop he had received from the Thing, his exoskeleton remained intact. "I fear no weapon of your devising. Ask the Human Torch and your mate just how effective your armaments have proven against me so far!" He faced them without any sign of trepidation. "And draw no comfort from the fact that you now stand united against me. The Thing's crude attack caught me unawares before, but still I am more than a match for your entire quartet!"

"That may or may not be the case," Mr. Fantastic replied. "In any event, I'm about to render the question academic."

Without further ado, he pulled the trigger on the Distortion Ray. A disorienting blend of lurid colors and flashing lights washed over Annihilus, who recoiled instinctively, then relaxed his posture as the polychromatic beam appeared to have no visible effect on him. "Is that it?" The insectoid laughed mockingly. "Your vaunted new weapon? It doesn't even tingle!"

But Reed looked as intense as Sue had ever seen him. "Now, Sue!" he said urgently, before the psychedelic radiance could begin to fade. "Encase Annihilus in a skintight force field sheath . . . to save us all!"

Huh? Sue didn't understand, but she trusted that Reed knew what he was doing. Even though her overworked brain still throbbed painfully, she draped an invisible curtain over their perplexed adversary, tightening it around him like a second skin. She suspected that Annihilus could easily break free from this thin and delicate field, but it was intact and skintight, just as Reed had insisted. "Done," she told him. "But I don't understand."

"Nor do I!" Annihilus said indignantly. He tapped the back of his left gauntlet with his right index finger, feeling the paper-thin force field covering every inch of his exoskeleton. "What are you playing at, Richards? If you expect me to suffocate, you shall be gravely disappointed. I can survive in even a total vacuum!"

"That's not my intent," Mr. Fantastic said. "Didn't you recognize those colors and patterns, Annihilus? It's the Distortion Effect, the same preternatural process that transmutes matter into antimatter, and vise versa, whenever one of us crosses from one universe to the other. You were converted into positive matter when you first traveled to our universe via Samra Qury's Posi-Portal." Reed smiled slightly, pleased with his own ingenuity. "I've just reversed the process."

What? Sue tried to grasp Reed's meaning. Was he saying that he had turned Annihilus back into antimatter? Was that even possible? And how was it a good thing? *I always thought that antimatter would explode if it came into contact with matter from our own plane of reality.*

"Let me spell this out to you, Annihilus," Reed said, lowering his weapon. "Right now Sue's force field is the only thing that is preventing you from being consumed in a matter-antimatter reaction of catastrophic proportions. The minute she drops her field, you will be irrevocably destroyed . . . unless you return to the Negative Zone at once."

"You're bluffing!" Annihilus accused Reed. "Such an explosion would surely kill you as well." His Cosmic Control Rod glowed in warning. "I have the advantage here. Use your so-called Distortion Ray once more, change me back into positive matter, or I will obliterate both you and your mate before another minute passes."

Reed shook his head. "I wouldn't do that if I were you. The instant Sue dies, her force field dies as well, and that's all that is keeping you alive." Reed's face and voice grew ever more somber. "You're correct that the chain reaction will destroy us as well, but you should now by now that the Fantastic Four would gladly die rather than let you or Blastaar invade our reality."

"What he said," Ben confirmed. His shrugged his rocky shoulders. "I'm in no hurry ta cash in my chips, but there's a lot of decent, ordinary people out there worth dyin' for, even on Yancy Street. And nobody's gonna miss a Thing much anyway."

"For once, I'm with Ben," Johnny chimed in. He landed on the fireproof floor beside his teammates. He kept his fires low to avoid singeing them. "I'm willing to go up in flames if that's what it takes. Just try me!"

"Reed speaks for all of us," Sue said. "For myself, I'd die content knowing that my children would never have to fear you again." She gave Annihilus a withering gaze. "Although I suspect that the very concept of such a sacri-fice is totally alien to you."

Annihilus quivered in rage. He clenched his fists at his sides even as he allowed the menacing glow around his Cosmic Control Rod to gradually subside. "Madness!" he declared. "What sort of lunatic beings welcome death just to spare another? Death renders all other considerations meaningless. It is the ultimate predator—and life is the only prize that matters!"

"For you, perhaps." Mr. Fantastic handed the Distortion Ray to Ben. Unwinding his arm from around Sue, he took his place behind the control console. "But if that is the case, then you truly have no choice. Now that you are antimatter once more, you must return to the Negative Zone to survive."

Annihilus threw back his head and railed against the heavens. "May the Vortex consume you, Richards!" He glared murderously at Reed and flapped his wings in satanic wrath. "You and all your despicable kind. I will rid the multiverse of humanity if it takes me a million years!"

The sheer intensity of his genocidal hatred sent a chill down Sue's spine, yet she dared to hope that all this sound and fury signified that Annihilus had genuinely accepted his defeat for now. Her prayers were answered when, his outburst concluded, he draped his wings over his shoulders and strode to the sealed pit in the center of the chamber, where he stepped onto the adamantium plates guarding the entrance to the Negative Zone.

"Very well, Richards," he hissed. "Do what you must. But know that you have not heard the last of me. I am the Living Death Who Walks, and none who live can escape me."

Reed activated the Nega-Portal, then hurried them all out of the chamber. They watched through a protective pane of clear carbon poly-lattice as the pit opened and consumed Annihilus, who disappeared into the swirling colors of the Distortion Area.

Sue wondered how long it would be before they encountered him again.

Not long enough, she knew.

• • •

Later, after the Nega-Portal had been locked down once more, and the interdimensional monitors had confirmed that Blastaar's armada was still on its side of the Vortex where it belonged, Johnny picked up the Distortion Ray from a counter in the laboratory, where he and the others were busy mopping up the mess. "I've got to hand it to you, brother-in-law," he told Mr. Fantastic, giving Reed an enthusiastic thumbs-up. "This new gadget of yours sure did the trick. That's pretty slick work, even for you. I'm impressed that you managed to whip this bad boy up while traipsing around the Zone at the same time."

"But I didn't," Reed stated calmly.

Johnny blinked. "Come again?"

"The Distortion Ray is a fraud," Reed explained. "It's all smoke and mirrors, engineered to do nothing more than mimic the bizarre visual sensations observed in the Distortion Area."

Ben and Sue, who were also helping to straighten up the lab, paused in their efforts and stared at Reed incredulously.

"You're joking," Sue said, raising her eyebrows.

"Not at all," Reed insisted. "I wish it were that easy to generate an nth-dimensional phase transition with nothing more than some polished lenses and circuits! As is, I'm afraid a fairly impressive light show was the best I could manage under the circumstances."

Ben scratched his head. "So you're sayin' we won by a fib?" He frowned, seeming somewhat deflated by Reed's unexpected revelation. "Gee, that's kinda a letdown."

"It was more than a fib, Ben," Reed assured him, his voice growing more serious. "The true key to victory lay in understanding Annihilus's alien psychology—and taking advantage of his mortal fear of death. I knew that in any sort of standoff that appeared to place his very existence at risk, he was bound to blink." Reed looked back over his shoulder at the Negative Zone Chamber, where Annihilus had come so close to the ultimate victory. "In the end, his obsession with his own survival is what defeated him."

"SEE, I TOLD YA WE'D HAVE OUR PICNIC after all. It's just a day late, is all."

"Yep, you called it, Uncle Ben."

The Richards family, in strictly civilian garb, were stretched out on beach towels and picnic blankets in the middle of Sheep Meadow, a lush, fifteen-acre lawn near the southern end of Central Park. Lost in a sea of green, along with countless other New Yorkers and tourists taking advantage of a beautiful Sunday afternoon, the Richardses *almost* blended in completely.

Okay, they got a few curious stares when Reed's arm stretched six feet across the blanket to retrieve Valeria's misplaced pacifier. And, yeah, Johnny got some wide eyes and giggles when he toasted the hot dogs with his bare hands, mostly to get the attention of whatever unattached cuties might be jogging by, while Sue inadvertently startled the family next door when she started rocking Valeria in an invisible cradle to quiet the restless infant. And, yeah, sure, there were even a few clueless losers who didn't know any better than to gawk at an unassuming orange rock pile who was minding his own business, just sitting on the grass with his favorite godson, but, hey, a couple of funny looks never killed anyone.

"Did they actually have sheep in the Sheep Meadow when you were a kid?" Franklin asked Ben.

"Are ya kidding'?" he answered. "How old do ya think I am?"

Oak, elm, and maple trees bordered the sprawling expanse of grass. Beyond the trees, the Manhattan skyline rose up around the park on all sides. A cool breeze and the warm sun made for nearly ideal picnic conditions. Frisbees soared across the meadow, occasionally sharing the sky with kites and pigeons.

The Thing leaned back on his petrified elbows. *Man, this sure beats the Negative Zone.*

"So, Stretch, what we gonna do with those Nega-Zone critters down in the basement. With the wings and the jaws, ya know?"

Reed gave the matter some thought. "On a day like this, I'm tempted to donate them to the Park Zoo, but I suppose the most sensible and humane solution would be to return them to their native habitats, under carefully controlled conditions, of course."

"But not today," Sue stressed forcefully. "We owe the children this picnic after taking a rain check yesterday. Besides, the longer we stay out of the way, the more repairs the maintenance droids can make to the building."

"You got a point there, Sis," Johnny said. He stuck his finger into a marshmallow, toasting it from the inside out. "Me, I don't want to even think about the massive cleanup job that's going on back home."

"Figgers," Ben commented. "I always said you wuz a slacker at heart."

Johnny snorted. "Says the guy who is too lazy to zap a frozen pizza before he swallows it whole."

"Just doin' my part to save energy," Ben maintained.

"Can I help it if we ain't all walking barbecues like you?"

Bored with the grown-up's good-natured bickering, Franklin tugged on the Thing's arm. "Hey, Uncle Ben. Let's go play some Frisbee."

"Whatever ya say, squirt. You're the boss."

Maybe I ain't as cut off from the human race as I get ta thinkin' sometimes, Ben thought as he lumbered to his feet and chased after the excited eight-year-old. He glimpsed a strolling couple walking hand in hand and felt a pang, but only a pang. Even though part of him couldn't help wondering what might have happened between him and Samra, he knew that life on Earth still had its own rewards. *I'll never really be alone, as long as I'm part of this crazy family called the Fantastic Four.*

"Go long, kid! It's frisbeein' time!"

ACKNOWLEDGMENTS

First off, I owe a huge debt to Stan Lee, Jack Kirby, and all the other talented Marvel Comics writers and artists whose work I shamelessly pillaged while working on this novel. Rereading all those old and new comics, sometimes over and over, was definitely one of the perks of the project.

Also, many thanks to my editor, Ed Schlesinger, and my agent, Russ Galen, for making this book possible. And to Sean Kleefeld and the staff at www.ffplaza.com, whose website was an invaluable reference source. Plus, an enthusiastic shout-out to Joe Murray and Paul Stikik at Captain Blue Hen Comics in Newark, Delaware, the first place I go to in search of back issues and trade paperbacks, not to mention my monthly comic book fix (I'll be by to pick my latest batch any day now, I promise).

Finally, as ever, thanks to Karen, Alex, Churchill, Henry, and Sophie for providing me with plenty of support on the home front (even if Sophie sometimes wanted to play "mousie" instead).

ABOUT THE AUTHOR

GREG COX is the *New York Times* bestselling author of numerous novels, including the official movie novelization of *Daredevil*. Other Marvel-related books have included *The Gamma Quest* trilogy, starring the X-Men and the Avengers, and two Iron Man novels.

In addition, Cox is the author of ten *Star Trek* novels, including the recent *To Reign in Hell: The Exile of Khan Noonien Singh,* as well as books and short stories based on such popular series as *Alias, Batman, Buffy the Vampire Slayer, Roswell, Spider-Man, Underworld,* and *Xena.* His official website is www.gregcox-author.com.

He lives in Oxford, Pennsylvania.

Not sure what to read next?

Visit Pocket Books online at
www.SimonSays.com

Reading suggestions for
you and your reading group
New release news
Author appearances
Online chats with your favorite writers
Special offers
And much, much more!

POCKET BOOKS
A Division of Simon & Schuster
A VIACOM COMPANY

POCKET STAR BOOKS
A Division of Simon & Schuster
A VIACOM COMPANY

10421